# Unnatural Selection

# Unnatural Selection

by

Simon Whitmore

This is a work of fiction.

The events depicted in this story are entirely products of the author's imagination or are used in a fictitious manner and should not be construed as fact.

Where factual information is portrayed, it is intended to be as accurate as possible, and any mistakes thereafter are the author's own.

**ISBN:** 9798529985434
**Imprint:** Independently published

*In memory of Enid*

*"Be sober, be vigilant; because your adversary the devil walks about like a roaring lion, seeking whom he may devour."*

**1 Peter 5:8**

# Prologue

The sound of pounding feet echoed through the streets, boots not made for running slapping aside remnant puddles as leather uppers with man-made soles battered the tarmac, the grey block walls and solid concrete of the empty buildings exacerbating the natural, yet unnatural, acoustics of the ever-quickening footfalls.

The owner of such awkward footwear was a man, perhaps thirty-five with signs of grey hair around the temples, his face drawn, ragged. Ahead of him his ten-year-old son was faltering, slowing. For a moment he recalled his schooling, the stitch that youngsters seemed to suffer from on track days. Days like that tended to be bright and sunny, not nearing dark and overcast as it was now. He swore to himself, feeling his own legs struggling, like dragging lead; why had he not been watching the clock? *Stupid.*

The man pushed the young boy ahead. "Quick. Go." He looked back, saw nothing. "Keep looking ahead. Don't wait for me. Now. Go, go."

The boy ran in front, obediently, his gait improving at his father's words, renewing his vigour.

Behind them now, the tick-tack-tick of another's feet, chasing them; definite footsteps, becoming more pronounced, were getting quicker, louder, echoing through the barren streets.

Closer.

"Go on, boy," the man strained through heavy breaths, concern now entering his voice.

Rounding a corner the man stopped and threw his back against a wall. Out of sight. Breathing hard, he spat and craned his neck around the edge of the brickwork, the sweat on his skin causing his clothes to cling to him. He chanced a look round the edge and back up the dark and deserted street. He scanned the road, could still see damp footprints where he and the boy had been only moments before.

Bleak buildings towered above them, huddled together, grey and lifeless, all taking solace as they stood their ground in the grimy wasteland, their windows smashed, curtains billowing through like enormous cloth hands waving a final farewell. Rubbish, paper, tin cans, polystyrene food containers with rotting half-eaten kebab meat, filled plastic bags, cigarette packets and crumpled clothing littered the roads and pavements, blowing about innocently, unaware. Abandoned cars with doors and boot lids open, chassis burnt out and wrecked, sat alone, keys still in the ignitions, their passengers long gone.

Two bodies, ravaged and mutilated, lay still, half in and half out of a silver and black car, once one of those hybrid or electric vehicles, the hideous and agonising expressions on its passengers' dead faces telling something of their demise.

It was a fine city. Once. Now it was a desolate and dangerous playground for those few who were left. A real-life set for Laser Quest or Urban Paintball. Only toys guns had been replaced by crude weapons designed to split heads or pierce torsos at close range.

The man gulped down dry spittle as his breathing returned. He heard the pursuing strides closing in. *Damn it*. He pushed the boy's back gently, urging his son forward again and started off himself, both now moving better for having stopped for a moment; they needed a safe place, a sanctuary they had not yet been able to find.

A faint crash of glass sounded behind them. *Shit*. He turned, listened, his eyes on the edge of the building where he had stood only seconds before. In the still of early evening cool air caressed his neck, pricked his skin. He shivered. *Easy now*. He slowed his breathing, trying to regain some composure, silently exhaling through his mouth. All was quiet—the boy's shuffling footsteps ahead of him the only real discernible sound. His lips taught, the man sniffed, attempting to calm himself, the ozone in the air raking his nostrils. Maybe he was becoming a little too edgy. Being overcautious wasn't a bad thing, but it wasn't good either for his stress levels, constantly living on the edge.

Their job earlier had taken way longer than expected—there had been no windows in the building they were exploring—and now he and the boy had found themselves caught out by the time. Evening had come earlier than expected, the clouds making sure of that, the sun long gone. Blood rushed through his ears, a demonic tattoo beating in his head, as he strained to listen. Was he imagining the noises closing in behind them? Surely it couldn't happen the only time they had been caught out; were they really that unlucky?

The answer came to him immediately as someone—a man in once-smart but now dirty clothing—came hurtling around the corner into the strewn street behind them.

*Fuck.*

Whoever it was, their pursuer obviously meant business; as the man looked at him, allowing his senses to process what was happening, he saw the pursuer's face was twisted somehow—was it a trick of the shadows or was he grinning?

*Double fuck.* The man turned to the boy and screamed at him. "Run, son. Faster."

His legs and heart pumping harder, faster, the boy responded to his father's frantic shouts. Saying nothing, short legs took on the strength of an Olympic runner as he tacitly understood. The man followed, hesitating, unsure of whether to follow his son or turn and make his stance here.

Behind them the speeding stranger with the malignant grin continued in his pursuit, relentless, untiring, his pace increasing.

Much closer now.

The man stopped. Running was something he had not done for some time now. Age had taken its toll. Getting back before dark was always the easiest option. He knew the running man behind them was not running from anyone else, he was pursuing them, was after them, his grisly grin simple evidence of the joy of the chase. *Who is this freak?* In truth, although the man did not know his pursuer, he knew exactly what the man—or thing—was. He closed his eyes.

It was time to defend himself.

The man checked on his boy, seeing him take refuge behind an old bus, then grabbed for the back of his jeans, the long pocket draping down to his knees, its contents his only salvation. Cricket stumps. He fumbled for one. Sharpened to a point, the lethal sporting accessories had become his weapon of choice since he had, quite accidentally, pinned one some time ago with a steel rod after being caught while they searched for food—for some reason the thing was lying behind the counter of a deserted supermarket. As it lumbered to a stand and came at them, he and his boy had fled into the rear storeroom; reaching for the first thing he came across, a steel rod, he had crammed the rod forward almost blindly. It served a purpose, of sorts. The thing had fallen back, flaying around in apparent agony, grabbing at the rod aimlessly, its body writhing in its dead skin, its deader eyes showing nothing. The thing was dying; its body had finally found peace. At least that is what he had hoped. As the thing battled against what he assumed were its final death throes, he and the boy had made their escape. Had they stuck around, they would have seen the thing pull out the steel rod from its body, the steel rod a mere—and uncomfortable—impediment, and continue in its own search for food.

Perhaps for them again, one day.

The man pulled out the makeshift, but not so deadly, he now realised, homemade stake. He stopped, exhaled heavily, and turned, ready to face it.

"Come on then, you mother—"

The forceful push seemed to come out of nowhere even though he had expected the rapid assault and he reeled backwards, slamming hard against a wall, winding him. Through the heaving of his own breath, he heard a rattle of timber against concrete as he crashed down. He squeezed his hand closed, feeling only fingers and thumb, realising what the rattle of timber had been. He had dropped his weapon. Although it may have hindered the thing for a moment, essentially the improvised weapon was useless. However, being without any weapon at all left him feeling naked, vulnerable. *Oh shit.* He turned away, struggling for air, scurrying on his knees; he scrambled for something, anything.

The nimble and powerful stranger stepped into view. Black clothing topped by a ridiculously white face, abnormally deficient in colour, looked down at him, the grin still there, the eyes red, almost black, detached from humanity like a reptile's, revealing unrelenting hatred.

Using the wall as a bolster the man pushed himself up and stood straight. His thighs burned, lactic acid seared his side. *Stitch.* He caught a glimpse of his boy through clouded eyes as the boy headed into the doorway of a building some way off. Safe. For now. *I love you, son. Keep going.* Turning to face the stranger, the man looked at the thing directly in the eyes; one last act of defiance.

The pale-faced stranger regarded his prey. And took a step forward.

*This is it.* Hoping dearly that his son would be fine, would get away and live to see another day, the man closed his eyes and began mumbling: "Our father, who art in heaven . . ."

The crunch of stone beneath advancing feet seemed peculiarly loud as he felt the stranger come at him. The man hastened his prayers, grimacing, his eyes still shut tight. This was it. The man stood still, waiting for an end to it all, an image of his son's once-happy face emblazoned in his mind's eye. *Goodbye, my boy.*

An unfamiliar sound pierced the night: a solitary and slight gust of wind.

". . . Lead us not into temptation, but deliver us from evil."

The strange noise had not been the death knell he was expecting; to him, nothing had happened. Instead he heard nothing, only silence. A second or two passed. Then came a dull thud. *Thuck.* Something heavy had hit the ground in front of him. He opened his eyes.

In front of him something certainly had happened; was still happening in fact. The stranger's body trudged forwards, towards him, headless, still in the act of pursuit; muscle memory going the extra mile, or few inches at least. The man dodged sideways to avoid the grasping clutches of the hands, now on spasmodic auto-pilot. Catching his heel on the raised pavement, the man fell back and onto his side, cursing loudly.

Beside him, a heavy round object, eyes peering up at him above a fixed—but well dead—inane grin. The thing's head had come clean off. Black filth, an excuse for its blood, oozed thickly like years-old molasses from the cleanly severed stump.

Climbing to his feet, the man shook his head, wiped his palm across his face, and sighed heavily. *Fuck me backwards.* He brushed himself off, checked to see where his boy had got to.

"I'm over here, dad," the boy shouted.

*Thank God.* He waved at his son, his guts inside churning over and over. The man turned, lowering his hand as the boy approached, two men now at either side of the boy. One of the new strangers had his hand on his son's head as if ruffling the boy's hair. As they neared, the man was about to ask the two new arrivals just who they were when one of them smiled, his ashen face sporting a strange, warm glow under the last of the sodium street lights.

The sharp swords that hung at their sides were not so inviting.

## Chapter 1

Randell sat back, leaning his bulk against the wall. He sighed, the sigh becoming a vast yawn. Morning had finally come. Even though, at six-feet-two tall, over eighteen stone, and only twenty-two-years-old—a pup really and in the prime of his life—he was shattered. He leaned forward, resting his arms on his knees. Feeling like shit, he closed his eyes and dropped his head.

Staying awake night after night was tough on them all, and was beginning to take its toll. Last night had seen the most activity yet, had left him, and he was sure the others, feeling tired and listless. His legs, in fact all of his limbs, felt heavy. Randell yawned again, wiping at his eyes, thinking of easier times. His previous job had been as a labourer for a local builder in London. Heaving concrete blocks around along with eight-by-four plasterboards and bags of cement meant he was fit, a naturally strong young man, but that all seemed so long ago and now, well, he did not want to admit it, he was out of shape. To top it all off he had never worked night shifts either. The body took time to adjust. But all that was behind him now. Everything had changed. Not that the shifts were actual work, the shifts had come about as a basic necessity for survival. But they were as draining as work. More so in fact. At first, staying mentally alert at night was not too bad. Until three or four in the morning came round. Then it became really tough. Then you had to really dig in. At any moment you may be called upon to physically protect yourself and those of the household who were doing much the same and feeling just a knackered as you.

He looked down at his stomach. *Gross.* A slightly less-than-corpulent mound greeted him. He had put on weight, the others in the house nicknaming him Randy from the all-but-forgotten American comedy show My name is Earl; it had been insufferably repeated on the television in the UK for years. He raised his hands, clasping his head, ran one hand through his thick black mane of hair. It felt greasy, and needed a cut. He sighed, his stale breath arrested by his knees lingered provocatively around his nostrils. *Rancid.* He needed to drink, to eat something, something more than just canned food. Running his tongue around the inside of his mouth, trying to create a little saliva, he attempted to moisten his dry throat. He swallowed, raised his head and looked about.

The house was a dump. It was supposed to be plush—or once had been. Houses in the Belgravia area of London were once hugely sought after and terribly expensive. It was, after all, just a stone's throw from Buckingham Palace. The late 1830s house had been constructed to celebrate the start of Queen Victoria's reign and was situated in a small and quiet residential square, part of the Grosvenor Estate, alongside about twenty-five others, all similar in outward appearance.

Way too much furniture swamped the front room, each of them heavy wooden pieces, many brought in from the surrounding houses which now stood empty, none of it matching. They were all placed carefully, pushed to the outside of the room, covering windows, doors, any and all apertures. In the centre of the room the expensive Axminster carpet was worn, fluffed and fouled, and coming away from the floor beneath. Randell remembered giving a helping hand to install it only a couple of years before after a mate of his had landed the job; his mate had gone on and on about it for weeks. The owners of the house had chosen the carpet for its trendy and stylish chequered motif. It was quality stuff but Randell had hated it, wondering just why the owner of a house in Victoria Square would want a carpet not-so-aptly-named Grosvenor Square. It had been heavy and really awkward to lay.

In all there were five of them living in the great house. All of them living like dogs in what seemed to be little more than a grand but forsaken kennel—the most robust house in the neighbourhood, certainly in the square—scrounging for food by day and fighting for survival at night. And now, it really was beginning to get to them all. Along with the now stark and disrupted innards, the house stank of piss; an eternal odour of sour ammonia permeated the air. During the day it was not so bad, it was bearable; they could open up the windows, let in some fresh air. At night though, all doors and windows were sealed tight, locked and barricaded, nailed shut and boarded up. It kept them out. Mostly.

Dawn now brought roll-call, something they had established without thought or discussion. The shouts went up, each of the residents calling out their own name one by one as they had done every morning for about the last three weeks.

He heard the girl first. "Ulrica."

Then from upstairs, two more voices, one female, one male.

"Seffi."

"Ralph."

The final voice was further away, somewhere either higher or deeper within the house.

"Connor."

Randell called out last.

All five present and accounted for; everyone was all right. *Suppose that's something.* He stood up slowly, pushing himself up from a mahogany chest of drawers, and walked through the large hall to the front door. He reached for the key from the ledge and unlocked the heavy, reinforced door, working on the locks, finally swinging it wide.

A gentle breeze met his face, mixed with that early morning smell of cool damp he had always enjoyed. He breathed it in, the fresh air soothing his nostrils and what he knew was an oncoming headache. Outside, the rising sun shone, brilliantly ignorant of the nightly terrors, unaware of the unabated and vicious attacks that had taken place relentlessly while out of sight as the planet did another of its aeons-long revolutions. A streak of brown and grey caught his eye and he turned to see a dunnock to his right, sitting atop some debris. It made a few shrill remarks, its head flicking rapidly left and right, and flitted off towards the hedge that surrounded the square.

As he looked at the bird he spotted another movement in the corner of his eye. It was Ulrica, coming out from the kitchen. She paced through the hall towards him. Randell turned, still squinting, and saw she was carrying two glasses of water. She handed one over to Randell. He took the glass, nodded at the smaller girl, her hair deep auburn and raggedy, then swallowed the lot in one gulp, rubbing his sleeve across his mouth as the water dripped down the stubble of his unshaven chin.

"Thanks."

He looked at her. She was lithe and strong—she had been a dancer and Zumba instructor—and, Randell reckoned, about the same age as himself, perhaps a little younger by a year or two. She was pretty—or would be if she cut her hair and styled it a little instead of dyeing it bright red all the time—in a little sister kind of way. She would need to take off that garish dog collar that encircled her slender neck; he had never seen her without it and found himself wondering if she even took it off when she slept. He noticed she had a long cut along her forearm, angrily red. It ran perpendicular over a series of shorter scars, all lined up one after the other, some healed many moons ago, others still pink, raised and healing.

"You OK?" he asked, pointing at the fresh cut.

Ulrica raised her arm, examining it in the early sunlight. The deep gash was more black than red, smeared, dry and crusty, after an intense night.

"Oh crap," she said, shrugging her shoulders. "Suppose I'll live."

"They didn't get you anywhere else?"

"No, stuck him good. He ran off with the others."

He nodded. "Good girl."

He poked his head out the door, having a good look around. The once-beautiful square was now a mess; rubbish and broken glass lay all around. The two-dozen or so grandiose four-storey houses were some two-hundred-years-old, and all

Grade II listed—at least they were before the local council, the government, the population, and anybody else who gave a damn about history and architecture had been about. They were now a row of lifeless ruined blocks, looted and deserted; more like the common lodging houses of the ramshackle East End, not quite that of 1888 Spitalfields but bad all the same. In all there was not a complete window left intact. Piles of glass and dusty white stucco filled the pavements, brickwork on show in great patches, black iron balustrades now redundant, curtains torn and mangled, household contents scattered and crumpled. In short, having suffered permanent nightly attacks since things had horribly altered, and with the residents long gone, the whole area had become derelict. More like a building site with little regard for health and safety.

In the centre of the square a recreational seating area formed an elongated roundabout of sorts some twenty-five metres in length and eight metres wide, a one-way road encircling it. Car parking spaces were full, many cars damaged, the vehicles redundant without any drivers. Ten ornate lampposts, all at evenly spaced intervals, lit the terraced area— the boxed-hedging now tatty and overgrown—their bases acting as natural breaks for the four-foot high railings which surrounded it. The park benches inside had long been vandalised. Two trees, once both trimmed and tidy, stood solemnly, one at either end. Within the square's black railings, in the centre and facing predominantly south, a statue of a young Queen Victoria looked on serenely, a rose in her left hand, untouched. Randell eyed the statue. She would not be amused if one of those night-prowling sharp-toothed bastards decided to attack her one of these nights.

Peering past the square, he scanned further. The house he and his new pack of lost souls inhabited sat at the west side of the square, facing due east, and the sun was now breaching the Nova building on Buckingham Palace Road, right in front of him. Randell had once sheltered himself in one of the plush penthouses in the Nova building shortly before the building's ground- and first-floor defences had been breached. It had been hard to tear himself away from a life of relative decadence— living a life in a place he could never have aspired to, or dreamed of—but even a fortress without its defences was just a building. And buildings were subject to attack from unwanted and unnatural forces. He knew he would have to find somewhere else, somewhere smaller, more adaptable. The next day Randell had vacated the extravagant-but-bland-looking building, reluctantly leaving behind the residents' cinema and fitness suite. Before leaving, and in daylight, he had thoroughly searched every room, finding nothing useful other than some tinned food and extra clothing. It was one building among thousands; he would keep moving on, keep searching. London was a huge city, but appeared tiny from where he currently stood. He knew perspective could easily be distorted.

Somewhere out there was his brother. *Where are you, bro?*

He shook his head as he saw an image of his brother being dragged away by several unruly fiends. *Fuckers*. Not wanting to relive the memory, he headed outside to re-attach any broken lines that ran out and along the perimeter of the house. Empty tin cans of all varieties, clustered together, hung from the line, acting as a primitive and early warning system for what he called 'approaching sucker-fucks'. Hatfuls of garlic cloves hung about the windows and doors, some of it stamped upon, crushed and mashed into the walls and floor. He hated it, its stink upon his nostrils, and disliked the mess it left behind, but in some respects it was good, it exuded a deeper aroma than a whole clove. It did, however, mean they used more and would soon need to forage for more of the pungent bulbous herbs.

"We'll need more garlic," he said, knowing Ulrica would still be watching from the front door. *More shit we've got to hunt for.*

"That's if we can find any," Ulrica said, clearly thinking along the same lines.

Randell nodded, happy the tin lines were set once more. It was only morning but he knew it would not be long before night fell again. At least he had done one job which meant less work to do later before they locked up. He turned back and wedged open the door, allowing the breeze to do its magic and clear the fusty inner air of the house. Ulrica let him by.

He looked down at Ulrica's arm once more as he passed. "I'll get the first-aid kit."

Inside, the others were milling around—their daily chores just beginning after a sleepless night—and opening up other windows, prying off timbers and stacking the wood close by. Because of their nocturnal existence breakfast had been moved on several hours—to lunch time. After the house had been aired, and the defences checked, the five occupants, including one with a freshly bandaged arm, her wound beneath cleaned and disinfected, all retired to their beds. That was after a quick external search of the immediate vicinity to despatch any hidden nightly-assailants who had been caught out and left behind by their so-called family, seeking refuge in a darkened corner.

It had not happened often but in the last two weeks they had found at least two of them, reeling in the recesses of a nearby doorway or stairwell. After several attempts at interrogating them, none of the things had revealed anything— they either did not want to tell them anything or genuinely did not know about his brother's whereabouts—Randell killed them swiftly, wondering why he had even bothered asking them in the first place. It was pointless, he knew, but necessary. Just in case. *Who knows, one day . . .*

Killing the things had become easy; he no longer saw the person they once were—the paint-daubed decorator, the suited solicitor, the cheated-on housewife or the cheating husband (or vice versa), the bus driver, the retail assistant in his gender-neutral polo shirt with logo, the lesbian barista from the local coffee shop, the hard-hatted builder, the transvestite who walked proudly down the street. All he saw was the infection: the lifeless eyes, the teeth, the hunger, the hate. He had learned the hard way though. A big movie buff, he had soon found out that they were wrong—a stake through the heart did not work, and dragging them kicking and screaming into the daylight did not seem to work either. It only rendered them stupefied, charring the skin and disabling them momentarily. That was often his window of opportunity as they scrambled about in disarray; sharpened sticks or stakes disabled them or, with enough force, impaled them, keeping them in one spot.

Lighter fluid and a trusty Zippo was all that was needed for the final part. And a bit of distance. No point starting a fire in your own lounge or hallway. Death and cremation came all at once. Although beheading always worked, it seemed too grisly for him to carry out. After all, he was not an animal just yet—not quite. The girls of the house, Seffi and Ulrica, would always disappear if that bit needed to be done, preferring to go and prepare some food or clean up, prep their weapons, check on or do anything so they did not have to witness it. Somewhat fortuitously, one of the other residents who lived with them, Ralph, was a veterinary surgeon—or had been before the world as they knew it had turned into a warzone between what they had since found out to be the so-called Mictlani and the Urbat—and he, too, treated a dead, toothed fiend with the same care and attention as one would a diseased and plague-ridden sewer rat, and put it down instantly.

Randell sent them all to their own private hell with the same thought: *One of you sucker-fucks must know something. Friggin' Mictlani scum.*

The large house had five bedrooms so there was more than enough space, a room each. Randell's room was on the second floor, a mattress lay on the bare timber flooring. Upstairs now, he kicked off his boots, crawled under a grey blanket, chucking his dirty socks aside, and immediately fell asleep, hoping his dreams would stay away just for a day. Any thoughts of his brother's whereabouts would have to wait until he had recharged.

On waking, Randell still felt tired but instantly sniffed the welcome smell of food cooking; the warm, strong odour flowing through the house. Something in his gut would help revive him. His stomach shouted up at him, letting him know it wanted filling. *Mmm. Smells good.* He dragged himself up, promising himself he would tidy his room soon, get rid of all the scrunched-up tissue that lay discarded around the mattress. He sniffed. He'd pick up some air freshener too.

Downstairs in the kitchen it was Seffi's turn to do the cooking. And she was doing a 'full English'. *Nice.* Up to her neck in frying pans, eggs and mushrooms were gently sizzling away while, under the grill, she was checking on sausages and bacon which were steadily browning and turning crisp. There was a loud, sharp ping as the microwave announced that whatever was inside was now hot and ready for consumption. Seffi popped open the door and pulled out a steaming bowl of baked beans.

"Hi Seffi." Feeling better as the smell enticed him, Randell announced his arrival into the kitchen. "Need me to do anything?"

"If you can put the plates out for me, I'll start dishing up." Seffi said as she turned a sausage.

Randell went to grab the crockery.

"You washed those hands of yours lately?" she added.

"Oops." He made his way to the sink and flipped on the tap, grabbed the sticky bar of soap. Turning the soap in his palms, the stench of coal tar was strong, he worked up a thin film before rinsing his hands thoroughly. He dried them on the tea-towel. Seffi glared at him and looked at the towel rail. "Oops. Sorry," he said.

Seffi sighed, waiting, there was hot bacon on her fork. "Throw it in the wash."

The plates clinked as he put them out along the worktop, doing as he was told. He touched the plates more than he needed to, fussing and fiddling until they were all lined up; it was his way of displaying to her his recently lathered and clean hands. He was reaching for a knife and waiting for her to tell him off for using the tea-towel and not the hand-towel when, to his left, there came a noise: a mechanical sound of red-hot springs in upward motion.

"Oh, can you butter the toast please," Seffi said, negotiating the eggs onto a spatula before dropping them onto the awaiting plates.

"Already on it," Randell answered, knife in hand, butter dish at the ready. He waved his hands in the space between them needlessly.

"Thanks sweetie." Seffi shook her head and walked to the door. "Come and get it."

She was doling out the cutlery as Ralph entered. A large stocky man in his mid-fifties, he was Seffi's partner, and had been for about the last ten years since he and Connor's mother had divorced.

"Thanks darling. Smells fab," he said, stretching over and kissing her cheek as she plopped his plate on the table.

"Using that rice bran oil you like. You know, the one with no cholesterol," Seffi said.

Ralph looked at Randell, his cheeks beginning to turn pink. "You mean, it's the one you like me to have."

Randell nodded at him, attempted to keep a straight face.

Seffi sighed. "Now, now, you eat too much red meat. What's wrong with taking care of oneself? You'll be thanking me one day."

Ralph sniffed at his plate again. "I'm already thanking you, my dear."

Ulrica came in next, towelling her hands dry. She threw the hand-towel on the side. Randell sighed.

"Hey," Seffi shrieked. "Don't put dirty towels where we prepare food."

"Yeah," Randall agreed.

Ulrica giggled morosely, then grabbed the towel and chucked it through the gap into the utility room.

Connor reached for it as he came through, wiping his hands on the towel for the sake of it, his hands still bone dry. Looking glum, he sat down.

Ralph watched his son sit, saying nothing but staring at the plates. Seffi looked over at Ralph.

Randell gave Connor a curt nod, one of simple acknowledgement.

"Hey," Ulrica said to Connor.

"Hey," Connor mumbled in return.

Seffi glared at them all. "Come on then you lot, eat up, it's getting cold."

In silence, slurps and burps aside, they ate.

Placing his knife and fork in the twelve-o'clock position in the centre of his now-empty plate, Ralph looked over at Randell and Ulrica. "You guys going to pick up some more supplies this afternoon?"

Randell nodded.

Connor watched them as his father, Ralph, the ex-animal doctor, nodded back.

"Can you get some more cleaning products this time, the place smells like a doghouse," Ralph said.

"Of course we will," Ulrica answered. "I need to get some girlie things anyway."

Randell gave her an obscure look. "Girlie things?"

"Never mind. Seffi knows what I mean."

"Yeah, might explain why they went for you with extra determination last night," Connor said, a pathetic grin on his face.

"Not last night, silly." Ulrica blushed. "It's . . . coming up," she said, her words hushed.

Ralph frowned at his son. "Connor, keep it clean, son."

Connor went quiet.

Seffi pointed to Ulrica's bandaged arm as she chewed her food.

The younger girl's face reddened. "Oh, it's just a superficial wound. Soon heal up."

Randell was already standing, his plate on its way to the sink. "Come on then slow coach, we've already wasted half the day. Won't be long before it gets dark again."

Ulrica jumped up, thanked Seffi for the breakfast and went about apologising for the day before's attempt which had quickly turned into a disaster. Heavily charred toast, not-far-off-pink bacon and congealed over-done beans stuck to the bottom of the pan. Ulrica knew her own cooking was not up to scratch, but she had tried so hard. At least everyone ate it and for that she was grateful. She walked up to Randell.

He already had his jacket on and was filling his pockets with small tins of accelerant and, knowing they always came in handy, he placed two knives in his back pocket. Finally he tested his lighter, sparking up a solid flame. *Good.*

Together, they headed for the door.

Shoving his hands into his pockets, Connor wandered away. "Thanks," he muttered.

Only Seffi replied. "You're welcome."

"Now, you two stay out of trouble," Ralph said. "Don't forget, we lock up just before sunset, so don't be late."

Randell nodded at Ralph, then looked down at Ulrica. He smiled.

She pulled a crucifix on a chain over her neck. "Right, let's go."

## Chapter 2

"Did you see that?" the man said for the third time.

The lad stared at him, mumbled something incoherent, then said, "It was pure luck"

The older man, looking pleased with himself, nodded. "Maybe, but would you have believed it if you hadn't seen it for yourself?"

"But it's a sword," the lad said, dryly. "It's supposed to do that."

"That's as maybe, but still."

The lad sat down on an old chair, the varnish peeling, flaking, having been left in direct sunlight for several months. "We should have killed them."

Ivan, the older one, the man with the sword who was doing all the bragging, looked across at his young protégé, Felix. What was wrong with the lad? "Are you stupid?"

Felix turned away, pretended not to hear.

Ivan stepped up to him, placed his hand on the young man's shoulder. His voice was quieter now, more settled, solemn. "Come on, Felix. How many times have I told you? It's our job to protect them." He felt the lad's body stiffen.

"But it's not our job," Felix answered, shrugging heavily. He pulled away and leaned forward, his elbows upon his thighs. "Well . . ." He looked up at Ivan. "I suppose. What else is there to do?"

"Good." Ivan said and patted the lad on the back. He turned and regarded his blade, stroking it gently like it was a tiny pet, a delicate kitten. "Anyway, seems she likes to be kept well oiled on the blood of those vermin."

"Here we go again." The lad kicked at the corner of a dusty rug. It revealed a dead mouse, its body crisp and sunken, almost mummified. The dust sparkled as it took to the air, a beam of sunlight shone through.

This time Ivan glared at Felix. "Watch your cheek, young man."

"I just think we should have killed them."

Felix was referring to the two humans they had saved last night, the man and his son being chased by the prowling vampire. Coincidence—or was it that they could simply smell them?—had found them passing closely by when they had heard the fearful and urgent shouts from the boy. As they had arrived on the scene they could see that the man had clearly given up, reciting his prayers like he was. How was that going to help him? They had ran towards the boy's pleas and found him hiding away in a shop doorway with his father about to be set upon by a lethally fast and rapacious Mitclani with only one simple desire. Like a professional Ivan had pulled out the *wakizashi*, his Japanese short-sword—he had taken it from a wall display in a private penthouse in Mayfair—and deftly removed the undead's head with a solitary but overtly accurate side swipe. They had then stayed with the pair they had saved from certain death by sharp teeth with their bodies rapidly leeched of blood, making sure they were safe for one more night at least. As morning approached, Ivan and Felix had said their farewells and headed for a safe hideout. Up all night they needed rest themselves and so they had found a quiet and out of the way basement.

That is where they were now.

The basement room was adequate enough; a little dusty, a feint odour of damp, but otherwise untouched and not too messy. There were two single beds, some four feet apart, and a small en-suite crammed into the rear left corner. In the opposite far corner was a tiny kitchenette and two wooden chairs, one already occupied by Felix.

Ivan pushed his bed up against the door after checking it was locked and sat up on the mattress. To the side of him, resting on soft cloth upon the Scandinavian-style bedside table, was his now treasured sword, safely tucked away in its scabbard or *saya*. He eyed his watch. The luminous face showed 8.24AM. They should be safe until dusk.

Felix got up and went over to look out through the tiny crack in the window. Thin slivers of sunlight cascaded through from the pavement and railings above. "I'm bored."

Ivan shook his head. He could barely ever remember being young, let alone being bored. To him, it all seemed like a lifetime ago, that it had happened to someone else who vaguely resembled him, someone whose only worries were to keep up with the mortgage payments and the bills, not someone who had to do what he and the lad had chosen to do since everything had changed. He realised the boy was restless but could do nothing for him.

"Please, get some sleep."

The lad's shoulders slumped. "I just want to go outside," Felix said.

Nodding, Ivan responded quietly, his tone that of a loud whisper. "I know, but you really need to get some rest. It could be another long night's hunting."

"But—"

"Listen, they're out there," Ivan pointed to the window, "without fail every night, searching, hunting, killing. We've managed to waste a few so far but they seem to be multiplying, and killing without thought."

"Yeah, that's because the Mitclani are basically vampires."

Ivan sighed. "Agreed, but if they used their brains they'd realise with every innocent life they take, they lose."

Felix frowned. He was tired. "What do you mean?"

Ivan thought for a moment as Felix trudged back to the chair. "Right, history lesson one-oh-one. Let's see. Back in the 1800s, don't quote me on that, in an attempt to defeat the Native Americans the American military decided to slaughter the buffalo. And slaughter them they did. It was bloody, heinous. You see, it was a major food source for the Native Americans and with millions of buffalo gone it left them with nothing to eat. The Americans knew that the enemy can't mobilise its troops if it can't feed them. Obviously, this was war, an unjust one at that, but can't you see, the vampires are doing the same to themselves, becoming their own worst enemy. By killing off their only food supply it means that one day, and that day is coming soon, there won't be any food left for them."

"So," Felix smiled, "you're analogy means that to defeat the Mitclani we kill their food source. I.e. the humans. Told you we should have waxed them."

Ivan nodded. "OK, bad analogy. But the fact remains that once the food supply is gone and, yes, I mean the humans, what will they do then? They can't eat each other."

Felix shrugged. "They go pescetarian?"

"Come on, don't be a jackass." Ivan turned to check the door again.

"Do you think they'll turn their full might on the Urbat, the wolves?" Felix asked, more serious now.

"Good question, Felix. That may very well happen but they can't drink Urbat blood, anything wolf is real bad for vampires."

"So, they run around for a bit and then just die of starvation?"

Ivan shook his head. "Think about what you've just said."

Felix turned away. "All right, then *we* kill all the vampires."

"Can't do that either, there's way too many of them. Anyhow, there's safety in numbers."

"True."

Picking up his short-sword, Ivan regarded it again, fascinated. "Look, I don't agree with what Man does in this godforsaken cesspit of a world, but I can't let humans go by way of the dodo either."

A perplexed look upon his face, Felix said, "Ain't a dodo a big fat pigeon or something?"

"Something like that. But seriously, the way things are going Man will be extinct soon enough, but just not yet, eh?"

"So what do you suggest?"

It was the question Ivan was waiting for. "That's easy. The Mitclani, the vampires, whatever you want to call them, they need to petition the humans, reach an agreement, accept one another and live side by side."

"In harmony?" Felix chuckled.

"No, not exactly, but enough to allow both sides to exist together, somehow. Maybe find a way to harvest blood. Legally, morally. And sensibly. It could be done. Let's face it, the hospitals are empty and they do have all the equipment necessary."

Felix wanted to argue the point. "Humans call themselves innocents, they cry woe is me all the time but they just want to kill vampires themselves. Hypocrites; Man and the Mitclani will never see eye to eye."

"They might if the Urbat have anything to do with it."

Felix nodded. "Maybe. But then we'll have to deal to them, too."

Ivan nodded slowly. "Yes . . . and no. They are already sympathetic to the humans. They should be easy enough to persuade, animals that they are."

Partially freeing his pre-owned *wakizashi* from its *saya*, Ivan studied the sharpened edge of the blade. He re-sheathed it and laid it down beside him, within easy reach, then lack back on the bed.

"Listen, we need to rest when they do. It's not as if we have a choice."

# Chapter 3

The rear of the house at Victoria Square ran onto Beeston Place, a one-way street which began at the south side of Buckingham Palace Garden and opposite the Royal Mews.

Ignoring the palace and its grounds—it had long been ransacked with no food or drink left, survivors living like kings and queens shortly before death had found them—Randell and Ulrica headed west. They passed the Goring Hotel, famous for its long-serving Royal connections—it was once the favourite hotel of the Queen Mother; a nearby bar with expensive hard liquor and a full top shelf, it was a place to hide for a few convenient hours. The flags outside were shredded and bedraggled, hanging flaccidly in the breeze. The year was 2023 and Randell did not really have a clue who the Queen Mother was, although Ulrica thought she had some idea, saying she had seen her on social media once. Or maybe it was some documentary or show on TV.

"Wasn't she a bit like Mother Teresa?" Ulrica asked.

Randell grunted, not really listening. "Who's that?"

Realising she couldn't quite remember, and feeling a little embarrassed, she shrugged. "Oh crap, never mind."

Randell scanned the road and its buildings, its doorways and windows. "Whatever. Keep your eyes peeled." He kept checking behind every now and then as they walked.

All five of them in the house had, at one point and by pure coincidence, the notion to stay at the Goring, to live for free in opulent surroundings. But the big hotel was far too open, and was quite impossible to barricade. Seventy-one rooms meant that at any one time more than ninety percent of the rooms at night could have been occupied by Mitclani. The only safe way of enjoying a night at the hotel was for all of them to share the same room. Even then it was way too risky. It did not help the ambience that, in the early days of what had become known as the Cacodaemonic Cataclysm—before the Urbat had time to gather their packs and force the Mictlani vampire hordes into hiding thus temporarily halting them—an entire wedding party had been butchered one dark celebratory evening by the Mictlani, the ruptured and bloodied bodies of those killed for food and not turned still decaying right where they had fallen.

"How was your brekkie?" Ulrica said as they walked, trying to inject some light-hearted conversation as they walked. It saved having to always think about their reality: the last of the survivors in London, perhaps the UK.

"Good." Randell continued scanning their surroundings.

"Mine was good too," Ulrica added, nodding. "Seffi's a good cook."

"Yeah. Ralph's a lucky guy. Except, what is it with Connor?"

Ulrica thumped his arm. "Hey, he's not that bad."

"OK. Whatever you say." He walked away, over-exaggerating his actions, frantically rubbing at where the small girl had tapped him.

She frowned, knowing it would probably take a bus to drive into him to actually cause him pain.

They turned right, going up what looked to be like a greener version of a war-torn Middle Eastern city. The streets were empty of people. Grosvenor Gardens was silent, deserted. Pushbikes and scooters lay in the middle of the road, discarded like large lumps of waste paper. A car, corroded and battered, sat at a forty-five degree angle to the road, its front end smashed into a roadside lamppost. Litter blew carefree down the street, a bright yellow M turning into a W before swiftly becoming an M again as it tumbled along. Dark patches of blackened blood quilted the street, the odd dead body scattered here and there, lacerated and maimed, lying beside the remnants of its drained life juices. Redder yet, bloodstains graffitied the walls in what seemed random yet deliberate splashes. The two ignored it all as they went by; they had seen the same thing for some time by now. Other than a few more vehicles, one a black taxi cab, and a few limbs dotted about, the scene was the same on Upper Belgrave Street.

"Crapping hell. Do you think, like, everyone is dead?"

"No, they can't be. There must be other survivors; we can't be the only ones left. No." Randell did not like to think of everyone being dead because that included his brother. He knew his parents had more than likely been killed in the first wave of attacks on humans; they were old, slower and weaker, but his brother, Sullivan, he was young and strong, cunning.

Not that the humans actually had any idea, but the war of *Eengurra* was a centuries-old battle between the Mictlani—ancient vampires, born to kill and feed on the blood of humans, and the Urbat—upright lycanthropes who lived honourably by a moral and martial code. During the full moon it was traditional for the Urbat to lock themselves away, in order to spare human lives. Now and again accidents would happen, particularly if a lackadaisical Urbat, in a crazed moonlit rampage, escaped its monthly incarceration and went on a killing spree. Individual Urbat who were caught deliberately flouting the ancient laws, purely on the grounds that they felt they wanted to exercise their right to go a-hunting, were severely punished, some being executed for crimes against humanity. The Urbat believed it to be their duty to protect the weaker life-form. Humans had no chance against their strength, their claws, their jaws. After all, what was a brown cardigan-cladded university professor going to do when surrounded by a group of murderous, large-toothed leeches on legs after a night out at the library? Lecture them until dawn? The Urbat leaders were true warriors, lethal and efficient; they fought in packs (as wolves do) but with the deadly accuracy and discipline of the Roman centurions of old.

In recent years the conflict had intensified to such a scale that it had finally spilled out onto the streets of everyday human life. Thousands died, caught in the crossfire of this, the Underworld's latest battle, before the police force and army even had a chance to be called in. Even with the latest technological and their expensive weapons many soldiers died too, promptly, uniformly, by teeth and claw. Just when the Mictlani were becoming desperate, were visibly losing the battle against the Urbat, the human armies had stepped in, thinking the

Urbat the main enemy and fighting on the side of the Mitclani; the idea to first get rid of the greater foe before turning on the other. However, it only served as a major disruption which, while adding to the chaos, had actually aided the Mictlani and confusing their sworn enemy. The Urbat had soon found themselves fleeing, attacked by the very people they were trying to protect. Hirsute caretakers of human life—there one minute fighting the Mitclani, the next chased off by tanks and missiles. It left the humans easy targets. To the merciless Mitclani. Until then humans had lived in ignorance, their attention glued to their mobile phones and reality TV shows; before all this there had only been terrible stories, gruesome fables, fireside tales, horrific myths of all shapes and sizes. None of it had been real.

Now, months down the line, the country, and quite possibly the world, was barren and depleted of nearly all human life, the mobile phone zombies having sent their final Snapchat or Facebook posts. Insta-death.

Randell thought of his brother. There was still a chance he was alive, there must be, he could almost sense it. And how could Ulrica just blurt out a statement like that: is everyone dead? Did she not realise it meant her mother may also be dead? After all, hadn't her mother, as well as Sullivan, been taken by the Mitclani too? He tried not to think about it.

Ulrica looked up at him, seeing him brooding. "Oh crap. Me and my big mouth."

He stopped and looked down at her. "It's OK, but . . . What about your mom?" he asked.

Ulrica's whole body stiffened as her shoulders collapsed and her face went blank, her eyes darting about.  Her hands fidgeted wildly; she began pulling each finger in turn until it cracked or popped at the joint. "Erm . . . She . . ."

Like a big brother Randell put his enormous arm around her and squeezed her gently. "Sorry."

The sibling-like squeeze did the job, she was lucid again. "Hey, hands off the merchandise," she yelled.

"Listen, we'll find her. One way or another."

"We'll find them both," she said. She smiled up at him.

She leant her head against him as they continued into Belgrave Square Garden, passing the statue of Simon Bolívar, the base of which was steadily becoming encapsulated by a thicket of weeds and wildflowers that had taken root in the cracks of the flagstones.

"Hang on a minute," Randell said, suddenly dashing off towards the Vetruvian Man statue. "What was it Leonardo da Vinci said? The root of the penis is at half the height of a man."

Ulrica wandered what the hell he was going on about until she heard a loud zipping noise as Randell unzipped his fly and began peeing up the corner of the plinth.

"No peeking now," he said.

She tutted and giggled, watching his back, as he overtly shook himself for a few seconds. "Men," she said.

He looked down at the rising steam of his piss. "That's mine now." He laughed and turned back to her.

Ulrica looked at him. "How come a builder knows stuff like that?"

"Stuff like what? Pissing? "

"No, you idiot. Leonardo da Vinci stuff. "

Big shoulders shrugged and he smirked. "Like you. TV."

As he went to walk on, a loud clanging noise came from one of the Embassy buildings over the road. He sighed, looked at Ulrica and put his forefinger in front of his lips. Ulrica had already gone quiet and was looking about, making sure there were escape routes if need be. Serious now, Randell slipped a knife from his back pocket. Some time ago he had tried using a crossbow—a Barnett Vengeance, courtesy of Woody's of Wembley—after watching too many films, but soon realised it was not for him. It was all good aiming at a target for fun or if you had time and distance on your side, but during a frenetic attack found it was rendered useless.

Knife in hand, he walked forward. "Come on. And stay close."

Like an obedient puppy, Ulrica followed. "I intend to."

Along with shopping (it was more like selecting and taking what you wanted than shopping because the shops were always open, and there were no proprietors) it was their job to locate any vampire nests during the hours of daylight and, as long as it was deemed safe, to exterminate any of the Mictlani inhabitants that they found there.

Fairly sure they were headed in the right direction of where the noise had emanated they came up to the front door of the Serbian Embassy, the only one with all its curtains drawn. A dead give-away. With his boot Randell pushed at the brass foot-plate of the big black door. A minuscule squeak of hinges filled the silence. He stepped in as Ulrica readied her sharpened stakes, one in each hand.

She looked at her bandaged arm. "This'll be payback," she whispered.

Inside was dark. "Leave the door open as wide as poss," he whispered back.

In seconds the two had scoured the ground floor rooms, the gentle pitter-patter of footsteps moving swiftly beneath elevated breathing patterns their only sound. With his knives at the ready Randell nodded towards the stairs, and then ascended. The small landing at the top led to another flight of stairs and several rooms, each door closed and latched. In the semi-darkness Randell looked at Ulrica.

"Be ready," he mouthed silently.

She nodded, her eyes set, lips taught.

Randell tried the first door. The handle let out a high-pitched squeal as he eased down the latch. *Shit.* The door swung inwards. No sooner was it open enough for a small body to pass through, Ulrica was gone. Into the room. She entered faster than a Jack Russell terrier that had slipped its leash, off in chase of some vermin or game, determined and wild. In seconds she had traversed the room and reached the curtains, snatching them away from their fixings and dragging them down. They tumbled to the floor in a heap, the darkened room now lit up in an instant. She spun around automatically to keep the daylight from blinding her partially-accustomed vision.

Nothing.

Just an empty room and a great big lug looking like an apprentice commando at the doorway. She blew out a sigh, her cheeks expanding. Randell nodded at her and tipped his head towards the next room. As before, as one, they moved. Same procedure, different door.

One after the other, they swept through the rooms, each one proving empty.

At the next door Randell rested his fingers on the brass handle, ready to go again. He looked at his sister-in-arms again. "You good?" he whispered.

The door exploded inward, leaving its hinges and crashing to the floor. Before he had even registered what had happened, his hand still poised to open the handle, something came at his neck. *For* his neck. He couldn't tell if it was male or female, but it was definitely Mitclani. And hungry. Teeth bared, the thing was snapping like an giant airborne piranha. The knife left his hand, clanging to the floor. *Fuck.*

Ulrica reacted quickly, and drove one of her shortened stakes into the thing's back as it clawed for purchase on Randell's bulk.

"Watch your own back," Randell screamed as he grabbed the vampire and brought it down to the floor in one almighty throw. A crack accompanied the expected heavy thud.

Just as he spoke, another son of Mictlani jumped out and came at Ulrica. She tripped and fell onto the other vampire that Randell had floored. She could only watch as Randell stamped down hard, narrowly missing her but caving the thing's head in with his boot. Beneath her the body writhed and twitched frantically.

Seemingly ignoring the big guy, the still-live (or still-undead) vampire came at her again and now there were three writhing bodies on the floor. She screamed, pushing the thing away, aware that she could smell its awful breath—or excuse for breath.

Randell scrambled and reclaimed the knife. He raised it, ready to drive it down. It was no good; Ulrica was in the middle of it all. He pocketed his weapon quickly and grabbed the rear of the attacking vampire before its teeth reached Ulrica's softer flesh.

He lifted it and swung the toothy-bastard towards the top of the stairs and let go. The vampire let out a strange gurgle as it careened down the steps, bouncing and tumbling, bones snapping as it went. Randell reached down a second time and hauled Ulrica up. Like a rag doll her body responded to his brute strength and in seconds she was standing again. Randell was stronger than he had thought, his fears of losing his strength unfounded.

"You bitten?"

She shook her head, panting wildly.

For such a big man Randell moved quicker this time. He took the stairs three at a time, following the vampire as it descended. At the bottom the vampire attempted to right itself, ready for another attack, but was unable to stand. Not thinking, and not even giving it a chance to see if it could walk atop busted shin bones, Randell punched it hard in the solar plexus, a grievous body blow. The Mitclani's body lifted and reeled backwards down the hall and into the doorway. As it hit daylight, the vampire's skin began to bubble and blacken. The strange gurgle returned, this time turning into frantic screams.

By now Ulrica was downstairs, had straightened herself, and was ready to go again. She kicked the creature in its midriff as it singed, its burning flesh tainting the air. Randell stepped forward and sprayed the lighter fluid in its face, then brought the Zippo into the game. The vampire's upper body and head erupted into flames. Again, it tried standing before its face distorted into a shriek from which came no sound, then, as the broken bones gave way, it tumbled backwards, the fire burning steadily. The stench of flesh slowly incinerating made them retch.

"Any more?" she asked.

Randell shook his head. "Don't think so. They'd be here by now if there were."

"Let's get out of here."

Regaining their breath and strength after the fight they stopped outside Mosimann's on West Halkin Street. Randell remembered seeing lots of smartly attired men in suits and beautifully women in fabulous dresses entering the old Scottish Presbyterian church which had been fancifully converted into an exclusive dining experience for the upper echelons of London society. Now, the doors to the club flapped in the breeze, the place bereft of its classy clientele and gastronomic delights.

"Where to?" he asked Ulrica, checking again that she was all right.

"Only one place for it. Follow me."

Each and every time he entered it, Harrods seemed to get bigger and bigger. It was big anyway but even more so when devoid of any customers. Other than the two of them. But they were not really customers in the true sense of the word because they were not paying; only taking.

"We stick together," Randell said as they entered from Basil Street.

"Yeah but I don't want you watching me when I get my stuff."

"No? Then be quick about it. We haven't got all day."

"Yes, master."

He let her have some space but made sure she never left his sight as she bagged up whatever it was she needed. He thought again of his brother, of the two they had just killed, how it had snapped at them. Is that what the fuckers had done to Sullivan?

With Ulrica's bit done Randell headed over to the food section and found an old lady's shopping trolley, polka-dot-red with a bright red handle. Ignoring Ulrica's strange looks, he filled it with some jams and preserves, some oil and seasonings. He was careful to choose some red wine—a reserve with what he thought was the best designed label—and a nice bottle of Johnny Walker for Seffi and Ralph respectively. Finally, he hauled one of the hampers into the trolley. A glimpse inside revealed tins of biscuits, cakes, cheese things and other brightly packaged foodstuff.

"We'll have to get some real food on the way back. This stuff's way too fancy for me."

Brompton Road had a supermarket; it was a Sainsbury's local. It was practically right next door to a little Waitrose so they had more than enough choice. It was one of the few shops they had entered over the weeks that appeared untouched by raiders. It was almost as if the staff had all simply stopped, turned around and walked out, leaving the tills and the lights on. Randell and Ulrica decided they would leave it until they had exhausted all the other surrounding shops. No one was going to beat them to it. And if they were, at least it would serve as an early warning signal that there were others in the area. Other survivors.

"Fill yer boots," Ulrica said as they entered beneath the dark grey banner with the words: Open every day 7am - Midnight. She spotted a pristine mobile phone upon the counter. It was a top-of-the-range model. "Always wanted one of these."

"No network so you can forget it."

She examined it. "Amazing, it looks so new."

Randell repeated himself. "No network." His voice was more high-pitched this time.

"I'll keep it for the camera." She shoved it in her back pocket.

Further inside, the store was worse than untidy (so much for untouched), its Unique Selling Point long since forgotten; half-empty shelves, rotten produce, smashed and spilt glass jars of pickles and tins scattered about the floor. Taking their time to read the best before dates (as if that mattered, food was food, they would wolf down anything as long as it did not smell too bad) they filled some bags with what Randell and Ulrica deemed 'real food', careful not to take too much—they could only carry so much and could always come back the following day. And the day after that, until the store was completely bare. Randell decided he might want to pick up an extra speaker for his room back at the house, one of those Beosound 2 wireless jobs, from B&O further up the road so he needed an excuse to return. He could always grab a bag of coffee beans from the Starbucks behind for Ralph, too.

He turned to the girl. "Right, we got enough?"

Ulrica nodded.

Heading back they took a different route, walking along Pont Street where they passed a line of large old trees, the foliage green and bright. They crossed Sloane Street and headed through Cadogan Place, the overgrown grass revealing the local council's lack of attendance, the park patiently waiting another child or a dog to pass through, all laughs and barks, and end the silence.

Soon they entered Eaton Square and continued checking for enshrouded windows and blockaded doors as they went, ignoring discarded pushbikes, prams and black cab, and any passengers that were slowly but progressively turning to dust on the back seats.

As they slipped into Beeston Place, heading once more towards The Goring Hotel, they did not notice two pairs of undead eyes watching them from the safe confines of a once-grand and darkened house near the junction on Grosvenor Gardens.

## Chapter 4

Steady in their hideout, the two pairs of undead eyes—those once belonging to a man and a woman—continued to watch the pair of walkers, a large young man with a mane of dark hair and a smaller possibly younger girl, from their temporary den on Grosvenor Gardens until they disappeared from view.

Near silence followed, no breathing, no pounding heartbeats; faint noises of clothing ruffling gently across fibrous muscles as bodies moved below them the only sound.

The man spoke first.

"Looks like today could be our lucky day." Serkan's deep voice belied his delicate body. He was slender, bordering on scraggy, as though protein had deliberately been omitted from his diet as he grew into a man. He had what can only be described as an ordinary face, plain with stark white sallow skin, short stubble upon his chin, the hair on his head full with a natural wave, dark but interspersed with white flecks; a man in his early thirties when he was turned, greying too soon. He leaned forward, too far, risking being burned by the sun's cauterising effect; he was lucky not to be seen from the blackened doorway. Brass nameplates to his right twinkled as the lowering sun caught them, causing him to squint. It was losing its heat but still posed a threat to them. It wouldn't be long before they could venture out unheeded.

"Mind you don't lean too far forward. We don't want your pretty face to burn," Hemma, the woman, scoffed.

Serkan ignored her, kept eyeing the corner where the pair had gone.

Annoyed at being given the silent treatment, Hemma raised her voice. "Tell me, what is it that's caught your eye?"

Disturbed from his reverie, Serkan uttered something incoherent. He turned and glared at her, his dark eyes narrowed, his face fixed. "What?"

The look startled her. "What is it?" she said.

Serkan stood and faced her allowing his face to relax a little. He regarded her for a moment, wanting to keep the words to himself, to martyr them almost, as if by telling Hemma the pain would go away. He could see the pair of walkers still, turning the corner, over and over, in his mind's eye. "Nothing now, but only a moment ago I witnessed the smug little bastard who killed my beautiful Agana."

Hemma's eyes widened. "Are you sure?"

"Of course I am sure, walking by as if taking an early evening stroll, as if nothing is on his mind. With a young lady friend no less. While my Agana is no more."

Hemma, Serkan's number two since the death of his lost lover Agana, frowned. "How can you be sure it is him?"

His face straight, he showed no emotion. "Well, if it isn't then I've just found us dinner for later." He went back to brooding, imagining himself watching the large man and smaller girl go on by, over and over, only to see them leave the vicinity in the safety of daylight. And still breathing.

She watched him closely. "Pining over her won't bring her back," Hemma said.

Rage filled him. Turning rapidly Serkan grabbed for her throat. She squirmed under his grip. He squeezed and shoved his face close to hers. "No, but killing him might bring me . . . Something. Closure perhaps."

Hemma's eyes showed little distress as she peered into the angry face of the speckle-haired vampire, her leader. She was unfazed at the throat grabbing. He could squeeze all he liked; it was never going to finish her. How could it?

He loosened his hold on her, allowing her a retort; he knew it would come regardless.

Eyeing him defiantly, she addressed him calmly. "If you say so."

His jaw crunched as he ground his teeth together firmly. He huffed, letting her go—his body language that of a runner with his feet in the blocks—wanting so much to just head out into the light and follow the pair down Beeston Place, to see exactly where they were going instead of just envisaging, imagining, filling in the blanks. No matter, he knew he would soon sniff them out once the darkness allowed.

"They're animals," he said, retreating back into the shadows.

"And we're not?" Hemma mused while she rubbed at her throat, straightening her attire.

He knew she would be goading him after his assault. "You know what I mean."

She thought about that. Throughout time, humans had shown their idiocy repeatedly, had acted as animals, raping, killing, fighting, taking up arms. She had been human herself not too long ago, but could recall little if anything of her former life. "Hmm. Quite. So, who is the girl with him?"

Serkan, uncaring, simply said, "I do not know."

"Well, while you're killing him perhaps you can let me have the girl."

"Whatever tickles your fancy." He grinned at her.

*There. That's better.* She rolled her eyes. "Oh, young blood, it's the best. Not tainted with age or prescription meds. I'm sure you've tasted blood tainted by analgesics, those cholesterol lowering thingies or blood-thinning drugs. It's like sour wine."

"Rat poison. Surprised we don't bleed out."

"Wouldn't matter if we did, now would it?" she said. She was referring to the last thing she could clearly remember, the time she was taken from her family and her daughter.

She had been ready to leave her abusive husband after years of struggling with her marriage, so when Serkan had killed him it had saved her a messy job—or at least had saved her the cost of a drawn-out divorce. However, when Serkan had then gone after her daughter, Hemma had gone berserk, coming at the vampire with such vehemence that he had fought hard with the crazed mother, only to let the daughter slip away unnoticed into the night, to stay in the land of the humans. Instantly admiring the mother's mettle Serkan had decided to turn her instead of killing her and leaving her cadaver to rot on the kitchen lino. That meant bleeding her out to a particular state, ensuring enough Mitclani venom entered her system to make the body's necessary changes from human to vampire. It was an agonising experience but then the pay-off was great— immortality, as long as one was happy to stay in the dark and give up sunlight. Shades, heavy makeup and thick clothing with a good hat or helmet helped but it limited a vampire's movements, got in the way of a clean kill. It was always best to wait until dark. Yes, Mitclani ruled the night.

That had been almost a year ago—she had only known Agana for a few weeks—so she found it difficult to feel any real sympathy for Serkan. Agana had been a night stalker for centuries apparently, high up in the Mitclani line, and had experienced things Hemma could only dream about; they were on totally different wave-lengths, from dissimilar backgrounds, so it was hard to even empathise with her death.

Agana had been known for her hot-headed arrogance and an apathy that often got in her way, clouded her mind, and because of that (and her hubris) she had been caught, and her heart had been aggressively punctured and pulped by something large and gravely sharp. A vampire's death was nothing if not brutal. Enough said.

After her death Serkan had gone mad. Brainsick and unhinged he had ended up killing two of his own kind; the two lieutenants who had been serving alongside Agana had abandoned their duties and had let her enter an unknown and secure house on her own. Serkan blamed the two lieutenants directly because they should have swept the area first, declared it clear, even though he knew Agana was an elder, their superior, and had most likely dismissed her subordinates in her arrogance before charging the citadel as it were, and meeting her end.

Even so, and for a long time, he wondered why she had entered before them, and on her own. It was only because of his position and standing—that, and his unbalanced mind at the time of the misdemeanour which declared him temporarily insane—which had saved him being put to death after he was hauled up in front of the elder judges, the *Amiqui Ixmati*; the normal sentence of being hurled straight up into the daylight by an ancient ballista only to land upon a bed of tightly-packed spears, or *tepoztopilli*, to finish you off. That is if there was anything left once the sun had done its thing.

"We go tonight," Serkan said.

"Should we not wait, regroup, send for support?"

"No. The sooner he is dead, the better."

"You know, we could turn him; he would be an asset against the Tecuani."

The Mitclani had their own name for the Urbat, a name from their own language. Tecuani meant Wild Beast. Of course, they were aware that the Urbat did the same. Centuries ago the Mitclani had been given the moniker of Summa Nura, or Deprived of Light. It didn't sound as derogatory as Wild Beast but when one considered that over the ages many tribes and peoples have revered the light, had taken it as a sign of purity, of beauty, that the sun lit their way, warmed them and boosted their crops, then, all those years ago, it had been a most grievous, almost blasphemous and disparaging word. Hurtful. Maligned.

To gain immortality as a vampire, one had to give up the light. It is the one thing that any Mitclani regrets, no matter how impetuous or angry they were, or how much they argued or protested that they did not care.

Nowadays it was mostly ignored (sticks and stones and all that) but back then Summa Nura, two simple words, had caused the war to endure. Tecuani on the other hand meant little to the Urbat. The name referred to the Dogs of Death, which they were, as they were, too, essentially, Wild Beasts. Perhaps it is their idea of ignorance or maybe they even liked the sobriquet but the fact remains thus: the genus *Canis* is generally more interested in food or sex and has little interest in words or name calling.

"No, I won't turn him." He glared at her. "I haven't seen any Tecuani around here lately, and I'm not offering him eternal life after bringing dear sweet Agana's to an end." He shook his head. "Not now. Not ever."

Hemma thought about his words. Earlier on Serkan had described his dead lover as 'beautiful' and Hemma knew she could never disagree with that; Agana was beauty personified, stunningly so, although what she ever saw in Serkan she would never know. But *dear sweet* Agana? *That's an oxymoron if ever there was one.*

She turned to him. "It would be better—"

Serkan cut her off, glowering at her, his eyes dead, detached, numb, showing no fear, only uncaring apathy, like those of a white shark. "No, tonight I will kill him."

# Chapter 5

Since Randell and Ulrica had left the house to go in search of supplies, Seffi and Ralph had left Connor to his own devices and gone about their own duties during the day.

Ralph knew the boy preferred it that way; however, it always left Seffi feeling bad, as though she had stolen his father from him. It meant an easy life for Ralph who knew it was often a somewhat strained relationship between his son and Seffi, mostly because of Connor's attitude. Especially since Seffi was not his mother. Seffi said and did all the right things, was always eager to accept Connor and include him, but the lad seemed to enjoy his own company. Seffi had resigned herself to the idea that time would bring him round. Only then would she be truly happy with Ralph and the situation.

They checked the house over outside, the doors and windows and roof—he and Randell had barred up the loft hatch on the first day of meeting up in the house—for any major damage. Minor damage just meant that they would have to keep a close eye on it, make a note, and then pick up supplies in order to repair or bolster the damage in the next day or two. Major damage meant a busy day for all. Today, after last night's assault, he house was sound. It was how they liked it. Good.

Back inside Ralph found Seffi had washed up and put away the crockery and all the cutlery, and she had wiped down the kitchen surfaces and generally tidied up. There was still the faint whiff of cooked bacon and baked-bean sauce. Ralph went up to her and placed his arms around her waist and kissed the back of her neck. She rested against him, a moment's warmth and peace.

"You all right?" he whispered to her.

She smiled, then realised he could not see her face. "Yes," she said. She turned, her yellow gloved hands wet, and attempted to clasp his ruddy face.

"Whoa, you can keep those away from me," he said, laughing, gently pulling away and avoiding the rubber gloves and tiny bubbles.

"Pity, you could do with a shower," she said, smirking.

"Really? What, you mean after a long night's graft protecting the house and then a morning's work checking everything over I don't smell as fresh as a daisy in a luscious green meadow?"

She sniffed at him. "Let's just say that there's nothing fresh about you, mister."

He raised his arms, allowing his armpits some air. "Thanks for your honesty, my little flower," he added.

"I would say you're more like a week-old withering lily." She laughed, fondly recalling the powerful stench of old lilies, a time when she used to get flowers, real flowers, and not just a bunch of snatched forget-me-nots from Ralph when he was feeling romantic. "Why don't you go have a shower and get the bed ready for when I come up?"

He smiled at her. "Yes, dear. Whatever you say, dear." He turned and headed for the shower. "You can put your wet paws away now."

"Go on, I'll be up in a bit, once I'm done down here."

Seffi turned back to her chores; she was good like that, house-proud, even in light of their situation. She did not want the men, or even herself and Ulrica, tripping over stuff in the house. She would find a place for it and put it away. Like a crafty spaniel hiding a bone she would always know where it was, as and when she needed it. Professionally Seffi was a psychiatrist, or had been in an earlier life. She specialised in adolescents, working with teenagers. In twenty-five years of practice she had treated and counselled many young men and women, helping them with things like body dysmorphia and eating disorders, gender issues, obsessive-compulsive disorders, mood disorders including that of bipolar and personality disorder. With society's problems seemingly worsening, and with medical funding dropping, Seffi had no idea that things could get any worse.

But they had, immeasurably so.

Once her brain had processed and accepted that vampires were indeed real, she soon realised that they also had a plethora of the same disorders that she had worked on daily with humans. For instance, she had seen how a Mitclani's mood could change on a sixpence. And what was drinking blood if it was not an eating disorder? And talk about OCD; they would not let anything go. Their vanity would not allow it. That was why she knew they would be back again tonight, and the night after, and that she would have to leave Ralph to get on with his duties, to ensure that the house was secure. She might fool around with him after catching up on some sleep before Randell and Ulrica got back; she would have to be absolutely certain that there would be no chance of Connor hearing them. That was not fair on the lad. Then again, she might just settle for a kiss and a cuddle; Ralph could tuck his urges away for the time being.

She realised that whatever happened the human race was still essentially doomed. It was not a crazy notion; she had a straight and clear mind. One only had to look at the people who had claimed power around the world: egotistical maniacs, the power hungry, the greedy, prejudiced and racist bigots. At one time the world had been a global village, then, almost at once, world leaders looked inwards. Hate crimes against those of a different race were perpetrated around the globe, presidents and prime ministers ignored the effects of capitalism and the words of scientists and naturalists, letting the world suffer. Temperatures were increasing year on year, water levels worldwide continued to rise. Because of that the body count had risen as environmental disasters left thousands dead. A tsunami here, an earthquake there, sinkholes swallowing up small parts of the neighbourhood; these were brushed aside in favour of making money. The rich becoming richer, the rest swept away or buried under rubble. But that did not matter to the rich, they knew better, surely? They had schooling, degrees from the best universities, intelligence beyond the simple masses. But no, greed blinded them, their egos massaged by wealth. They were untouchable, on top of the world. What could possibly happen?

But it did happen. The unthinkable—to them anyway, anyone with half a brain could see it coming a mile off—occurred just when they were counting a new pile of freshly printed bills. When those they had trodden on to get to the top had finally had enough, the lower classes and workers turned to the only place they could, and literally stormed the castles. In days the wealth-crazed rich were out on their ears, living on the streets, their material things taken, their bank accounts seized. And then this demented struggle for the Underworld had literally spilled out onto the streets. The once-rich-but-now-destitute with no place to go were some of the first to be bitten, either turned, left for dead, or placed on the menu with only their bones and gristle left. A turned politician was an extremely dangerous animal, whether vampire or wolf, the rapacity they had in human form only exacerbated by large teeth, hairy backs, or an aversion to the sunlight. And at that point, even if Seffi had been able to offer up her services instead of running for her life, they would never agree to psychotherapy or counselling, and six weeks of cognitive behavioural therapy would never be the answer.

In the meantime she hoped to bridge the ever-widening gap between Ralph and his son, Connor. She had little sway over either of them, she knew, but it did not stop her wanting to try. She thought of Connor, how he was, his apparent indolence. Was this because Ralph's chosen profession had frequently found him working long hours, often caring for a frightened or stricken animal into the late evening and weekends, and so had not been around to care for his son? Did Connor see work as a hindrance, something in the way of family, of relationships? That was all very well if the money is coming in; just where did Connor think his father acquired the means to support and raise him in such relative comfort? Did he feel neglected because of that, and now the gulf between them was simply too wide? She knew of Connor's sexuality issues; had spotted it instantly. She hoped he would talk to them when he was ready although she was not sure how Ralph would take it. It did not matter to her; she would be on hand to help both when the day came. She did have a distant idea that maybe Ralph or Connor was somewhere on the autistic scale and both found it difficult to engage. Or maybe Connor did not like that his father had found another love later on in his life and now she, Seffi, was in the way. It was always possible that he just did not like his dad, or her, or even the both of them. She felt sorry for them both, father and son. She knew Ralph could be impossible at times, pigheaded and stubborn—he was male, go figure—and that he was often quick to anger, having a short fuse, but he was also gentle, kind and caring. Then again, were we all not capable of that, even if only in some small way? Perhaps the son was too much like the father and it took opposites to attract. She sighed at the sound of someone banging at the door.

Because it was still light outside, a loud rattle at the door meant only one thing: Randell and Ulrica had returned. If it was them they were back much earlier than anticipated. And put paid to any frolicking she and Ralph had planned.

With Ralph upstairs and Seffi still tidying around it was Connor who let them in, reeling back the locks and steels and timbers that reinforced the front door.

Randell entered, no words exchanged.

Ulrica followed. "Hi Connor."

"Find anything?" Connor said after securing the door again.

"Food," Randell said.

"Yeah, more crappy tins of food," Ulrica said. "Suppose it makes dinner easier." She spied Seffi through the doorway. She was smiling. "For me anyway."

Connor regarded them both as they headed into the kitchen, dropping their bags onto the worktop with a clunk.

"Be careful," Seffi said.

"Why?" Randell said. "Worried the Joneses won't like it if it gets damaged?"

Seffi sighed. "No, it's good stuff is all, not too many repair men out there these days." She headed to check the state of the living room; she had heard Ralph come down earlier.

Seeing Seffi deflated Ulrica dug her elbow into Randell's side.

"Ouch." He looked down at her. "Watch it."

She beamed up at him. "Why, worried I'll do it again?"

He had been angry since waking up, and had been fired up since killing those sucker-fucks earlier. There had been no sign of his brother, no trace, nothing. He looked at Seffi as she lolloped away, realising he had been too blunt with her and had possibly hurt her feelings. None of this was her fault.

"I'm sorry," he said loudly, looking at Ulrica for approval.

"Don't tell me, tell her." Ulrica pointed towards the living room. "You can be like a snarly dog sometimes."

"It's because . . . Sullivan." It was his turn now for shoulders to give in to gravity.

"I know, but we're in the same boat. Don't be like that with Seffi," Ulrica added.

"Yeah, you're right." He placed his hand on her shoulder and squeezed gently.

"Ouch," she squealed

Randell stepped back. "Sorry, forgot you bruise easier than me. Are you OK?"

"It's all good," Connor answered, butting in, leaving Ulrica rubbing at her arm, both hands deep in his pockets. "Dad's in there with Seffi and I'm rummaging around the house on my own, bored." He had no idea that Ralph was upstairs.

Randell had nothing against Connor, not really, but it just seemed he could not to relate to him, so he did the gentlemanly thing and put up with him being around. He was Ralph's son but unlike his mostly-affable father there was just something about Connor that did not sit right with Randell. It was not his arrogance, it was deeper than that. Connor was self-important for all the wrong reasons. Before the world had turned upside-down he would only land a job because of someone he knew, not because he had any particular skills. Admittedly, the lad had done some study but only after being left a considerable inheritance from Ralph's oldest brother who had died after a long career in Whitehall and who had no children of his own. Apparently Ralph had tried guiding his son with such money but Connor insisted on going out and buying designer-named clothing and accessories. Even fakes were passed off as the real thing. He was the kind of person who name-dropped at the right social gatherings, made out he knew certain people who, for all intents and purposes just weren't nice, some of them criminals. And not only that, he revered them, as if knowing someone of such standing elevated him to some kind of super-stardom. They all knew, could see it, that Seffi was his step-mum, and because of that Connor only suffered her; it didn't help when Ralph took her side each and every time an argument or disagreement occurred. Connor resented her for that. She had taken away any favour his father felt for him.

To top it all he could be pretentious, vain, and considered himself precious; Randell had not seen Connor leave the house in a while. Was he too good when it came to scavenging for food or killing vampires? Or did it mean he might get his hands dirty?

"Great, go and be bored somewhere else then," Randell said, going off to find Seffi.

Being alone, her mum gone, Ulrica needed as many people around her as possible and she felt no animosity to Connor. Yes, he came across a little lazy but she had seen how wiry and strong his body was after accidentally walking in on him while he showered one day. So it wasn't because he was weak, it was something else. Her instincts told her that Connor did not hate Seffi, nobody in their right mind could, so there was good in him, she just knew it. Was he rebelling? Was it just a father/son relationship? Just what was going on with him?

Connor was alone in the basement of the house.

The basement was the lower-ground living area in its own right and accessible from the outside front of the building via a small gate and some steep stone steps. Or used to be. The door had since been blockaded thoroughly from inside and out, with the steep steps outside filled with heavy junk; two industrial sized washing machines and a large American double fridge-freezer blocked the way. They had thought about leaving the truck that they had used to 'deliver' the white goods in place, or drive it up and over the basement entry aperture, to leave it virtually sitting atop the stone steps to really hinder access. The idea was that Randell and Ralph would then take a knife to the tyres and most of the engine's hoses and cables so it could not be moved. It sounded a good idea but meant that there would be a great deal of work to move if again if need be. And, more than that, it hindered the general view of the square from the house. The view was important, they needed to see who—or what, and how many—was approaching the house at any given time.

The house had been designed, at some point in its history, with internal access to the basement rooms. In recent years this had been cleverly covered up, decorated as though nothing had ever been there, the area on the ground floor now used for extra living space. Taking it upon himself, Connor had opened up the internal access, giving himself some much-needed privacy.

No one but himself ever came down. He was not so stupid as to realise that nobody in the house really cared much for him. Randell and Ulrica had come into their circle some time ago—one at a time they had found others of their own kind, seeking safe digs, and had been invited to stay—disturbing the already disturbed family unit. Since finding Seffi, Ralph had all but turned his back on his son and no matter what Connor did to revive his father's feelings for him, nothing seemed to work. All he ever heard about was how wonderful Ralph's other friends or acquaintances were; how they had done something, whatever that 'thing' may be, far better than him. It did not appear to matter to his father that he was trying his best; had taken himself off to Nottingham on a foundation course studying biology and chemistry after realising the A levels he had passed were not going to help him much. The year away had probably been bliss for his father and Seffi. Upon completing his course, the fight between the Mitclani and the Urbat had changed life for good and put paid to his and anybody's job progression.

Survival was the career of choice these days.

The first room was a kitchen-diner, kitsch—he actually liked its garishness, the strident colours—with enough space for a 3-seater sofa that was highly-stylised and finished in deep purple (the kind of colour which would show up any dog or cat hairs immediately and present the owner with a constant battle of hair removal) on which he often found himself spread out on. The second room was a living area-cum-bedroom with its own en-suite. This second room he kept locked, the only key out of sight, below his clothes around his neck like a collar.

He had spent most of the day in there while Ralph and Seffi had been caught up double-checking the house's defences and while Randell and Ulrica were out gathering supplies. The evening was now fast approaching and he decided to catch up on some sleep before the night's trouble began again.

He stared at the locked door before curling up on his sofa and closing his eyes. As long as he survived the night, he would venture in there again tomorrow.

## Chapter 6

Footsteps behind him made him turn rapidly.

Reflexes honed, the Japanese sword stopped inches from Felix's neck. "You bloody fool. Don't sneak up on me like that. Announce yourself first. Shit."

Felix eyed the sharp end of Ivan's lethal blade, the wrong end to be staring down at. He shrugged, knowing Ivan really knew it had been him and was just being showy. This little snippet of knowledge saved him otherwise he would currently be a staggering corpse, nerves kicking about instinctively, blindly searching for a lost and vitally important body part. Even in the semi-dark of dusk he noticed Ivan looked perplexed, sad as he lowered the steel.

They were in the zoo at Regent's Park. The buildings had been left as they were; only the on-site shops and cafes had been ransacked. Ivan stood with his head down. Behind them the display and picnic lawns were a mass of weeds and wildflowers. To their right, the long thin snout of an aardvark peaked up from an emaciated mass of grey-brown. One look into the pens revealed decay, abandonment.

"What's up?" Felix asked.

Carefully sheathing his *wakizashi* Ivan stared down at the lion's cadaver. The lion was male, its mane limp and dry, the skin of the skull receding heavily, the eyes long since pecked out, gone for crow food. The body was flat, myriad maggots and bacteria having done their obligatory duty, rib bones sticking into the air as if unhappy to lie down and accept their fate.

The stricken animal had not been attacked and killed by Mitclani, Urbat or human; it had simply been neglected along with all the others. Starvation was an age-old affliction that never ended well. Ivan found it hard to believe that people of power from the past could often sit by and watch people starve, let alone animals. With the London Zoo's staff either dead or turned there had been nobody left to feed the animals. The Land of the Lions had been a remarkable achievement for those involved; the high street of India's Gir National Park, Sasan Gir village, replicated for an authentic-but-hybridised India-London feel. Apparently it helped make the lions feel at home. Ivan wondered if the actual lions at 'home', those still roaming wild throughout Africa, had all met the same fate, the outbreak affecting the whole world. There was a chance that the natural food chain was still intact in more remote areas but with a population of over 1.2 billion in that continent alone it was also highly probable that enough people had been turned into wolves who would venture out for meat, wherever it may come from. Any surviving humans would also need protein too. He gave up on the idea, his thoughts too distressing.

He was certain the zoo was the same all over, perhaps only the spiders at the B.U.G.S exhibit and the Aquarium left unaffected. Maybe some of the birds still had a natural source of food available and were still alive. Fearing the worst as he approached another pen he spotted a grey foot, the uncanny shape more human hand than foot, sticking through the tattered undergrowth of the Gorilla Kingdom; he had shook it away, choosing to ignore it. The lack of any noise, no yelps or yaps, no grunts or growls, no squawks or squeals, told him all he needed to know—the silence all informative.

"These . . . animals are . . . were important."

"Why?" Felix asked, shrugging. "It's not like they did anything."

"What? These animals were beautiful, some of them rare; they deserved a place alongside us, not beneath us. Certainly not this."

"Yeah, but you eat meat."

"Yes, but farmed animals: pigs, cattle, sheep."

"You mean, piglets, calves and lambs. What's the difference?"

Ivan stared at him.

Felix was quick to respond. "Look, we've all been affected. If there's one thing I remember from school about wildlife, it's survival of the fittest. We've both lost people, there isn't time to mourn. None of this makes sense. All we can do is keep killing. Or be killed. Then we go by way of that lion over there."

Incredulous, Ivan's jaw dropped. After a while he spoke. "That's, well almost, the most mature and intelligent thing you've ever said."

"Whatever. Just some crap that's still in my head. And since all this began, any anxieties I felt being at school or around my peers have all but gone."

He placed his hand on Felix's shoulder. "Thanks." He was about to praise the lad further when a loud banshee-like screech ran through the evening air.

"Sounds like they're awake," Felix said, turning to face the way the squeals appeared to have come from.

Ivan nodded, thinking of the lion, once king of the jungle. "Time for us predators to go do our thing."

Felix browsed the shelves at Starbucks; nothing much left, coffee beans littered the tiles, the strong scent steadily fading, the few pastries and biscuits left mouldy and rat eaten.

From within the shop on Euston Road they studied the entrance to the building opposite. It was an act of caution, to check out the lay of the land before you entered. After leaving Regent's Park they had tracked the raucous howls to here, The British Library, and were convinced that the racket was coming from within the same building which housed the Magna Carta, Leonardo da Vinci's Notebook and the 1964 audio recording of Nelson Mandela's speech while he had been on trial at Rivonia. An impressive inventory; just not appreciated by the current visitors.

Satisfied that nobody was hanging about, they headed out into the street. Outside now, the lad close behind him, Ivan scanned the road. The darkness was like a kindly spirit; it shrouded the damage, the sense of abandonment gone, the streets feeling eerily similar to that of walking home in the small hours after a party. One could be forgiven into thinking this was just another night after having been out drinking with friends. To his left was the Pullman Hotel; to his right, the gothic towers of Saint Pancras Renaissance Hotel. Together they put the nearby Premier Inn to shame. The City was full of lodgings of various means in a place with no travellers left to grace their doors.

Broken glass crackled and crunched underfoot as they crossed the six lanes of now-redundant tarmac. Felix ignored the urge to kick at a fading more-white-than-yellow tennis ball, left behind by a dog or child. The smell of old diesel still hung about. They closed on the library's entrance, the brick edifice tomb-like. Ivan ignored the sign; it was a building, a grand statement, not a portent of things to come. Wasn't it? There were no lights, but their natural night-vision was now at full strength. Paper drifted around the entrance square, the statue of a bowing Isaac Newton to their left fiddled with his dividers ad-infinitum.

Trying the doors, his weapon at the ready, Ivan tugged at the handle. The door inched open, silent on its hinges. *Good.* It was one less thing to worry about. He nodded to Felix who entered first. Ivan followed allowing the door to close quietly behind him. Inside, the library was cavernous, with stairs and escalators leading to a multitude of levels, the levels themselves holding well over 150-million items. There were lines of desks and reading lamps, and a terraced restaurant on the first floor. That was where the noise seemed to be coming from; the sound of hissing, cajoling, the yakety-yak of a vampire's threatening words once he (or she) had cornered their prey. It was always the same; the bloodsucker's 'disease' more like a verbal version of restless leg syndrome, it gave them an incessant urge to move their bottom jaws and utter bullshit of all proportions aimed at self-aggrandisement, of just how powerful and wonderful they were, and to scare their prey at the same time. As if a regular human would not be fearful at the sight of a night-stalking human-blood swallowing undead fiend with pallid skin and wretched claws who—for want of a better term, no more resembled a bat as a bunch of pedalling ducks resembled the Spanish Fleet of the Armada—was hell-bent on killing them. About to meet their maker, they then did not deserve to listen to the verbal bunkum that flowed from between sharp and oversized canines.

Clearly the initial screech they had heard from the zoo only meant that the chase was on. And now the vampires had found what they were hunting for, and had it—he, she, them?— somewhere near the food hall. Being vampires, Mitclani liked to toy with their prey, like a kitten with a soft toy. That, along with super-sharp blades and age-old fire, was now looking like it may be their downfall. In their frenzied haste, too tied up massaging their own egos, the three vampires had not heard Felix and Ivan approach.

In front of them, behind a serving counter, a smashed till beside them, was a man. He was brandishing a smashed bottle, upturned in his hand, pointing the jagged edges towards his three assailants, swaying it left and right. Seems they had made it just in time.

Using the loud verbal diarrhoea as cover the two hunters moved at the same time as all three Mitclani went for the man. In the time it takes to grab a tray and line up at the till, two blades cut the air, their owners moving with an agility with which they had only recently gained. There followed a thud, together with a sickening gurgling sound. It was this sound that stopped the third vampire in mid-attack. Looking to his left, the bragging and boasting long since forgotten, the final vampire spotted a neatly severed head. The gurgling continued as the vampire turned to his right. His other friend, colleague, fellow-worker, brother-in-teeth, whatever they were called, was gurgling because his neck was only two-thirds severed, with his head toppling to one side, dark blood dribbling out; the thing had recently fed, but would feed no more. Unhappy with his first blow, Felix hacked again at his victim with his blade. He missed, watching the vampire's lolling head as the body performed an unholy two-step. He felt ill, or would have done had he not been running on pure fear. The samurai sword that Ivan had picked out for him was longer, meant that he would not have to get so close to his prey; it also meant it was more unwieldy with a greater margin for error. This was proved by his first modest attempt at beheading in one deft stroke. Obviously he would need a little more practise.

He brought the blade down again and this time, the third swipe, he removed the thing's head. The dancing, jigging body fell away. Felix kicked the head in disgust, in hatred, in anger, watching it barrel along the tiled floor, a red trail in its wake. The third Mitclani, now alone, bared its teeth, hissed at them.

Unfazed, Ivan stepped forward. He looked at the idle grimace, its pathetic threats.

"That's like bringing a pea-shooter to a gun-fight." He lifted his blade allowing the vampire to see it clearly, the instrument of its soon-to-be demise.

The Mitclani showed no emotion, simply turned and faced Ivan, sibilating again, instinctively, as a cornered cat might hiss at a threatening canine.

After double-checking their surroundings, confident there were only three and no more, Felix sat on a chair, wiping at his own blade with a soft cloth as instructed by Ivan: "Always treat it with great care, with gentleness. Be confident of what you hold, let it speak for you. You are in control and with experience you will see it as an extension of yourself and together, man and blade, you will be invincible." It was trite, it was daft, probably something Ivan had half-remembered from a movie, but Felix allowed the older man to utter it proudly. Felix had scoffed at Ivan's words at the time but now, after his latest kill, he could see what Ivan meant. Sort of.

He was now the one sitting there cleaning and caressing his sharpened steel, and he felt good. It may have taken three blows but it had done the trick—and he was getting fed up at having to forage for new knives when his old ones snapped during a fight. The blade gave him a confidence he never knew he had; he had felt it. Was this a good or a bad thing? Once upon a time, in another life, he knew it would be considered bad, heinous in fact. Immoral and wrong. Now, as one fought daily for one's own survival he accepted it. He would do it again and again. To survive. In the past he would have been frozen, his body overtaken as panic set in, his anxieties getting the better of him. No longer, and no longer would he attempt to kill the innocent. Just why he had suggested to Ivan that they kill the man and boy which they had just saved was lost on him now. It was time to grow up and get used to his situation, no matter how difficult it seemed. He looked up at Ivan who now had the final vampire backing off.

The next bit happened quickly.

The Mitclani's chest exploded in front of Ivan. He could only stand there in shock as Felix sat forward, ready to jump up. After the vampire had turned its attention away from its prey, the once-hunted man, emboldened by his new 'aides' and that their odds had come crashing down (along with a couple of heads), had casually picked up a steel-legged chair and rammed one of the legs through his would-be killer's back. The steel tube pointed towards Ivan, leaving specks of blood on his face.

Relieved, Felix stayed put.

The three eyed each other, the man breathing heavily after the attack, as the Mitclani fiend crashed to the ground, the chair jarring up and to one side as the should-be murderous foot of the steel leg met the tiles, almost jumping from the undead's dead back. Not finished though, the vampire only thrashed about on the floor, trying to gain purchase on something, to right itself. Giving it no time or mercy Ivan stepped up and rammed his sword though its head. He reached for some hand sanitiser which sat on the counter top, unscrewed the pump lid and poured it onto the skewered vampire.

"Seventy percent alcohol," he said to Felix. From his pocket he plucked a cheap lighter.

Felix nodded back.

"Stand back," he said to the man. In moments the vampire was ablaze.

The man stared, twitching—was he getting ready to run?

Ivan looked at him. "We need food. Know where we can get any?"

The man looked up at the signs that adorned the eatery, its images of succulent bites, of families happy and smiling, and florid menus.

"Not that, I mean real food," Ivan added, stepping towards him.

## Chapter 7

The yawping and screeching outside was growing steadily louder.

It was getting closer. They were getting nearer.

They were in for another night's trouble. It would be yet another night defending and protecting the house, each other. This particular gang of Mitclani knew they were there, holed up inside the house, and were not about to give up any time soon. This time though, it sounded like there were more voices, different intonations, new words yelled out.

Randell sighed and wiped himself down. After waking with a hard-on he had masturbated frantically, trying to get the act over with quickly, and to ease the pain he felt in his balls. It had not helped taking a shopping excursion with Ulrica earlier in the day; he knew she was on her period and had once read somewhere in a magazine or on the internet that a woman's libido was highest during her 'fertility window' which apparently was anywhere from around three or four days before ovulation and then some days after. He had no idea what it meant really but it had had a strange and awkward effect on him. To him she looked better, more confident perhaps, flusher in the face. She even smelled better. It was female pheromones, he had read.

And then they had found and together had killed a couple of frenzied fanged fiends and his adrenalin had not helped his situation. He could sense the change in her body; it had given him twitches he never realised he could have. For her anyway. He knew she would be horrified if she knew. And disgusted. Ulrica had become like a little sister to him, and he would protect her for all he was worth. So why the strange feelings? And why was his brain connected directly to his dick? The answer was simple. He shrugged. *I'm a man, and there are no women.* Besides, as long as Ulrica never found out, he did not see the harm. She was attractive enough, she would see it as a compliment . . . No, maybe not. She really would be disgusted. He decided to pick up an adult magazine next time he was out, without Ulrica. And he vowed to clean his room sometime soon; it stank.

He entered his en-suite and tried pissing but missed the pot and sprayed the rim, the tiles to the side and himself. *Shit.* He wiped himself down, cursing some more, then flushed the toilet and washed his hands on a tiny sliver of soap that had stuck to the sink along with bits of toothpaste. After dressing he headed downstairs to meet the others, to discuss their strategy for the night to come, the impending attack. He found them all sitting at the table, and in front of them the usual weapons were laid out for distribution. Ulrica eyed him. As if sniffing out his earlier exertions, she asked him if he was OK.

Privately embarrassed from his earlier antics he nodded at her, hoping she wouldn't notice his awkwardness, his reddening cheeks.

Connor meandered up to him. "You ready, big guy?"

Randell grunted at Ralph's son; he hated being dubbed 'big guy', it made him feel simple. Admittedly he had done some labouring but more recently he had engaged in proper building work, and figured that not all builders were simple. There was a lot of technical stuff to get your head around. Some builders had huge houses, mansions almost, particularly around London. They had managed their professions and workers well. They had paid well and left men behind on jobs snagging for weeks just to get the job perfect and keep the client (some of whom parted with extravagantly large sums of money) happy. However, for all their fine building prowess and conscientiousness, plenty of them had died in their wealthy pads with their riches intact, their inheritances dying with them as their children were slaughtered in front of their eyes, unless they were lucky enough to go first. Millions of pounds had been rendered worthless by one destructive maul or keen and lavish bite.

"You two mind doing first and second floors tonight?" Ralph pointed at Randell and Ulrica.

Randell looked at Ulrica. "That OK with you?"

She nodded, her face solemn, knowing that while there was generally less activity on those floors it meant that whoever guarded those floors would be isolated from the others. If the floors were breached you would be on your own.

Randell knew what she was thinking, his shame abating. "Don't worry, we'll be fine," he said.

Initially the attacks had occurred on the ground floor only. Now, with more and more junk being deposited outside the house each night, the attackers in effect erecting their own jury-rigged siege tower (against common belief, vampires did not turn into bats and were certainly unable to fly in human form), the first floor, with its low concreted half-moon balconies, was now being probed more readily. And certainly more often.

Randell said he would guard the first floor, leaving the second to Ulrica where activity had so far been nil. That left Seffi and Ralph to cover the ground floor, with Connor backing up whoever needed bolstering at any one time, be that upstairs or down, wherever the attack was heaviest.

As always it began with shouts, taunts, name calling, and imagined tales of how soon they would get in and get what they wanted, of how they would devour them and relish their delicious and bloody innards. It was a tactic designed to scare, to intimidate. Well, they had been trying for around three weeks now and still they were being kept at bay, no matter how much they talked of their ooh-look-at-how-immortal-I-am-and-yes-I-know-I-need-a-visit-to-the-dentist-but-please-remember-I-don't-much-like-to-go-out-during-the-day superiority.

Randell wondered how they had all ended up in this particular house. For some reason—had it been fatigue, no time to think, the constant battle for survival?—he could not quite recall the events accurately enough. Surely there were safer buildings in the city? In reality he knew that the buildings of the Ministry of Justice, the M.O.D. and New Scotland Yard, along with the local prisons, had all been torched a long time ago. They had burned for weeks, lighting up the city landscape an eerie orange while darkening the surrounding buildings, the roads and the sky. Even No. 10 Downing Street and the Cabinet Office had been fire-bombed beyond recognition, although this had been done during the first 'turnings' and was more symbolic of a fed-up population than that of demonic warfare. With most MPs either dead or turned it had not had the desired effect; nobody, after all, was listening to those who were left. The economy, London's most prized possession, was dead and buried along with its residents.

A loud crashing noise outside caused Randell to alter his thoughts and think about his imminent situation. He shouted up to Ulrica, asking if she was good. Her reply was one of affirmation. *Good.* Objects thrown, with some force, added to the taunting; the noise outside increasing as more of the wretched gang appeared. It was only when the tin can warning system rattled that nerves became unsettled. It meant they were on top of them. Last night they had counted five, the odds even, and they had killed one at least one Mitclani or so they had thought. A quick peek through slatted timber revealed five again, with two more approaching.

"Oh, crap. Like vultures circling, here come some more," Ulrica said.

Randell stepped up to view. Two vampires—one male, one female—had entered the fray from the right of the square.

"Thought you said you stuck one of 'em?" Randell said. "Can't see any injured."

Ulrica shrugged. "I'll put ribbons and bows on the next one." She looked again. "Anyway, there's seven of them now." Ulrica stood at the gap, staring down into the square. She jigged up and down on her feet. "Aw, crap."

"Get ready," Randell barked, instructing not only Ulrica, but loud enough to warn Connor, Ralph and Seffi downstairs.

Serkan eyed the house, Hemma at his side.

"Ah, so this is where he is." He smiled at Hemma. "What a quaint little house. Looks like there are more of them inside." He turned his attention back to the house. "Feeling hungry?"

Hemma eyed the house, her head cocking from side to side, slowly and deliberately, making her appear more demented than she was. "Oh, yes."

Seeing the new participants approaching, two of the existing five Mitclani turned and climbed down from their vantage points.

"Who are you?" one asked.

"What do you want?" asked the other. Both sentences were accusatory, threatening in tone.

"I would have thought that was obvious." Serkan's reply was calm, even. He bared his teeth.

"This is our—"

Caught mid-sentence the first vampire's words where abruptly cut off, his Mitclani throat severed, taking flesh, sinew and vocal cords with it. Serkan rammed his hand into the freshly made slash and ripped the head back. A loud snap indicated the fight—for one vampire anyway—was already over. The body collapsed to the floor, the head draping down its back like a hood, still attached by tendons and skin.

The second one stared at Serkan. "You're of the Mitclani?"

"How very astute of you." Serkan replied, wiping his soiled fingers down the his front.

The second one continued. "That's punishable by death."

Serkan waved his mostly-clean hand. "Yawn. Yes, I've heard that before." He turned to Hemma. "Now dear, tell me, where have I heard that before?"

Seeing the brash newcomer distracted by his bravado, the second one stepped in, teeth and claws bared. Two feet from Serkan, he stopped. The slam in his chest was unexpected, it had come from nowhere. On looking down, an arrow jutted from between shattered rib and skin. Bloody muscle adorned the thick arrowhead.

The second one's face was one of puzzlement. "What? A fucking arrow?"

An arrow in the chest was a mere inconvenience but one in the eye or the brain, well, that could finish off a vampire no matter how strong.

Serkan and Hemma dived for cover. Someone from the house was firing upon them.

Inside the house, Ulrica shouted down to Randell. "You seeing this?"

Outside, the vampires were having a confab with the two newcomers. Within seconds, and with barely half-a-dozen words uttered, one of the vampires was down on the ground, dead, his head sitting neatly upon his upper back.

Randell had seized the opportunity to create some chaos, rather than simply sit and watch. He raised his crossbow, nocked the bolt, and fired through the gap. He knew it would not kill, but provided he found his target it would keep one or two of them out of the fight for a while.

He waited a moment, still holding his breath, and watched the vampire fall back, pulling at the unwanted object in his body, the others running for cover.

He shouted to Ulrica. "That's how you stick 'em."

"Yeah, yeah, whatever. Still six left. More or less back where we started. Oh, sorry, one's sitting down now. Same difference."

"Good point." He waited. "Get it?"

A barrage of missiles hit the house, an immediate retaliatory strike, causing them to crouch and take cover in case anything made it through. The sound of people scuffling followed, there was the odd accusatory screech, and then it all went quiet.

"You good?" Randell shouted up at her.

"So far," came the reply.

Randell looked towards the stairs. "You lot down there all right?"

"All good here." Ralph's voice.

They waited. Still, quiet. Quiet was usually good, but quiet with vampires outside the door was not a good sign. And Randell did not like it.

He crawled to the bottom of the stairs. "Psst."

"What?" Ulrica whispered.

Using his hands as words Randell instructed her to stay down while informing her that he would take a look. He eased himself up, finding enough space to get a better view.

The vampires who had originally been attacking the house had either fled or died trying to protect their killing zone. Like outmatched vultures they had faced the two newcomers only to be chased off.

Where are the other two? Randell leaned closer to the timber. He crept back, looking up at Ulrica who was face down with her face over the top stair. He shrugged. "Can't see anything," he mouthed. He pointed at her to go and take a look from her floor.

On all fours Ulrica inched herself towards the window, bracing herself, ready for anything, the quietness all too convenient after weeks of relentless attacks.

"Be careful," Randell whispered.

A lithe white limb exploded through the batons of timber sending splinters everywhere, directly in front of Ulrica. Its grasping claws reached for her. Ulrica careened backwards, knocking into a small side table. The lamp on top skimmed away onto the once-plush carpet. She growled in pain. She called out for Randell.

"Connor, up here," Randell shouted and took to the stairs to aid Ulrica.

"Crap," she said, rubbing at her wrist, sprained in the fall. *How the fuck did they get up here?*

Her peripheral vision caught a glimpse of something at the partially exploded window. Something odd, almost glinting. An eye, looking in on her, the arm inside still probing. Ulrica felt violated, her private space invaded. Picking herself up she grabbed the claw-hammer at her side. She went at the hole, beating back the intruder's protruding limb. Along with the arm the eye disappeared, allowing its owner time to fall back, to realign its body, and stick its face to the hollow.

By now Randell was at her side. He watched as Ulrica froze, dropping the hammer.

The face looking back at her, it was the same face, her face, older, but different somehow. It was her mum's.

## Chapter 8

"Are you all right?" Randell held her by the shoulders. "Ulrica?"

She did not respond. She was just sitting, staring stared ahead, her eyes vacant. He shook her, gently but firmly.

Again. "Ulrica?" This time it was Seffi who spoke. The softer voice of the older woman did the trick.

The girl looked about, broken from the spell of her fright, the night's revelation unfolding itself, seen between broken timber, the face appearing in her mind over and over. One moment, all was quiet. Then, the attack, the eye, the face. That face. Her mother's. Cold sweat clung to her temples. Randell could smell her heavy body odour, expensive perfume—top-shelf stuff, taken freely from an un-staffed and finger-stained glass counter at Harrods no doubt— mixed with perspiration.

Even with Ulrica out of the fighting the night had ended up being easier to defend with only two night-prowling aggressors. After appearing on the scene, this new male vampire had proved to be a tough battler, more than making up for the others who had fled or been killed, and with only two targets between the four of them it had proved a far more comfortable night than they expected to have. It had been a disconcerting sight for them all to watch the newcomer casually stroll back to the injured vampire, the one with the bolt though his chest, open up his neck with just his fingernails and pull at the skin and sinews before decapitating him. The newcomer had held up the head and smiled directly at the house, almost gleefully, as if relishing the act.

Eventually, the big orange blinking eye that always appeared rising above the horizon at dawn had seen the two flee, one of them now identified as Ulrica's mother. Randell only wished he could get the blockades down from the door fast enough and follow them, take them out while they were seeking refuge. It was a dangerous idea, to go out alone. Make no mistake these two new ones were trouble. Big trouble.

Thinking it best to stay put, regroup, plan the next move, Randell found himself wondering why the sunlight only debilitated them. He knew it burnt them, would end up disfiguring them almost if it was a hot day—he had seen one of them practically melt right in front of him. Had he not watched so many vampire movies where they had erupted into flames, their ashes glowing red as they disintegrated into the breeze? Of course, he knew the answer: back then vampires had only been in books and movies, they were the things of folklore, long told tales to keep children in bed. Now he knew different. The Mitclani had revealed themselves as real. He supposed it made sense that a stake through an already dead heart would not do a damned thing. Severing the brain from the body made sense, as did burning them. And in a body without oxygen, how and why did the brain still function? He shrugged, resigning himself to the reality. At least the light did hinder them, and kept them away during the day if nothing else.

"Connor, fetch her some water," Ralph said.

"Why me?" he said, arranging an array of knives on the sideboard so the points all faced the same way.

"Because you're my son." The words were curt, patronising.

Connor looked at his father. "That's a fact, not a reason."

"Connor."

It was always the same answer: "Because you're my son." What the fuck did that mean? That he should do his father's bidding at his every whim? Just because he had spoken? Make it so Number One. Connor thought his father sounded like that bald geezer from Star Trek: The Next Generation. He could hear it now having watched the countless re-runs on TV. Ah well, Shatner was the best.

With his tail between his legs—he knew his father would only get angry—he padded away slowly, warp factor one, hoping that once (just once) his father could appreciate something (anything!) he did and accept him as an equal, as an adult. At 21 years of age, it was the natural order of things; he was not a small boy any more. He grabbed a glass and headed for the kitchen sink. *I'll show him, one day.*

Randell repaired the windows, padding and bolstering them further until he ran out of timber. Now he would have to get some more. There was plenty of it around, real good stuff too, left over from any number of the plush house and hotels in the city. There would be mahogany, ash, maple, cherry, teak and walnut. And real oak, ancient and hardened. It meant he would need some new drill bits, real sharp ones, and lots of them.

Ralph licked the back of his hand. He had sustained yet another injury during the night; the blood had stopped but now the wound was watering. The metallic taste from earlier was now salty. He would brush his choppers later.

Seffi stroked Ulrica's head and neck. Concern showed on her face; she was worried for the young girl who was still more than a little shocked.

"I . . . I thought she was dead," Ulrica managed to say after some time.

They all regarded her, watching and waiting. Connor shrugged.

The realisation that her mother was actually dead had not yet hit her. Like Randell searching for Sullivan, she had always hoped she was still out there somewhere, alive. She spoke softly, calmly, her features numb. Yes, her mother had been turned it seemed, she told them, but did it mean she would turn back to being human if they managed to find and kill the vampire who was responsible for turning her? Ulrica shook her head. That really was for the movies. The best she could hope for was a swift end. To put her mother at peace.

When Ulrica said it, Randell's gut twisted at the thought of him having to do the deed. Things often fell to him. He was the biggest, and strongest. However, if it was to be him would Ulrica, even once she had faced the horrible truth, ever forgive him? Perhaps he could persuade Ralph or that slacker Connor to do it; she could hate one of them forever instead of him.

After helping Ulrica to bed, Seffi spoke quietly. "Looks like it's me on breakfast duty again."

"Thanks, girl," Ralph said, attempting to inject some humour.

"Girl?" Seffi's pitch was much higher. "You'll be getting scraps if you keep that up . . . Boy." She forced a little smile, and headed off.


Bacon was fast becoming scarce; there was only so much of it they could find that was still in date.

They had initially found plenty at The Stoke House, a restaurant in the Nova building which boasted (straight from Google): Meat dishes & colourful salads are the stars of this stylish, all-day modern carvery. They had even come across reserves in the freezers there. Now though, they had taken to rummaging around for it at supermarkets and corner shops, the salty cured meat only good for so long. Both Randell and Ralph liked their meat so would happily scour the local area for some time until other duties beckoned. Apparently nitrites were bad for you. Neither of them cared.

Today was not about bacon; today was about finding the lair of the male vampire and Ulrica's mum.

"They couldn't have gone too far," Ralph said, feeling positive.

Randell stared at the built-up area, buildings of all shapes and sizes, every spare inch a prized property with land at a premium in the country's capital. He had searched some, plenty really, but who was to say that any one of those could not now be tenanted by vampire, human or wolf.

"So which way then?" Randell said, a little dazed.

Ralph looked about him. "Um. Not sure."

"Funny that. Better get sniffing then boy." Randall smiled at him.

Nodding at his friend, Ralph said, "Yes, very good."

They started in the first building they came to, Grosvenor Gardens Mews East, passing under the small brick archway searching for signs: fresh footprints, blood trails, newly broken windows or forced door frames. Rubbish and paper lay about the yard. Outside there were cardboard boxes that had spilled onto cobblestones from a garage, its up-and-over door at half-mast. A dead cat laid at the bottom of a whitewashed wall, stretched along its base, its body appearing uncannily long, the stench of death long gone as it desiccated in the mild morning air. None of it looked newly disturbed.

It was the same story at The Goring, their efforts rewarded in the ornate red bar once they had searched every room. After pouring themselves drinks from the still-intact bottles along the top shelf of the bar, the red decor too much for their eyes, they decided to sit in the rear conservatory. It was bright yellow with velvet tub-chairs. The grass outside was still surprisingly green, unkempt without its gardener tending to it, but a better view than bricks and concrete and tarmac. The room was musty with a faint odour of alcohol mixed with furniture polish.

Ralph had finished his drink by the time he sat down so he turned back to the bar for a refill. Back in his seat with a fresh and filled glass he saw Randell's eyes were closed. He decided to join him, the drink warming his innards and making him a little drowsy. They should be all right for a while, both of them sitting out of sight, surrounded by glass in the full sunlight. If not, well, they would die in their sleep. Peacefully. Perhaps death would be a good thing. It would end the boredom, the everyday search for food and the constant nightly battles. If it was not vampires trying to get at them, it was werewolves, elders of the Urbat pack able to change upon will, which would come sniffing around. Could those savages not wait for a full moon? As if they didn't have enough to contend with. He could understand if the wolves had found a vampire nest and needed to deal with it quickly and efficiently. He supposed attacking before a full moon gave them an advantage, with surprise on their side, the vampires caught cat-napping—just like he was about to do. He shrugged, and closed his eyes.

Ten minutes seemed more like an hour. Randell looked at Ralph who was stirring.

"Afternoon."

Ralph nodded.

"Time to get back?" Randell asked.

Ralph nodded a second time. They both stood and stretched, facing the private grounds. Getting up to leave had given Randell a slightly different perspective of the garden. From his new height he spotted what looked to be a shoe at the bottom of a short set of stairs, something he had not noticed when he had sat in his chair eyeing his single malt. He headed outside to get a better look. The shoe was still attached to its owner, the owner's torso and upper legs beneath the garden's lush overgrowth. From the knees down the legs were charred, in some places ash stained through the trousers. The body was face down and had been there for some time. A closer inspection revealed several puncture wounds in the back along with an object sticking neatly upwards from the top of its spine, giving the body the look of someone who had been going to a fancy-dress party as a prostrate but back-to-front dalek. Only it was not such a reveller, it was a plain and simple Mitclani, the best type of vampire: the dead kind.

"That's not going to kill it," Ralph said, leaning closer to inspect. He pulled back the untended foliage. "No, but that would do it." He pointed at the body, holding back the leaves for Randell to get a better look.

No head. Or at least no upper head. The jaw and chin were intact; the rest sheared off neatly as if a wide axe or spade had been used. It could have been either a cracking shot, well aimed and deliberate, or a really bad fumble with a weapon that the user had no reason to be wielding. Whichever it should have been, either one had had the desired result.

"Yep." Randell could not help thinking that the corpse had been deliberately hidden; it had not crawled away, half burned and half headless, and hidden itself with a stake through its back—death by unnatural selection—or had it? Was the sucker-fuck attempting to get out of the daylight and had then been attacked? And if so, by whom?
"What do you think?" he said.

"Dunno," Ralph said. "It's dead, that's all I care about."

Randell looked at the veterinarian of old. "And here's me thinking you liked animals."

He snorted. "That . . . thing may be many things but I assure you, it's no animal."

Randell agreed. "Yeah, just a shame it's not our friend from last night."

## Chapter 9

With everyone either out or catching up on their sleep Connor had once again retired to his basement rooms.

He sat, slouched at a stool, elbows on knees, his chin in his hands. He thought about his mother, about whether or not she had made it. He feared he knew the answer: she was long gone. She was always the unlucky one; had come out worse off with the divorce. His only hope was that she had died quickly and painlessly and that she had not been left to forever stalk the night. Unlike Ulrica's mum. He thought of his ex, of better times. He wiped at his nose and looked down at the floor, counting the bits of fluff and odd shapes of tiny detritus that he could see embedded in the carpet. He made a mental note to find a vacuum cleaner one of these days and deal to it. In front of him was a table, six feet long and about three wide. It was covered in an old bed sheet, badly stained. Forgetting the others for now he turned his mind to his own tasks.

He sat up and pulled away the sheet. Revealing a body. It was strapped down, heavily, head to toe, and covered in tubes and valves. Around it lay catheters, small bottles, discarded rags. Through its chest, pointing severely at the ceiling, the stake which had pierced its heart was still there, embedded deeply. It was one of his more ludicrous tests, done initially when he had first caught the damned thing. As they had all since found out, it was nothing but an inconvenience for the thing but it did at least have the effect of keeping the vampire from writhing about so much, making his other trials easier.

The smell of alcohol and decaying flesh permeated the room, like an abandoned abattoir left to fester in the heat. To his side sat Petri dishes, a large microscope, vials with brightly coloured tops, and circular holders, syringes, conical flasks, a kidney tray of small tools and scalpels; there was even a Bunsen burner and a set of oddly shaped callipers. A laptop beamed up at him, on all the time, at the side of it all. It sat next to a large desktop analogue clock. Batches of dried blood stained the worktops.

The vampire on the table squirmed beneath its bonds, its mouth cautiously bound in thick leather reminiscent of a Victorian asylum's restraints, its hands and feet fettered. It was alive—undead, but living the life of a blood-loving sponge. After an earlier test attempt on another Mitclani, of which had failed miserably, he had wound up killing the host. That was no good on a few accounts: he could not garner any results from a dead test subject but, more than that, it meant he had to go out and risk his life to drag a new one in. The latter he did not relish the thought of. After all, this one had been a tough case, first to capture and second, to get it back to the house unseen by the others. But he had learned some things about the wretched creature and, ever fearful of being bitten, Connor had come to the simple conclusion that in order to succeed or even get close to succeeding he needed to keep his subjects still in the land of undeadedness as it were.

His latest idea had some potential. At least he thought it did after reading all the supportive papers he could find. He had come to the simple conclusion that it was definitely the right avenue to explore. The theory that he was working on had to do with a particular protein, TIMP2, which was found in the umbilical cord of human babies. The thinking was that the TIMP2 protein may actually rejuvenate live cells. It had been a discovery of fascination to him at the time and the early results showed apparent restoration to elderly and depleted brain tissue. At the same time the protein seemed to inject youthful vigour into the new patron; the winter of life becoming a second childhood all at once to the recipient. Some years ago researchers had found that blood from teenagers was capable of restoring memory and cognition in aging mice, likely due to the protein in the plasma. The TIMP2 had boosted the mice's hippocampus—one of two complex parts of grey-matter that was shaped like a sea-horse—and improved the tiny rodent's maze navigation skills. What was known was that TIMP2 inhibited the group of enzymes known as matrix metalloproteinases, some of which are involved in the progression of Alzheimer's. So, the research would help dementia sufferers, and perhaps help treat those with Parkinson's disease, multiple sclerosis or motor neurone disease. Trouble was they did not know why? It was just another unanswered question; the medical research world was peppered with them.

Take that University of Nottingham! His School of Life Sciences course should have been the precursor to better things: a career in haematology or blood sciences. He had originally gone for it because it looked like easy work—after all, how heavy could a test-tube of red stuff be? Not only that but all the brochures and website bumf always depicted a pristinely-clean laboratory and lovely young men and ladies in white lab coats. Yes, clean, easy work, surrounded by attractive people; who could ask for more? And the chance of becoming famous, perhaps rich (his uncle's money would only go so far), if ever an important breakthrough was made. And since the population had dwindled taking with it all the medical research boffins along with any funding, that breakthrough would now have to be found here, in his basement, at his hands, using his brain. It would make his father proud of him. *He'll see.*

So, he thought hard, the gist of it was easy enough to grasp: something to do with combining babies, hippos and sea-horses which resulted in granddad mouse coming away with the brain of a teenager, and with superb map-reading abilities. It was all good for the mice but, really, so what? It was not as if the elderly mouse had a walking stick with which it could prod one of its annoyingly (and naturally) young and handsome rivals, and it did not need to remember any of the details about the holiday it took with the wife and kids only last month. It almost certainly had no fangs, feeding exclusively on blood ingested through its gut. Moreover, it was not scared of sunlight, only Man and his incessant rodent-related experiments. So the question was simple: would it work on humans, on the undead?

The breakthrough Connor needed—of which he wasn't altogether convinced could be achieved—involved stimulating the memory of the host; only that would shake the vampire from its undead slumber, regenerate it, and hopefully return it to human state. Killing the host, the one who had turned them in the first place, would only kill that host and do nothing for the subject. Once a vampire, always a vampire, unfortunately. He thought of Ulrica's mum, of how the girl would be feeling now. He shook his head; he missed his own mum.

Always careful to stay clear of the head, its hisses muffled, Connor shoved the catheter deep into a vein in the back of its greying hand. The hand twitched under the strains. He'd have to be quick. Having not been fed for some time, there was little blood to find in Mitclani subject's system. He drew what little blood he could and placed the tiny vial to one side. He would need before and after samples if anything—*hope, hope*—was to happen. He tried for another vial, ignoring the vampire's incomprehensible complaints. After a few more minutes he managed to draw another two. The vials clinked quietly as he put them on the counter top, ready to be put through the centrifuge.

Finding the refrigerated centrifuge had proved difficult initially—at first he was not exactly sure what one even looked like—however, once he had scoured the local hospitals and found one he then had to conceal its return so he could get it into the house unnoticed. It was something he was naturally good at; people tended to ignore his presence. It had been easy in the end—after all, he had managed to get a live vampire back to the house without being seen or raising suspicion. And the others often left him alone, they were out or doing other things. And, he was sure none of them cared about what he was up to from one moment to the next. It gave him plenty of time—too much really—on his own, to do whatever he wanted. None of them ever ventured downstairs to see him or even check in on him. A shout from above was always enough. For them.

Satisfied that he had enough samples, he stopped, sat up straight and stretched. *Right, what now?*

He looked about. First, he needed the refrigerated umbilical cord blood from the. He reached for it. After defrosting a small amount, doing it carefully because he knew that his supply was getting dangerously low, he drew some into the syringe. He pumped it directly into the catheter tube, watching the deep red liquid descend into the vampire's arm.

He watched, and waited.

The Mitclani's body went rigid, began to twitch, to convulse, constricted as it was. Connor leaned forward. Was something happening? He checked the straps a third time, just to make sure, and hovered over the vampire's face, looking into its black cloudy eyes. The eyes being the so-called window to the soul, he was sure, would react first. *Come on. This time.*

The clock ticked by, its sound a metronome in his head, each tick and tock a second closer to his father's respect and affection. *Come on.*

The Mitclani's body ceased its thrashes, began to settle.

Nothing had happened.

He tried another syringe.

Again, more convulsions, more time passed and the thing began to calm itself once more.

No reaction. No changes to the eyes, the skin, the leather-guarded sharp teeth. They just hissed their objections from below their binds.

*Bollocks.* He sat back as the vampire's squirming subsided and it lay still. *Fuck.* He wrote down a few notes with a large red X next to it. He grabbed the sheet and threw it over his specimen. The Mitclani's eyes stayed on him before disappearing below the soiled cotton.

Leaving the room, careful to lock the door, he wondered if the day would come when he would have to perform his own version of parabiosis. Instead of using defrosted blood samples he could try splicing together a newly-birthed mother—umbilical cord, baby, and all—with the vampire. That was if he could ever find one. If not, he would have to find someone pregnant. He mused over the two women who lived in the house above him. And shivered at the thought. One was way too old, and he was sure his father would not be too impressed if Seffi was to get pregnant let alone be used in some diabolical experiment with her baby in tow. He realised the baby would be his half-sibling and almost retched at the thought. He did not need any more competition and, besides, he was certain Seffi had been through the menopause.

That only left one other female in the house but, being a gay man, he had no idea how he would do it. Would he do it for the hell of it? For the cause? No, he couldn't. It was not him. But what if he had to, in a bid to save humanity? He had the man parts after all. Just not the desire.

Then it came to him. It just might work. He could work out the details later. And she would make a great surrogate mum once she got over her grief. He shrugged, all he would have to do now, apart from continue his experiments in secret, was to borrow some more books about artificial insemination.

## Chapter 10

From the second floor of number twenty-three Victoria Square the two men sat, their two chairs pulled up just close enough to the bedroom's window, their eyes just clearing the top edge of the sill, allowing them both to view the heavily boarded up house at the far end of the square.

The rotunda-shaped bedroom allowed them a vista of the whole area, with Queen Victoria's back always to them as she looked over the square from behind bronze eyes. It was still daylight so they were not immediately bothered about any roaming troublemakers and their ever-hungry fangs coming back too soon. Before this, they had secured another, more robust, hideout on the south side of Lambeth and would usually head there before dusk. But it was their time now, to make their move—although they hadn't banked on anyone being at home—and so tonight they were in these less-than-secure temporary digs facing up to another night where they could not go out.

Prison had done that for them; it seemed wrong since they had escaped that they should still not be allowed out. Of course they could go out, whenever they wanted, just as long as they did not mind if they were bitten and turned, or bitten and killed, or simply murdered. It was twice as dangerous during a full moon when the thought of being brutally devoured and ripped apart by a lunar-consumed and unrestrained werewolf came second to a quiet night in. Getting into a drunken brawl back in the day was one thing, savage death by Mitclani and/or Urbat was not quite fisticuffs down at the local pub. Having said that, fist fights were a thing of the past; the new generation preferred guns, knives, or even acid. Heinous. Or they did, until they had all but disappeared, no longer casualties of each other but that of the Underworld.

"What do you think, Barclay-boy?" one asked. His name was Sani. He was of mixed race with a large build and still-dark hair, Number 1 buzz-cut all over, his smooth skin belying his real age and life's tougher experiences.

"Well, Sani, looks like someone's home," Barclay said, a man—and not a boy, being almost a decade older than his comrade—of little more than five-feet tall in his late fifties, his bearded grey face covering his scraggy and lined skin. Skin that, unless one looked closely, they could be forgiven for thinking they were looking at a bloodsucker. They were not. They would be looking at him, Barclay, career criminal, professional thief and picklock, although he liked to tell those he met he was a 'steal' magnate, careful not to spell it out as he beamed up at them from a leathery smile.

No, Barclay and Sani were less than regular Joes who had, over the years, shared their plunder and a cell at HMP Pentonville, in the inaptly-named C wing. The prison had an illustrious history with Doctor Crippen being hanged there in 1910. In more recent times it had been temporary homes for a few celebrities, footballers and singer-songwriters with a penchant for the name George. The ill-fated Oscar Wilde, wrongly imprisoned for his choice of whom he should direct his love at, had spent time there before being transferred to Wandsworth. Before its final downfall, the prison was dilapidated, with drugs and contraband rife, along with regular attacks from inmate to inmate. Any celebrity who chose to give up his or her charmed lifestyle, even for a week, and become more intimately acquainted with the aged prison's squalid cell rooms was most likely doing some serious drugs.

They knew the area, knew of all those households that potentially had loose cash lying about and those that did not. Having a nice house but with all the money tied up in capital was of no use to them. They could break in and make themselves a nice sandwich or rest up in luxurious silk bedding, but beyond that they had no use for the house, unless a nice easy-enough-to-carry-and-fence-on expensive painting adorned the walls. The problem with that was that there were no punters left to take it off their hands for a mutually beneficial price, a done deal, thank you very much.

One of the houses in the square had piqued their interest after they had somehow found out that Ian Fleming of James Bond fame had once lived there. Upon getting out of prison they had visited it only to find the house a pitiful excuse of its former self, the insides ruined and ransacked, the perpetrators bodies torn asunder and scattered throughout the house, caught in the act by someone or something more unhappy and violent than themselves, more Casino Royal-Red than Royale, and definitely shaken not stirred. They had not returned to the house but could see it now, almost opposite from where they sat in waiting, looking at the other house at the far end with the barricaded doors and barred windows, the basement stairs filled in with old household electrical appliances, now going rusty.

"It wouldn't be done up like Her Majesty's Pleasure if no one was in, now would it?" Sani said, his height making him sit further back than Barclay so as not to expose himself.

Barclay thought about that for a minute. He nodded gently. "Fair point."

"You think it's still there?"

"Bloody well hope so. All this is for nothin' otherwise." He folded his arms and sat back.

What they were both still hoping for was that the money and jewellery they had stashed in the house before being sent down was still there. Hidden and untouched, and waiting for them to acquaint themselves with it again. Several Post Office jobs and one high-profile—it had made all the headlines—jewellery heist had given them a stash that would see them and theirs into a comfortable retirement. But, like many a plan, things hadn't quite gone the way they were supposed to and they'd had to scarper, pronto. Getting wind that the Old Bill was almost upon them they had found themselves in the square and, seeing a window slightly ajar, had taken their chances and broken into the house's basement where they had quickly and efficiently secreted the hoard beneath the kitchenette cupboards; Barclay had slipped in, being the smaller of the two, deftly pulled down the kick-boards and slid the lot under.

Hours later they were in a police cell. That cell led to another cell which then led to court and finally prison. That was eighteen months ago; since then, the world had changed so much. And so they had bided their time, knowing only too well they would one day get out. It had come sooner than expected and all they had to do now was get into the house by stealth.

Now, they were watching it, seeing who came and went. If anybody. The place may well be empty, its residents having fled. There was every chance that they had been killed. They had come across several households which had slain owners inside. But there was something about the timbers, the boarding, the junk out front, the blackened windows, that told them there just might be life inside. Of course, it could be occupied by Mitclani, the state of the windows giving them away. They could just break in—they had done it plenty of times before—and deal to any residents, good or bad, but they were thieves, not out and out killers. And besides, one or both of them may get killed with a silly or impromptu move. No, for now they would quietly observe. And wait.

Barclay recalled the famous (and a favourite) Christmas ghost story. Scrooge had said the words: "If they would rather die, they had better do it, and decrease the surplus population." Obviously, Scrooge was referring to the poor, those in prison or the union workhouses, and not the most affluent of Britain's greatest and wealthiest city. Dickens' tale was one of fiction, but, in real life, it had not taken the help of the Ghost of Christmas Present to bring it into being, to decrease the surplus population, only beings from an otherworldly place, fangs and talons unveiled, extremities too large for the delicate human populace to bear.

Since time began, Man had installed himself as the self-imposed top predator, in one form or another he had survived close to two-million years; that was until a deadly microscopic bug or a tumorous cell dragged him unwillingly to his grave. If that was not enough he forged weapons and started wars. Over the ages acts of murder, even genocide, were perpetrated on his own kind. Death came in all shapes and sizes. The media moved on from one to the other, the former one forgotten in the next headline. Man could do no wrong, he was invincible. Even when landslides killed hundreds or tsunamis formed giant waves that filled lungs with water he would not believe the impact he was having upon the earth. And when mangled steel with four wheels crushed vital organs at the side of a road because he chose to ignore the safety signs, he still wanted more.

Arrogance, it seemed, had not yet beaten death. The world of today proved Man could be beaten, ridiculously easily. Had been in fact, driven to extinction almost. The biggest dodo of them all.

"Nobody updates their kitchen that often," Sani said. He frowned. "Do they?"

"Bloody well hope not."

Carefully, Sani eased himself forward a little and scanned the square below one more time. "What do we do with it once we've got it?"

Barclay looked at him. "Whatever we want. What does it matter, we'll be rich." He nodded, more at his own thoughts and words than anything else.

"Yes, but . . ."

"Listen, we're both gettin' on. Neither of us has ever had it easy. Don't your body ache in the mornings, even before you get outta bed? I've told ya, these vampire things'll give us eternal life. Pain free. All we gotta do is bargain with 'em." Barclay smiled, thin lips turning up, facial hair twitching. "Who don't like diamonds and cash anyway, and lots of it?"

Sani nodded. He rubbed at his knee.

## Chapter 11

"I do love Connor," Seffi said.

"In my own way. After all, I love his dad." She thought for a minute. "And like his dad, he can be infuriating."

Ulrica nodded gently, staring ahead though puffy eyes. She had not said much for some time, her tears in the way, her throat constricted by the inflammation of her grief.

As always Seffi was comforting the girl, trying to help, doing what came natural to her, and was offering up her counselling services, only this time there had been no appointment made. She knew that Ulrica wouldn't mind. In the year before the world had changed Ulrica had seen a number of counsellors and had finally ended up seeing a psychiatrist. She had wound up in Seffi's office several times after Ulrica's father had abused her; not sexually, but verbally and physically, often coming home drunk and beating his wife and daughter, blaming them for whatever had or had not happened in his life. Better than blaming himself for his own shortcomings. And lashing out at them was an easy target, it freed up any tensions he felt. He would then act out, playing mister-nice-guy and show care and love to them, often going overboard with what she now knew were false emotions, before sliding back into his bad habits with name calling and sarcasm. It was all too confusing for a young and growing woman.

So Seffi and Ulrica had a history, albeit a mostly one-sided one. Once the world slipped into anarchy and death, Ulrica had lost her mother, never knowing if she had fled in fear, if she was dead or turned. It was an event she replayed in her head most days as she tried to sleep. In her mind, her mother was alive and well—how could she think anything else? She had hoped above all, if she had made it through, that her mother had finally summoned the bravery to leave her father, one way or the other. The shitty bastard did not deserve her. Never had really. It had not helped her anxiety any, but since finding Randell, Ralph, Seffi and Connor she finally felt she belonged, and had somewhere to stay. It was a bonus that her old psychiatrist just happened to be one of the survivors. The thought of being alone chilled her. Knowing Randell was also suffering with the loss of his brother had the effect of strengthening her own resolve; she was not the only one in pain. She didn't feel it any less, more like she shared her pain with a friend, or friends, now Seffi and Ralph were there too. Connor . . . was Connor. She let him be but suspected he had his problems, too.

Instead of professionally guiding her from a hospital or private room, Seffi was now sitting with Ulrica as the girl succumbed to her truth in the living room of the house. Since Ralph and Randell had gone out Seffi had tried to console the younger woman as she sobbed. She had stroked Ulrica's hair, and removed the girl's dog collar as she finally drifted off, exhaustion getting the better of her. Seffi had decided to grab some rest herself at that point. Only disturbed now and then by

Ulrica's tiny and interspersed cries and murmurs, they had both managed to sleep for a few hours.

Both awake now, they could hear Connor rattling around downstairs somewhere. It usually meant he was doing something, keeping out of mischief at least.

"Ralph does too, obviously. He just has an odd way of showing it. He's a sweet man but he's not always the romantic sort," Seffi continued. She passed Ulrica a glass of water.

"So, no roses then?" Ulrica said, lapping at the water fiercely, getting it on her nose and cheeks. She wiped her sleeve across her wet nose.

Seffi halted, thought for a moment. "I'd get dog roses, sometimes. He'd pick them from the hedge on the way home."

"Oh crap. Suppose they're pretty enough though. A bit scrawny compared to the real deal." Ulrica stared at the floor.

Getting Ulrica to finally engage in some conversation, Seffi chanced her luck. "You know sweetheart, she's not your mother anymore." It was a statement.

The room fell silent once more. *Damn.*

"I know," Ulrica said, her tears starting up again. "But, I suppose I've always assumed she'd be all right, that I would eventually find her. Not this . . . crap."

Seffi didn't know what to say. "Come now, you've not had time to accept it yet, let alone begin the grieving process.."

Ulrica cried again, unable to stop.

Seffi held her for a few minutes, then caressed her reddened cheeks. She looked at her younger friend. "Cuppa?"

Wiping he sleeve across her nose yet again, Ulrica sniffled and nodded.

By the time Seffi returned with two mugs of hot tea, Ulrica had pulled herself together a little. They sat quietly, with various gulps and slurps their only conversation.

"You won't want to hear this but we can at least give her peace," Seffi said as she placed her empty mug to one side.

Still staring into her mug, Ulrica knew Seffi was right. Her mother had gone. In the exact moment that whatever fucking greedy Mitclani had clasped their venomous choppers around her mum's slender neck, she knew that her mum had been lost. Gone forever. But not gone in the correct way. No, she had been turned. Turned to live life as a night-prowler, never to witness the sun rise again, never to be around for her daughter when she needed a cuddle. Like now.

"I'm sorry you had to find out this way."

"Yes, but at least I know. She deserved better than that . . . after my dad. "

Seffi nodded, staying quiet so the girl could continue.

And she did. "Better than poor old Randy. He's been searching for Sullivan everywhere."

"That's true. And with each passing day it will get easier. But Randell is determined. I can't say I hold out much hope. As far as I know Sullivan's not as strong as his brother and I think if he was still alive he would have found his way back by now."

Ulrica looked at the door. "Hmmm, maybe, maybe not. He could be holed up somewhere else in London, in another city or town even, depending on . . ."

"It's a possibility, I suppose. Problem is we can only go so far before having to return, before it gets dark."

"Yeah. Crap." Ulrica stood. "Unless we continued walking westwards, like, forever." She walked off down the hallway.

"Where are you going?" Seffi asked.

Ulrica looked back. "Oh, didn't I just say?"

Seffi frowned, trying to think back to the conversation.

"Crap. I said crap. I really need the loo." Ulrica scurried away, slamming a door behind her. Seffi heard the latch engage.

"Wonderful." Seffi sat in silence. She thought she heard Connor curse somewhere within the house. "Hey," she shouted towards the toilet door. "Don't forget to use the spray, stinks in here." She silently reminded herself: I'll have to say something to those boys. Show them where the bleach is.


Ralph and Randell had expanded their search area. The air was cooler now in the late afternoon, the blue of the sky turning more a shade of grey; they should be heading back soon. But first, Elizabeth Street beckoned. They strolled past the Thomas Cubitt pub, resisting the urge to go inside; they had had their fun in The Goring earlier.

The famous pub was named after the former Brighton man who had designed practically everything in one of the wealthiest districts in London. Few people knew that way back, in the seventeenth century, the now-exclusive area was exclusively a marshland of boggy proportions, ran by thieves, robbers and those known as scapegraces: reckless and unprincipled reprobates. Not necessarily a nice place to hang out, even during the day. But that was before Sir Thomas Grosvenor had got his sticky mitts on it, by proxy. Ralph explained the story to Randell.

Randell found it odd how Man professed the world as his own, but in this case, the man had gained it only by marrying a woman. A super-rich woman at that. He knew wedded bliss also meant wealthy bliss. It was simply theft of another kind, but done right out in the open, in front of all, the words 'love' and 'I do' passing a few lips and, well, that's all right then. It was, "Woman, do as you are told, I'm the boss now," as Man had a tendency to do. He was a stand-up loveable miscreant, with a posh accent and a white collar, but just as devious. Of course that was all history, the family were now celebrated—just not in the East End, or anywhere north of Hyde Park for that matter.

"Here, look at this," Ralph said.

They had clambered over and through vehicles and boxes, scooters on their sides, scratched and dented helmets cast aside, and reached a pet shop. He held up a dog lead.

"It's over a-hundred-and-twenty-five quid," Randell said peering through the door, its window put through. Glass crunched beneath his feet. "Wouldn't want to walk your expensive pooch with this."

"That's just the lead, the collar's extra." Ralph winced.

"Let's take it back for Ulrica. She's already got one."

Ralph stared at him. "Randy?"

He looked at him. "What?"

"Are you as stupid as you are big?"

"Huh?"

"She's not going to take your dog jokes after she's just found out about . . . you know."

Randell's shoulders visibly drooped. "Yeah, sorry. Wasn't thinking."

"I know, kid." Ralph knew the big lad would only be thinking about finding his own brother, especially after the latest development, what with Ulrica's mum still . . . around.

"We'll find him," Ralph added as he, for no reason whatsoever, placed the lead down carefully, as if afraid to mark the overly expensive and everyday item.

"Yeah, dead or alive." Randell looked at Ralph. "Or undead."

## Chapter 12

After returning home they had found the house quiet, the atmosphere subdued.

Randell had taken himself off for forty winks before the night began. He had a bad feeling about these two new Mitclani. The male had a vicious streak; after all, they had watched him quite contentedly kill his own. And then there was the problem that Ulrica's mother would be fighting alongside him. Something told him tonight things could get a lot worse.

There were several peepholes which dotted the timbers that covered the windows, allowing him a view of most of the square. He had glanced outside before retiring. The square looked dirty, dingy; the grey sky of earlier had drifted in rain clouds and these had since opened up, the square outside covered in a fine drizzle.

Now he was awake, feeling no more refreshed than when his body had the mattress, he stole another look outside. It was meant to be a quick scan, before night fell and they had to get ready. The clouds of earlier were thick and heavy, black almost, and had blocked out the sun as though dusk was already here. It was muggy and the rain of earlier had stopped but was still threatening to fall. He looked at a clock. Still nearly an hour until . . . He stopped as he turned to view the square again.

There were now two figures outside, standing in the shadow of the murk of the square.

They were staring at the house, not moving. They looked like two pale skinned mannequins, their intentions clearly set on the house. On its current residents.

He shouted out. "Er, guys."

It was Ralph who replied first. "What is it, Randell?"

"Take a peek outside."

He did as he was asked as Seffi joined him. "Damn," he said.

Ulrica came out of her room, rubbing her eyes. She was wearing only a vest top and her knickers. Taking her in and not knowing where to look, he felt awkward. He said nothing, only pointed outside.

"Crap it." Ulrica reeled back, not ready for the sight, let alone a night's fight.

"Need you with us right now, Ulrica," he said going to her and holding her up. He felt even more awkward than before.

She pushed him away, her face fixed. Seeing a determination in her eyes he had not seen before, Randell nodded at her and turned his attention back to the two figures who were watching the house.

"What are they doing?" Randell, whispered to himself.

"Come to finish what they started," Ulrica said, her voice monotone.

"You OK with that?"

She shrugged.

"Best get ready."

"Yep," she said, turning towards the stairs.

She met Seffi at the top of the stairs; she was panting after having carried up some weapons for the two of them. She put Randell's crossbow on the ground, then handed Ulrica a wad of knives all rolled up. Finally, she unslung the shotgun from her shoulder. Ulrica thanked her, realising how ludicrous things had become, Seffi had once counselled her, a tiny coffee table and pot plant the only things in the room with them. Now, she was handing out weapons like she owned her own arsenal.

Randell's eyes were still on the square and its current occupants. As Ulrica and Seffi turned to go their respective ways, the two vampires turned and walked away. He watched them go, unconvinced they were leaving.

At the same time, Ralph shouted up. "They're leaving," he said.

"Leaving?" Seffi said.

Ulrica stepped up to the window and watched as the mother she thought had long since disappeared turned and walked out of the square. She and the loudmouthed male her mother was with had not long arrived, were clearly preparing themselves for another attack, but had now simply turned and left. And they didn't think it was the pending rain that had deterred them. It was something else. Had to be. What else did they have in mind?

"Anywhere behind us they might exploit?" Randell said, loudly so everyone could hear.

"Not that I'm aware of, unless they start knocking down walls," came Ralph's reply.

"I wouldn't put anything past this lot," Randell looked at Ulrica. "The man, I mean, your . . . mum . . . she had no choice."

"She's not my mum."

Randell nodded. "No. I'm sorry."

"How's the roof?" Seffi said.

Ralph had checked it earlier. "Razor-wire's intact," he said.

"Hope you put up health and safety warning signs for that stuff," Connor said, his attempt at humour falling flat on a cold audience.

The rest of the house wanted to know where the two had just gone. Had they left because they were going to attempt a surprise attack from somewhere the rest of them had not yet thought about? Had they felt threatened? If so, by what? It was a long time until sun up. It was not as if they were scared of other Mitclani, they had proved that. It had begun to rain outside now, the dark clouds too heavy to bear their load had now opened up. Had it been the rain, were they vulnerable to it?

A noise echoed through the brickwork of the surrounding houses; a low guttural bellow. One of distaste, hatred. Of superiority.

It could only mean one thing. Like humans, vampires only had one true predator: Urbat. Wolves. The full moon was still a few days away so if any were out tonight it meant they were of the old guard, ancient walking wolves that could change from human form to wolf at will.

Then it came, loud, louder than they had heard before, meaning it was close.

A deep prolonged howl, designed to put fear into the listener, echoed around the buildings outside. It was definitely Urbat. Their appearance was, in one way, welcomed. The Mitclani had gone, for now at least. But it meant they now had to contend with a completely different set of potentially dangerous teeth.

"Lie down, now. All of you," Ralph whispered. "Stay still, and quiet."

As quietly and calmly as they could they all did as they were instructed.

Ralph was kneeling, about to lie down himself when, with one last glance he spotted the wolf, one of them, alone, entering the square. It walked steadily through the rain's mist, its snout pulsating as it sniffed at the damp air.

"What is it?" Seffi whispered.

"Urbat. A lone wolf," Ralph said. He looked at Seffi. "And it's coming towards the house."


Ignoring the rain outside, the wolf leapt over the railings.

It stepped forward, its gait light, its limbs long, and stopped in front of the statue of Victoria. It pushed forward its snout, the hairs around its nose slick and grey, the hide gnarly. It did a quick look left and right and behind itself again before turning back to look at the stone-cold face of the old Queen. Saliva, thick and glistening upon its teeth, covered its muzzle. At over six feet tall, with the head of an enlarged and enraged wolf, it was a formidable beast. But its mouth was ungainly, overlarge, and its wet fur and hunched upper spine gave it the appearance of an upright hyena. And an ugly one at that. The crossbreeding of this man and wolf had not been kind. Its chest heaved as it breathed, covered in drool, the effort of hunting evident as it moved. This was a hungry beast, already salivating, expectant of flesh, of meat. Even weakened as it was it would still easily rip apart any foe that stood between it and a potential food source.

Sensing its presence, the vampires that had fled as the wolf entered the square were safe, as prey at least. The wolf would only kill the Mitclani, it would not eat them. No, this wolf was out, for whatever reason, not adhering to the unspoken agreement. In that case, there was every reason to suspect that there were no more humans left alive or, more likely, this old wolf was starving. Which made it extremely dangerous. Unless it found a local butcher's—they had been pillaged long ago—or a lost cow or sheep meandering the ghost-like streets of London, then only human meat would suffice.

Sniffing closely at little 'Drina's bronzed face, the beast exhaled. If the tiny royal had been real, she would have in all likelihood let out a sound of glee. Having been raised to a strict timetable where the young royal had little time to interact with children her own age, constantly supervised by adults, she would no doubt have welcomed the inquisitive animal in as a playmate. She may have wanted to avert her face from its deeply unpleasant breath. Letting out another howl it stepped back, its face darting around the square, its nose twitching rapidly. Something had brought it here. Something was here. Its delicate amber eyes, belying its ferocity, settled on the house at the end of the square.

On two legs it marched forward.

Their instincts had paid off after they had indeed observed two men, one older man with a younger, bigger man return to the house late in the afternoon, each of them carrying bags of stuff.

Barclay guessed it would be supplies from the many surrounding shops, hotels and restaurants.

"One can live like a king around here," he had said to his friend, Sani, poured hot water into a king-sized chicken and mushroom Pot Noodle.

"Can't they just," Sani had replied, holding up the tasty hot snack before realising he did not have any cutlery.

That was earlier and Sani had ended up having to drink the noodles from the plastic container, once it had cooled a little. He had got it everywhere and even now he still had yellow stains on his chin. Now the rain had started and they were beginning to feel cold and bored.

Sani went to ask something else when his words were cut short. "Wha—"

"Shush."

Sani froze, his mouth still agape.

"Get down now, and don't move a bloody muscle." Barclay was whispering, his voice almost gone. Slowly, he pointed at the window indicating downwards, careful not to reveal himself. He gulped and held a finger over his lips.

Sani mouthed his next word and looked at his friend questioningly. "What?"

Barclay inched backwards and lowered himself to the floor. "Wolf." His voice was barely audible. He pointed towards the door of the room. They had locked, bolted, and barricaded the door as best they could, given the time restraints and the need to be hush-hush, all because they had decided to stay around just to see who came and went and if there was to be any vampire activity. Get the layout of the land before making your move. They had been almost right about the Mitclani, they had come and gone in a matter of minutes. They hadn't, however, counted on a visit from an old hungry wolf-man.

Barclay assessed the door again. It was more heavily shored up than he thought; it would take a team of men from a professional house moving company a weekend to shift all the junk that held it shut. It gave him some comfort. Unless the Urbat smelled them and decided to scale the outside of the building and enter through the glass window then they were all right. It occurred to Barclay that was exactly the sort of thing the werewolf would do if it did sniff them out. With nowhere to go if that happened, they would be sitting ducks. They would be slaughtered and eaten in a cruddy second floor bedroom. They could forget any prize they had their eyes on as their visual orbs slipped down the hungry Urbat's throat, a wonderful hors d'oeurve for the beginning of its feast. They would only be able to hear it gnawing on their flesh, tearing and ripping, as they lay blind and in agony until death gave them peace. He shuddered at the thought.

As if reading his thoughts Sani was already crawling across the carpet. Barclay followed. In the far corner of the room was a thick bedspread. It was made of a heavy material, luxurious in feel with a brightly coloured pattern. Upon entering the room for the first time they had encountered a body, a decaying cadaver, still in the bed. The rotting corpse stank and so they had torn some bed sheets into long strips and made simple masks for their faces to cover the foetor. They had both retched as they moved the cadaver into the corner of the room, wrapping it in as many sheets as they could find. The bedspread was the last thing to go over the corpse, keeping the smell out. Of course, all this work had to be done quietly and had taken a long time. By the time they were done they had become somewhat accustomed to the stink. Now, that same stink was to be their ally.

Sani was already unwrapping their grisly find by the time Barclay got there. He passed him a piece of shredded cloth. He tied it around his neck and then pulled the material up to cover his nose. Doing the same, he and Sani looked like two modern day highwaymen. Only they were grovelling on the floor. Nodding at each other, and freeing the last of the sheets, they slid their bodies under, joining the heavily decomposed occupant. Immediately they gagged, conscious not to make a sound, and nuzzled up to the corpse, the stench of death camouflaging their natural (and living) bodily odours, keeping them from being sniffed out. Barclay coughed, and Sani covered the smaller man's mouth with his hand, careful not to smother his friend.

"Shhhh," he muttered.

The werewolf shifted its bulk towards the front door of the house.

Inside the house, the five occupants stayed absolutely still, breathing slowly into the floor. Seffi was wide-eyed, staring into Ralph's; Randell had his hand on Ulrica's back in an act of reassurance but also to keep her down just in case the grieving girl got flighty. Connor lay on the stairs, prostrate, the treads needling his chest and legs, the rough carpet scratching at his cheek.

A soaked muzzle, water dripping from the jaw, closed in. The Urbat craned its neck and let out a grunt; had it caught the whiff of an odour in all this rain? It stopped and eyed the barricades, its head twitching, thick neck muscles rocking from side to side as it 'tasted' the air. There was a reason the door and windows were so well protected. Curiously, it probed the door with its nose, searching only for a particular odour. It backed off as the heavy aroma of garlic assaulted its nostrils. It sneezed, its large snout flexing forward as a spray of snot and saliva shot forth. Shaking its head, its nose now clear, it sniffed and looked up, eyeing the small ledges which made up the first floor shallow balconies. It reached up, like a man, and jumped, grabbing at the first ledge, swinging its grey and hairy body upwards.

The crescent-shaped balconies with their tiny balusters were only for architectural embellishment really; there was barely enough room for a plant pot let alone an inquisitive man-sized hyena-looking wolf. Ralph had meant to ask Randell to help him demolish them but, like several other jobs that could do with being done, they got left, partly due to more important and immediate work which needed doing and partly because Ralph felt loathe to attack the building's bold look and destroy its aesthetics. Doing that and then coming home every day to a partially wrecked house (on the outside at least) was a way of admitting defeat; one more thing to demoralise them, the post-apocalyptic landscape taking over inch by inch and slowly crushing their spirits.

The wolf examined the securely fitted boards, the fixings deep and deliberate. It jabbed its claw at a small crack where two boards had not quite come together. The gap was too small, the thing's large claws great for tearing flesh, just not so good at close up finicky work. Instead, it moved closer, letting its snout almost rest on the small gap. It took deep gulps, grunting as it did so, sucking in air through its nose. After a while it stopped and shook its head. Once more it let out a loud sneeze, its body jerking backwards as the loud yammer reverberated through the square. Quickly, it turned—had it heard something?—and, forgetting all about the house, it scanned the square once more. Instinctively it crouched, bared its teeth and stayed still like an out of place grotesque, amber eyes flicking left and right. If something was there, it would not be there for long. From its perch it already had the high-ground and, dark as it was, would go unseen until it was too late.

The square was empty.

It turned its attention back to the windows of the house, and slammed a curled fist into the wood.

Dust fell from the window inside, drifting onto Randell's face.

He lay on his back, his body now tight up against the skirting, parallel to the wall. He held the shotgun; it was pointed directly up towards the window. If the wolf got in it would have to lean in to see him. It would give him a second's head-start. Randell knew the shot would not kill the wolf-man if it did get in but it would be enough, particularly at such close range, to scare it off, and maybe remove an ear or an eye. Another bang against the timbers, louder this time, caused more dust. His eyes watered as an uncomfortable tickle grew in his nostrils. He lifted his left hand, the gun still raised and in place in his right, and grabbed at his nose. Like it or not a sneeze was coming. Ulrica was staring at him, knife in hand, frantically shaking her head. He squeezed hard, stifling the sensation.

The Urbat kept at it, hammering its mitts against the wood, clawing at it, ignoring the splinters that attacked it on a miniscule level.

Its yawls filled the square now, but not in anger. It was frustration. The thing was confused. Had it heard something? Sensed something with its canine nose? The way it the thing was acting, it was as if it could not be sure. Teetering on the useless balcony, pounding at timber, the rain was now coming down straight and hard, dampening its senses. It sniffled, unsure that it had smelled anything now. The man-wolf ceased doing what it was doing, breathing heavily, its breath a thick vapour in front of its muzzle. It let out a long howl. And stopped, its ears pricked. Slowly, it turned to look behind it, this time eyeing the second-floor window of the house on the corner.

Ignoring its original target it jumped down from the first floor bay, careful to avoid any debris, and railings that posed a threat. As it landed, its back fell into a natural arch as it crouched, its forearms supporting it, ready to spring off again like a one-hundred metre sprinter. In seconds it had taken off at full speed and leapt at the building sitting innocuously behind in the dark. Like a free climber on performance-enhancing drugs it scrambled up towards the first floor window, clutching for small cornices and crevices, its claws slipping and unable to gain proper purchase. The building was too sheer, with no architecturally satisfying add-ons or protrusions, just smooth render. That, and the increasing rain which now ran down the front of the building like a thin flat stream, had foiled its rabid ascent.

Inside, Barclay jumped in Sani's arms.

He had coughed a little too loudly as Sani had loosened his grip on him, the cadaver's body odour too much to bear at such close quarters. They had both heard the frustrated howl and felt the house shake as the thing threw its raking body at the walls. As careful and quiet as they had tried to be, they had been heard, sniffed out. One single cough had sealed their fate. Death would be here any minute, drooling steadily, growling and stinking like wet dog. It would only be a matter of time now. Once the thing reached the window, there would be a crash, a shattering of glass, a few steps and then just teeth and claws, and blood.

Sani pushed Barclay away and threw the covers back. It was not time to be giving in; they may as well at least try to defend themselves. Kill or be killed. Neither of them wanted to die in a stink-hole smelling of weeks' old decaying flesh. Better to go down fighting than to roll over and surrender. It was the first lesson they learned inside, that anyone ever learned if they knew what was good for them. Barclay followed, covering up their dead associate once more. They stood there, unsure of what they should do for a second or two, barely able to hear themselves think as the rain increased, loudly pummelling the roof and windows.

Then they heard it, or rather felt it. Another yawl, a snap of teeth and a thud as demented claws raked at and embedded into the masonry. And again. Barclay gulped as Sani readied himself. A hispid hand, canine yet still part human, appeared at the bottom of the window. The hand-paw tightened its grip and the two men approached the window. Fear gripped them, and they hesitated. They should kick at it now, not give it a chance to climb any higher, but they would give themselves away for sure. The thing would never give up. Once the rain had stopped, or slowed perhaps, it would be at the window. Then, as suddenly as the hand had appeared it abruptly disappeared, gone from the ledge. A roar followed as the thing slipped back down the wall.

Relief followed for a moment until they heard another thud as the thing's hand-claw reached up again. In panic Barclay turned to reach for his sawn-off but Sani had beaten him to it. The bigger man pointed his own shotgun at the window and, without turning his gaze, he passed the other weapon to Barclay. The two stood there, guns loaded and ready, the rain their only ally as it battered both the building and the thing below.

And then it was gone again.


Serkan hated the rain almost as much as he hated, what his race called, the Tecuani.

It was a good job he was inside. From the top floor of the Goring Hotel he watched the wild beast's attempt at scaling a smooth flat wall in such conditions. *Such simple things.*

Speaking quietly, he said, "It will give up soon, once its dilatory brain has caught up with all that violent flailing. All that exertion isn't worth the pay off."

"And what is the pay off?" Hemma stood behind him.

Silence. He continued to watch the futile attempts of the saturated hirsute beast. It gave one more try, leaping at the waterlogged wall again before crashing to the ground, narrowly missing impaling itself on the upright decorative finials of the metal fencing. It let out an eldritch whine, a scalded puppy's yelp, and stood, returning its gaze on the other house for a moment.

Serkan watched it as it shook itself, its large bowed upper torso shimmying unnaturally in the rain, before turning tail and running out of the square.

"That's a good question," he said after a minute. "I'm not quite sure."

## Chapter 13

Seeing the lone Urbat the night before, frightening as it was, had been a kind of blessing in disguise.

Yes, it had been alarming—they were lucky that only one turned up—but it had made it an easy night for them in the end. It had the strange effect of turning Seffi on somehow. Watching it prowl, feeling its presence and seeing its raw power had aroused her. And the night had been a long one. All she wanted to do was get Ralph in the bedroom. She may be post-menopausal but she was a female with desires and needs.

And she was there now, finally satiated, lying by his side, her body pulsing with delight, breathing heavily and her hair was matted with sweat.

"Hope the kids didn't hear us," she said, smiling at her lover and partner.

Ralph grunted. "I'm sure they're all old enough to understand."

"That's not the point." Seffi slapped his thigh beneath the blankets. She tried thinking back to the moment she had reached climax—had she been too loud?

"Shame Connor can't get himself a woman," he said, resting his hands behind his head and sinking back into the pillow.

Seffi looked at him, her fulfilled state turning sour at Ralph's throwaway comment. "That's not a nice thing to say."

Ralph eyed her. "What do you mean?"

"You know Connor's . . . well . . ." Her words trailed off as she thought of how to say it. She looked around the room for inspiration. The walls were a primrose yellow and, although it made her feel better, it said nothing to her. It was of no help.

"Well, what?"

She decided to be succinct. "You know he . . . likes boys?" She said.

"It's just a phase."

"It's not *just* a phase." She sat up. "I work with a lot of young and confused individuals. Sexuality is an important thing."

"So is sex." He smiled at her, smugly.

"You know, for an educated man, you're a little simple at times."

Ralph sat up, gave her the what-have-I-done look.

"Listen to me," she said. Her voice took on a serious tone. "Do you love your son?"

He pulled a face.

"I asked you if you love your son. Don't clam up on me now, mister."

He shrugged. "You know . . . Of course I do."

It was her time to be smug. "So tell him."

"I don't need to. He's my son. He knows. It goes with the territory."

"Piffle. What goes with the *territory* is a natural urge for procreation of the species. Sex. That's the natural order of things. Love doesn't necessarily come into it. An egg, if it's lucky gets a sperm donor; there isn't much love to be had from a miniature tadpole on auto-pilot."

"And you would know all about that, eh."

"You're an idiot. Look, you say he's your son but you need to show him. Love is about caring, listening, being there. Sex is just that; sex. Being a parent is special—do you not think Connor wants your approval, your unconditional love? Whatever he is? All this butch, keep your distance bullshit or the old 'one day he'll grow up' attitude is harmful. He needs to know."

He looked at her knowing better than to cross her; she knew way more about the human psyche. He only knew animals, and his own animal instincts. "OK, OK. I'll tell him."

She eyed him closely, looking for tell-tale signs on his face. Her own face was straight-lipped, blank. "Please. Promise me you will. Before it's too late."

"Too late? There's plenty of time. He'll always be my son."

She turned away. This man, the man she loved, could be impossible at times. She wondered how his parents had treated him. Why was he so standoffish with the one person who mattered most? She had seen it so many times in her career. She knew the young were vulnerable, what with hormones flying off in all directions and pressures from society and peers. It came to them at different ages and stages, many in fear of acceptance. Connor was gay, so what? As long as he did not go around deliberately hurting others, what was the issue? Love was love. A man can love a man just as much as he can love a woman. And vice versa. She was sure that Ralph did love his son, but for some reason he found it difficult to express. Why? It was not as if he had a complex personality, something like that of the narcissist with such an ego that he couldn't love anyone else— including his own son—but himself.

"You'd better."

She got up to go to the toilet and have a wash, hoping that Ralph would finally listen to her; in fact, not just listen but act on it as well. After all, he had always shown such care for his ailing animals. She made a mental note to approach Connor more often and engage with him, to break down any barriers that he, and she herself, felt about the awkward relationship between them; they both needed someone to talk to so why not each other? Whether through divorce or death, whichever way you looked at it, the poor lad had lost his mother and that was hard for any child. Seffi realised she was good at getting what she wanted, had a knack for gentle persuasion; Ralph would come round to her way of thinking soon enough. And then there was her own family.

"Do you think they've had it this bad in Scotland?" Seffi returned from the en-suite.

There was no reply.

"Ralph?"

He was asleep. *Great.*

While in the bathroom she had turned her thoughts to her sister.

Was she all right, still alive? Seffi could not recall seeing or hearing any reports from Scotland when the television and radio stations were still up and running. She had tried calling her sister's mobile phone but had just got a dead dial tone. And then, not long after, all the mobile communications masts had gone down.

Sadness washed over her as she reminisced: her sister and her making sand castles on a pristine and beautiful but freezing cold Scottish beach with the help of their father as they squealed with joy, their teeth chattering involuntarily like their own dental version of the Royal Edinburgh Military Tattoo. The two of them playing at dressing up, rummaging through their mother's wardrobe and drawers, putting on oversized dresses and high heeled shoes. It was only when they plastered their cheeks, eyes and lips with mum's favourite lipstick, getting in on the clothes and the carpet and the walls that they had been told off and sent to bed early. They had giggled all night eventually feeling guilty that they had potentially damaged their mother's makeup to the point where she would have no choice but to replace it. Seffi remembered the feeling of when, shortly after the lipstick debacle, she had torn her best skirt while climbing trees only for her mother to immediately condemn it, cut it up into strips and use it as rags, cloths for cleaning.

Then they were older, going out, holding boys hands, and kissing said boys. All this after being grossed-out by the thought of boys for years. Now, all they suddenly wanted was to smear their lips all over the boys' faces. It was exciting regaling each other's stories of their nights out with boys.

And then, in what seemed an instant, they were young adults, going to college, getting married, and heading off to work. That work, along with a man, had brought her to London, her career keeping her busy during the day, with the delights of what was always on offer in the capital occupying her at night. They went to see West End shows, concerts at Alexandra Palace, events at Hyde Park, parades around Piccadilly Circus, and the many street artistes in Covent Garden. It left little time to visit her sister.

And when the early reports first made the news headlines telling of beasts and demons killing each other and that it was escalating rapidly with many people already dead, she realised she had not seen her sister for more than seven years; her parents' funerals the last time she had been back. The guilt she felt was ridiculous; how could she blame herself for what had happened? Her sister could have come down to visit her just as much as she could have gone back to Scotland. And what now, caught in the crossfire of this strange battle? Otherworldly creatures had risen up, and taken over. How could she have ever predicted that? It did not, and would never, stop her worrying about her family so far away.

She could only hope for a good outcome, that somehow they had escaped and were, like them, in hiding and safe. As safe as one could be considering the enemy.

Perhaps she could persuade the others to travel up there. If they were careful, planned it properly, they could do it. Not easily but there were always options. There were hundreds of good-sized family wagons, even camper vans, dotted about the city; they may even have the choice of make, model and colour. Better than buying off the forecourt. Also, there was every possibility that they could be safer up there, the population much sparser and potentially more isolated and therefore untouched and still alive. The Scots had a knack for keeping unwanted types out. Or was the weather responsible for that? It would be good to see her sister, visit her parents' graves, and take flowers.

She climbed back into the bed, feeling the warmth from Ralph's body.

She laid her head on the pillow, draping her arm over him. She would first catch up on some sleep and then tomorrow, after another night of defence, she would put her idea to the rest of them. Regardless of their situation, getting away from the city could be the best move for all of them; give them a chance at life.

## Chapter 14

Seffi perished almost immediately.

As a coruscant sun twinkled with the last of its fiery delights, one more day coming to an end, a white-grey hand with lethal talons punched directly through the first floor window's timbers. It was no random shot, no flailing as before, just fast and straight, targeted. The target was one of the residents and it happened to be an unsuspecting Seffi who was standing by the window. Wrong place, wrong time. She had been readying herself for yet another night's onslaught, not her own funeral. The claws simply pierced her chest cavity and with one flick jettisoned Ralph's partner's heart from its warm and cosy and oxygen-rich environment.

Now, it lay, still beating on the polished wooden floor, the final throes of Seffi's life, the rich muscle not quite sure where it was or what to do other than the job it had done for decades. Her sister came to mind and in that instant she knew she wouldn't be going to Scotland anytime soon. Her body slumped to the floor, with eyes darting about, the brain attempting wildly to catch up with recent events; the last thing she would see being the air freshener in the toilet, still in its wrapper, in the same place, unmoved and unused from days ago. Ulrica had not utilised it. Aw, crap.

Ralph dropped to his knees and Randell came up from behind to stab at the vampire's intrusive and murderous arm. Ralph held Seffi as blood pooled about them. He cried out, attempted to ask her not to go, not to leave him, but she was already gone. The cold-blooded arm withdrew and Randell grabbed for some timber. He hoped the battery-powered drill was still charged, at least enough to drive some lengthy screws into the hard wood. The drill was right in front of him, but where were the screws?

"Connor," Randell shouted.

Connor came up the stairs, spotted his father on the floor, saw him holding something covered in blood. He looked over at Randell who had his back to the wall, supporting the timbers behind him.

Ralph was howling, rocking back and forth. "Where the fuck were you?"

Looking for support, Connor looked to Randell. "I . . . Er."

"You were supposed to be with her," Ralph screamed, his son backing away.

"But, I . . . I was . . . fetching stuff." Connor's last two words were mumbled.

"It was your only job." The tears fell down his face. "When I'm not with her, it's you . . . you're supposed to . . ." Ralph gulped. "You're my son."

Randell watched the father-son scene play out, knowing it was shock and grief at play. Connor could be a pain but to be fair to him he had at least been doing something for a change. Most nights Connor acted as a go-between from floor to floor, fetching and bringing whatever was needed and acting as back-up to whoever needed it most. As it was, Seffi had simply asked him to bring her up a glass of water. Which he was doing; he still had the glass in his hand. With Ulrica on the second and Randell on the ground floor it was Ralph who was also on the first floor and he had only turned his back for a second.

Ralph was hurting, lashing out verbally, but the situation at hand was more important. Angry words or blame wasn't going to bring Seffi back. She was gone; her heart lay on the ground in front of them all, left like a slab of meat for an obedient hound. Outside, the frenzy was only likely to increase now they could smell blood. And the ground floor was uncovered. He yelled at Ulrica to go downstairs and keep watch, but to keep away from the windows and yell out if anything happens. He heard the girl's rapid footfalls as he turned back to the job at hand.

Randell pointed to some tools in the far corner, and shouted. "Connor, grab that drill and get some more screws. Quickly."

Connor dithered, eyeing the drill, thinking of where the screws might be, whether he should go to his father. He put down the glass of water ridiculously carefully so as not to spill any.

Randell shouted at him. "Connor. For fuck's sake. Now."

This time, doing as instructed, Connor ran to get the screws. "Where are they?"

"Try back there, near . . ." He was pointing to a place behind where Ralph and Seffi was, by the far window. "If not, try downstairs. Be quick, I can't do this all night."

He found the screws in a small cardboard box up against the skirting board some four or five feet from where Seffi had dropped. Connor momentarily looked across at his father before picking up the drill. With screws in hand he began to work. Once he had driven home at least four screws Randell turned and held the timbers with him, pushing against a tirade of fists that still bludgeoned it from outside.

"More," Randell screamed.

"Bugger it, where's a wolf when you want one?" Connor muttered, knowing that the vampires outside would not be there if the same wolf had decided to return. Perhaps it would; hadn't it smelled something? "Now would be a good time," he said, answering his own question.

"What?" Randell looked at him.

Connor continued his frantic carpentry. "Nothing."

Downstairs, Ulrica was alone. She was shaking, too scared to even attempt a glimpse of outside for fear of seeing . . . that face. She had some idea what was going on upstairs but not really; she had kept her head down, meticulously eyeing the steps as she negotiated them at high speed upon Randell's command. The sounds coming from the first floor told her that whatever it was it was not good. She only hoped Seffi was all right, didn't want to think of the alternative. But Ralph's sobs? Her gut turned over. She had spoken with Seffi at length earlier, Seffi just sitting quietly, listening, hearing her worries and anxieties. Her fears. The biggest of them being that she now had to kill her own mum—or the thing that was using her body as a nightly killing machine. Banging began on her window.

"Crap." She swung her head round to face the stairs. "Could do with some help here."

No reply, only more banging, both upstairs and at her window.

"Randy!"

Hearing her, Randell shouted back. "Hear ya, girl." He turned to Ralph. "Ralph, really going to need you buddy."

Ralph looked up from Seffi's stricken body. "Whaa," was all he could summon.

Again, Ulrica's voice drifted up the stairs. "Only want one of you."

Laying down her head as gently as he could, Ralph stroked at Seffi's hair. "Be back soon, love." He walked away, machine-like, a mindless body heading for the stairs. The window secure again, Connor helped his father up and directed him to the stairs.

"I need to stay here with Randell, "Connor said, careful to direct his father away from Seffi's blood.

"Er . . . today would be good," Ulrica added before seeing Ralph coming down, his feet plodding, his eyes fixed on the space in front of him.

When he reached Ulrica, he stopped. "I'm here."

Ulrica gulped and stared at him, his face expressionless, his voice monotone, drab, his eyes wet and inflamed. It was then she noticed the blood on his shirt and trousers, his hands glistening with blood.

She grabbed his arms. "Oh crap, Ralph, are you hurt?"

He stared at her, lifted his bloodied paws, gawped at them. "What? She said she'd never . . ."

"What? No." She saw the blood again as the penny dropped. *Seffi*. She pictured the two of them talking over cups of tea earlier, mere hours ago, the softness in Seffi's voice, her propensity to just be there at the right time, to always say the right thing. Tears welled in her eyes.

Forgetting the situation at hand, Ulrica was about to console Ralph when there was a loud crash against the ground floor window. The timbers creaked and cracked.

"Crap." She grabbed a hammer, raised some more wood and began nailing. Randell had taught her to use screws over nails because they were stronger, would hold better. How nice. If she survived the night she would add some screws later. Until then . . .

"Ralph," she shouted, needing his attention, and help. "Ralph."

Approaching the window Ralph had already unbuttoned his fly and was poised ready, his penis in his hand. "This is my place, you ain't coming in, you bitch," he screamed, and let go his bladder.

Ulrica could only watch as the older man pissed up the timbers of the bolstered window. A flood of urine sprayed the windows, the wall, the floor.

Ralph spat at the window. "Fuck you."

Ulrica stood, aghast. It was going to be the worst night ever. If they survived.

*Seffi*.

## Chapter 15

"That were a rough one," Barclay said.

Barclay and Sani had taken a huge risk by stopping in the house for another night. They only hoped there would not be another late night showing of the wolf-man. If there was, they had readied themselves with weapons placed about the room in strategic positions: a shotgun in the corner, two steel blades on either side of the window, and a pistol holstered in the rear of Barclay's jeans. If it came to it Sani would use his bare hands and natural strength and fight the thing to its death. Or his. Anything as long as he did not have to go back under the blanket and play hide and seek with the rotting corpse.

As soon as the sun had set they had sat and watched as the vampires had appeared like two Jack Russell's ready to sprint down into a fox hole. Wasting no time—clearly the sharp-toothed aggressors of the house were all too wary of another Urbat visit and so wanted to get on with things—they saw the Mitclani attack the windows of the house almost immediately. The male vampire had breached the barricades on the first floor for only a moment but had quickly been repelled so it was difficult for Barclay and Sani to determine if any harm had been done. It didn't seem likely but who could tell. In his eagerness to get a closer look Barclay had almost ventured too near the window and exposed himself. Chances are that the two Mitclani, preoccupied as they were, would not have noticed him anyway but being spotted too soon, before they had any of the goods in their hands—their only game-play—would only put them in harm's way with potentially lethal consequences.

They would get the attention of the lead Mitclani when they were ready; he was clearly the one to talk to. Only then could a deal—and a favourable one to them—be done.

The attack had carried on for hours but the two vampires were repelled time and time again. Shots and arrows strafed the square. Screams and shouts continued into the small hours. Rooks lined the roofs and trees, the odd jackdaw among them, their peaked heads and thin beaks all eagerly awaiting the spoils, the chance of some carrion. They had no thought of prejudice or of taking sides, only partisan to themselves and their bellies; they would only be disappointed if at the end of the fight it meant feasting on the flesh of the undead, Mitclani meat not agreeing with their tiny and ages-old dinosaur-like innards. Conceding defeat as the night sky began to lighten, the two Mitclani had come together and after some wild gesticulating they had vanished from the square.

Sani stood quietly, intently watching the house. When he looked back into the square all was silent. He turned to his friend. "Did ya notice which way the vamps went?"

Barclay nodded. "Towards Bucko Palace."

"Ya think they'll be beddin' down there for the day?"

"Can't imagine it. Place is a dump now." He pointed at his own blockaded door. "It ain't like this. Ain't very secure either. Too big, too open."

Once the hellish beings had revealed themselves, the humans becoming acutely aware that the stuff of nightmares and terrible tales were all too real, mayhem had rapidly ensued. Man's idea that he was invincible had quickly led to riots and looting. He didn't seem to get it, that they were being picked off one by one by god-awful things; he could only see money, treasures. Buckingham Palace was just far too open, far too obvious a target, and full of decadent wares for it not to be touched. Nobody knew the whereabouts of any of the royals—if they had been airlifted to safety or quickly turned or even killed—but that thought was instantly disregarded as people began to murder one another in order to get at its treasures, some going as far as scraping the gold leaf away from the ornate decor. It may well have been the official London residence of the monarchy since 1837, but not anymore. The outside defences had held for a day or two but soon the changing of the guard was changed forever, and the *palace*—a place of interest—had dropped an A to become just a *place*, of little interest. Or complete avoidance.

The Tower of London had seen even worse carnage and had been stripped bare, the many victims thrown into the Thames. Soon after, The Battle of White Tower, as it became known temporarily to the survivors before they themselves perished, had seen a band of Mictlani holed up in the White Tower only to be assaulted by a massive tribe of Urbat one full moon, and slain savagely by tooth and claw, the white walls splashed red before the sun's early rays even had chance to shower it in orange.

Humans had sung the praises of the Urbat in the safety of dawn's light and had signed a treaty with them; the Mictlani were not only killing humans but were also turning greater numbers of humans to add to their army. Because of that the vampire population had grown exponentially, and greater numbers needed more food. And so on and so forth. And because they could only exist on the one thing, that one thing being human blood, the Urbat had been faced with no choice but to intervene; their moral code only worthy if certain actions were taken seriously and carried through.

Unlike the Mictlani, the Urbat were not too fond of their own voices; they were not brash or ostentatious. Killing vampires but living in peace with humans was the only way forward as far as the Urbat were concerned. Each full moon the Urbat would lock themselves away to keep the humans safe. The humans could carry on as if everything was normal; although, many humans never got over the idea that once a month there were giant wolf-men and wolf-women locked away in each city for the night. Once turned by the full moon the Urbat became crazed animals, a violent pack with no cognisant thought, and were not responsible for whoever they ripped apart. But that was the extent of the damage; they would not then go on to devour their victims and eat the meat of humans. Urbat could survive, quite literally, on dog food, however cuts of beef or chicken were much preferred; there was more protein and, besides, it tasted better. And humans could provide this, were good at this, if left alone long enough to rebuild their farms and replenish their livestock.

Having structure meant safety on the streets; an economy, people—and wolves—cared for with food and housing, security. Basic, yes, but far better than anarchy. Packaged as a model for freedom in many humans' minds, anarchy only equalled death. Lawlessness was not good for anyone and inherently - Man being Man—would soon lead to murder if people went unaccountable. Therefore it may not necessarily mean death by werewolf or vampire—it may be someone murdered for their belongings, their coat or a bottle of water—but death all the same. There was talk of the Urbat running blood banks in each major city and town where the humans could go to donate blood. This would in turn be used for their own medical purposes and would also provide an endless supply of food for the Mitclani. It was a win, win situation for all.

But, showing even more arrogance than Man, the Mictlani had instantly dismissed the idea and had stepped up their attacks—after all, the humans were mostly defenceless for twenty-seven days or so. And so it had gone on; one night a month the vampires died in vast quantities as man-shaped wolves sprung from soft pink flesh; the rest of the month the humans were steadily annihilated.

Barclay scanned the streets. "They can't have gone far; they left it pretty tight."

Sani nodded slowly. "Yeah. So how and when do we get in the house?"

As Sani spoke the door to the house across the square opened and two men, the men they had seen carrying bags the afternoon before, were now coming out. This time they were carrying a body. It looked like that of a woman. Following them out the door was a young woman and a young man. The young man was carrying two spades.

"Check this out," Barclay said. "Whoa. Not so close,"

Moving back from the window Sani stared over the sill. "I counts five of 'em, includin' the dead un," he said.

Barclay nodded. "Yep. Let's wait, see if any others come out."

They watched as the two makeshift pallbearers crossed the road with the body, walked down the road and entered the iron railings of the square. Turning back on themselves they faced the house from where they came. They placed the body down on the flagstones beneath a tree, careful to afford the body at least some dignity in death and avoid laying her remains in the bird shit. The older man stood mute for a while before crouching down, stroking the woman's face, and kissing her softly several times. As he stood again he lowered a sheet and covered the body. He lingered at the head, his chin dropping to his chest, before covering the dead woman's face.

Sani gulped.

Barclay looked on.

Below, the bigger man had grabbed one of the spades and was driving it into the flower bed next to the park bench. As if being held back by lead weights the older man stepped up and joined him, the spade moving tardily in his grip. The other two in the square looked on, the young man glancing back at the door every now and then.

"Why's he keep looking at the door?" Barclay said.

Sani shrugged. "Someone else inside?"

"Nah, they're burying one of their own. They'll all be out payin' their respects."

"He's just keepin' an eye on it."

"I ain't so sure," Barclay added.

It had been nearing midnight as Felix and Ivan slipped into a house at the far end of Victoria Square, unheard and unseen.

They had approached from Buckingham Palace Road, the Nova building behind them, and hearing a raucous ahead of them they had ducked into the first house on the left at the far end of the square; it was one of the few doors that wasn't actually painted black.

After leaving The British Library, and instructing the man they had saved to head north, they had themselves gone in the opposite direction, searching for signs of the living and the undead. Apparently they had heard news that the last of the known humans—there was also talk of a far off safe haven somewhere in the Scottish Highlands—had set up a safe house at Fawsley Hall in Northamptonshire. South of Daventry it was in the middle of nowhere, a rural hideout. So much so that many moons ago one Joseph Carey Merrick, aka The Elephant Man, had been granted respite there, far enough away from the curious and prying eyes of London. The north, east and south sides of the hall were not readily accessible by Mitclani because the reverend of the nearby Church of Saint Mary the Virgin had blessed the waters there—the area being a natural U-shape of lakes and ponds. It left only the west side that needed serious defence. Ivan only hoped he had informed the man correctly and had not saved him only to send him to his death elsewhere.

While venturing through Russell Square earlier in the evening they had seen the stricken body, or what was left, of a Mitclani, only trace elements left blowing in the breeze after being set alight. More human bodies, slowly desiccating, returning to dust, scattered the streets. It was a war-zone, or had been, the events only taking place under the still of the darkness, unencumbered, the daylight left to bear witness and uncover the night's atrocities with nobody left to collate the numbers, enter their names into the register, and bury the dead. Ivan shivered at the thought of ever having to enter Great Ormond Street Hospital; he knew it would be a scene of carnage, easy pickings, nothing left, the Grim Reaper having gone on a rampage for the hapless victims of the Mictlani and Urbat tribes all at once, the staff and the children suffering horrifically as Peter Pan looked on, unmoved and helpless.

It was while they were passing near to The Shaftesbury Theatre that they had got whiff of someone. Or something. They had been up all night and were looking for somewhere to rest; if not the theatre then they could try The Bloomsbury or Montague Hotels. Once inside the Shaftesbury, in one of the private viewing boxes, they had found a pair of teenagers nestled together, whimpering, clinging to one another with what little strength they had. One look told them that the unlucky lovers had been attacked and left to die, injuries and marks covering their bodies, blood smeared about the cubicle, on the floor, the upholstery.

"What should we do with them?" Felix had asked.

Ivan had looked at them both, at Felix. "They'll never make it."

Felix shook his head. He was young, not stupid; even he knew if they put these two out on the street, gave them a sat-nav with the exact directions to Northampton together with a nice new hamper from Fortnum and Mason, they would simply perish on the first night. They badly needed hospital treatment. At the very least, an IV drip each.

They had simply stood there, pitying the two victims for a moment before Felix spoke again. "We should just get on with it. Then be away. And, I'm hungry."

Ivan had only nodded. "It would be for the best."

Both feeling somewhat indifferent about their necessary decision, they had since made their way further south, only to wind up in Belgravia, once playground of the rich and richer.

Out of sight and hopefully out of mind they had watched the night's events unfurl. Two Mitclani, a woman and a man, had relentlessly assaulted the boarded-up windows of the ground and first floor with little interruption. Only now and then had they come together, words clearly exchanged, arms motioning in all directions, before attacking in a different spot; a ploy to catch the residents unaware. The house at the end was being well defended and there was little to see, the barricades doing their job. Ivan could only wonder who or what was going on inside.

After a long night's viewing, the unremitting attack finally coming to a natural end at dawn, the two vampires had scurried away. Careful not to expose themselves at the window Ivan and Felix had continued to watch. The house at the end appeared much the same. Felix was about to step away and bed down for the day when the front door had opened to reveal two men carrying a deceased woman. Only then did they realise just what had gone on inside. Those following were carrying spades. They looked glum.

"Five in the house?"

"Looks like there's only four now," Felix said.

Ivan shook his head. "Five minus one makes four; wherever in the world did you learn that?"

"You mean like when you say something is 'very tall' or to 'sit down'?"

"What?" Ivan was frowning, wondering what the boy was on about.

Sounding much like a teacher with little charisma, and without the dowdy and démodé navy tank-top, Felix spoke the words matter-of-factly. "Sit will do, you don't need to say down. Same as tall. Tall means tall, *very* tall means the same thing. Obvious as five minus one."

"So you did attend school. At least maths and English."

"Whatever." Felix swiped his hand through the air in-between them. "Anyway, what do we do now?"

"Don't know about you but I'd like to get a better look at those two in the window across the way." He pointed up and across at the second-floor window to the right. Number twenty-three.

"You mean the scrawny old guy and the big Asian-looking dude?" Felix said. "Saw them ages ago."

"It's not a competition, Felix. And why didn't you say?"

"Knew you'd spot them. Eventually." Felix said, the last word drawn out in mock derision.

"OK, OK. You'll be pleased to know I did. What I don't know is this: if they're holed up there watching then they're obviously not with the funeral parade, so why are they doing and what do they want?"

Felix smirked. "Now, that's a better question."

# Chapter 16

Serkan paced back and forth, dangerously close to the light that spilled in through the door's opening.

He did not care; the way he was feeling he could just go out, burn himself to a crisp if that is what it took, and finish the job. Finish them off for good. Rather than just sit by and give in to the day.

The day was shaping up to be bright and sunny as dark deep shadows from the surrounding buildings, their shapes cleanly defined and true, filled the streets outside. *Damnation.*

He had used every expletive known to the modern world and had now slipped into the Mitclani's ancient language of Nahuatl.

"Cuitlatl," he said, forcing the word through gritted teeth. *Shit.*

Hemma called out to him, trying to reason with him. "Serkan."

She knew he had survived this long only by keeping his cool; keeping his head when all around had turned to chaos. The calculated and calm mind almost always won the day. Hot-headedness led to mistakes. And that, for a vampire, often led to death. That was not the singular outcome she was hoping for.

Serkan's pacing continued. The morning air flowed through the building—a window or door open to the rear of the building that would need checking before long—now bereft of its contaminating smell, the heavy diesel fumes that threatened the delicate lungs of the citizens not so long ago. Death had many guises. Abandoned cars, with unrecognisable remains still in the driving seats of many, and buses, black taxi cabs and trains going nowhere; London had finally solved its pollution crisis only there was nobody left to appreciate it. The Mayor would have been a happy chappy if only his crushed and haemorrhaged respiratory organs had not filled up with blood as they killed him all those months ago. Chronic irony.

"Tzoyotl. Matoca." Serkan often used the ancient tongue when filled with ire. *Arse. Wanker.*

"Please Serkan, calm down. Someone may hear us." Hemma stared at him. "What does all that mumbo-jumbo mean anyway?"

He shot her a look, a look she knew that at any other time would have meant her instant demise. Getting away with murdering his own kind had only served to empower him, had given him some sort of god complex. Only he didn't believe in a supreme being, other than himself.

"Quemah," he said eventually. *Yes.* He stepped back, away from the light, and closed the door. It dragged on the floor, the hinges sprained and sagging.

"I'll go check out back," Hemma said, relieved that Serkan had finally calmed himself, not so pleased that she now had the whole day stuck inside with him again.

That was if they were not discovered—she would not be surprised if someone had heard them, what with the amount of peculiar cursing going on—and killed after Serkan's wild tantrum. Then again they needed to feed; maybe at least one fresh neck might come looking to see what all the commotion was about. She wondered how Serkan had survived all these centuries with such an attitude—was he stupid, lucky, or vividly shrewd? If dinner was not there for the taking, perhaps it was a ploy by him in the hope that dinner would come to them.

"All secure back there," she said upon returning back to the main part of the building.

Serkan showed his acknowledgement with a curt nod as if afraid that once he opened his mouth he would begin cursing and shouting again. A self-regulating vampire. Nice to see he had learned something; Mitclani were vulnerable during the hours of daylight and drawing needless attention to oneself when one should be bunking down in a shaded and safe spot was quite literally playing with fire.

They had taken refuge in the south side of the Buckingham Palace's Royal Mews where the royal collection of State Coaches once resided in their splendour. The Gold and Diamond Jubilee coaches had been ransacked and stripped a long time ago by looters ignorant of the deadly end they would soon meet. People had put gold and wealth over weapons and protection. Silly. Thanks to the war the economy had quickly dissolved and become superfluous. There were no workers left, no demand for property, and even money and the gold hewn from the coaches had become worthless.

It was like the NHS closing its doors and allowing the population to decline in health to such a point where nobody was well enough to go to work. No work meant no pay, and no pay meant no taxes paid. Of course, no workers soon meant no contracts or jobs finished, and so the big bosses themselves would disappear as their businesses collapsed, rendering everything null and void. Anarchy and violence would ensue for those left to survive. This exact scenario had happened, only much faster and on an unimaginable scale, once the war escalated and the Mictlani and Urbat had ravaged the towns and cities and much of the countryside.

Serkan had used this place as a hideout before, narrowly escaping one full moon as an Urbat pack descended onto the Mews slaughtering anyone still left alive, along with all the horses. Several large rib cages still cluttered the courtyard, a horse mausoleum, some lined up like oversized xylophones as though waiting for *Mictlantecuhtli*, the lord of the Underworld, to step up and play his own abominable version of Camille Saint-Saëns' Danse Macabre with his dreaded mallets. Perhaps he had already done so, in the Haras du Pin in Normandy, France; who knew?

Having shuffled to a safe corner and concealed herself as best she could Hemma closed her eyes. While the undead did not actually need sleep—that had been saved for the movies—she liked being able to switch off for a time. Only she couldn't. Her mind reeled.

"Which female do you think you got?" she asked without looking, knowing Serkan would always be listening.

"The old one, I believe." The words came out of his mouth matter-of-factly; he wasn't the least bit concerned that he had ripped out the beating heart from a woman's chest.

Something inside Hemma felt relief. *Why?* She had seen something in the young girl's face.

"I wanted that big bastard, the one with the arrows. Agana needs her revenge. As do I. Who does he think he is anyway, fucking Mad Jack Churchill?" Serkan could hear his voice growing louder as he spoke, expletives peppering his thoughts and words.

Hemma shook her head, forgetting the girl. "Instead of killing him, would it not be better to feed off him?"

"I'll not drink a drop from him. I'll bleed him out and crush his skull for what he did to Agana."

Here we go again. "Put it out of your mind, Serkan." She looked up at the ceiling, its clean and evenly painted surface contrasting all that lay beneath it. "Please."

"Never." The word came out more like a growl.

"Then don't be surprised when he outsmarts you," she said.

"What?" he snarled at her.

"Your emotions cloud your judgement; carry on like this and he may catch you off guard."

"Let him try," he hawked.

She shook her head again. *Impossible*. His anger was putting them both in peril. For a few brief seconds she thought she might approach the Mitclani Council, appeal to them to put an end to Serkan's private vengeance, his own little payback party, before realising that Serkan had, and always would, worm his way out and simply do as he pleased. He was too powerful and all too arrogant. After all, he had again killed at least two more of his own the other night with no repercussion. Had it even been reported? She doubted it.

"And what of the others?" she said, ready to give up for the day and sit in silence, let him stew.

"Well, you said it yourself. We feed."

## Chapter 17

Back inside the house Ralph immediately took off, leaving the others in the hallway, and locked himself in one of the four bathrooms.

Randell locked the front door, bolted and refitted all the timbers—ensuring each screw met a fresh hole and bit deep—as he watched the older man trudge away. Ulrica was weeping too, her nose and eyes red, fresh snot glistening on her upper lip. He nodded at her, a silent instruction urging her to follow Ralph and keep an eye on him. Half-heartedly, Connor had initially followed his father like a scalded puppy who did not want to get too near, unsure of his master. When he saw Ulrica approaching his receding father, he paced away, heading back to the basement.

Randell leant back, letting his weight hit the wall behind him. Sighing heavily he slid down and sat and dropped his head into his hands, resting them both on raised knees. He was tired beyond belief, his body numb and running on adrenalin. He knew his bulk would soon need sustenance; he couldn't keep going no matter how young. His stomach growled. He growled too.

"Food," he shouted. "We got any food?"

Hearing him shouting for the obvious—he was always scavenging for food—Ulrica scampered back downstairs. She had only made it halfway to Ralph's room before turning back on hearing Randell She entered the kitchen.

"Follow him. Do this, do that, go here, go there, heel, sit, lie down," she mumbled as she passed.

Her hands at her neck, she removed the dog collar and threw it aside. It landed on the worktop with a clatter. She wiped her arm across her eyes, her cheeks flushed and inflated as she let out a large and prolonged sigh. She knew Randell was a big lad and needed plenty of fuel in him, and she also knew how hard he worked to protect them all, so she did not mind. Not really. It would keep her mind occupied after what they had just done. And Ralph was safely locked away.

"I'll see what we've got," she said, her voice shaky.

"Thanks," Randell said, feeling shaky. "That ground out there is hard as hell."

He thought back on the night's tragedy. They were just readying themselves for another attack, had done the same for weeks and now, from out of nowhere, Seffi had been taken away from them. In an instant. Fast and brutally efficient. Randell could not remember a time when he had seen so much blood in such a short spell of time. Someone would have to clean it up quick-smart before the flies decided to play house with them. He could not ask Ulrica or Ralph to do it. As it was, Ralph could barely contain himself as they buried Seffi in the flowerbed, and who could blame him? That left him and Connor; he knew Connor would faff about, profusely complaining about why it had to be him who had to do it— conveniently forgetting that Randell was doing the lion's share—and expending twice as much energy than if he just got on with the job at hand.

Ulrica woke him. He had fallen asleep where he sat. She was tapping his shoulder gently.

"Randy, I've done you some food." Her eyes looked sore.

"Thanks, Pet," he said, dragging himself up.

Ulrica looked at him. "You woken up in Geordie-land?" She smiled through pink cheeks.

It had done its job. Calling her something unexpected had caught her off guard and she had forgotten her pain for a second. He might be tired but he would always look out for her.

"Nah, still here with you." He forced a smile but it came out as more of a grimace. He put his arm around her.

Together they walked into the kitchen.

"Better call Connor," she said.

"Yes, ma'am," he said, looking forward to getting some food inside him, before bellowing Connor's name through the hall. Again, a hint of a smile from her.

Ulrica had done justice to the bacon this time and the three of them ate in silence.

"I'll take some up for Ralph," she said, reaching for the spare plate she had set aside.

"He won't come out," Connor said.

Ulrica looked to Randell.

"Maybe so, but he'll need to eat. Besides, someone should check on him." He glared at Connor.

"Don't look at me," Connor said, going back to his food.

Randell frowned and turned to Ulrica. "Will you take him something? I'm sure he'll prefer seeing you to us anyway. Thanks."

She was about to go, bacon butties in hand, when she stopped. "Oh, crap."

Concerned, Randell dropped his bacon. "What is it?"

Ulrica shrugged. "I can't remember if he likes red or brown sauce on his bacon."

"Red," Connor mumbled, his mouth half-full.

"Brown," Randell answered at the same time.

Deciding for herself she grabbed the ketchup and headed for the stairs.

By the time Ralph unlocked the bathroom door the bacon was cold.

Ulrica handed him the plate.

"I'm not very hungry," he said, stepping back onto the landing. His face was puffy, angry red lines circled his eyes.

"You should eat something."

He closed his eyes, nodded gently. "I will."

"You promise?"

"I promise."

"It'll be cold."

He gave her a tiny smile. "Nothing wrong with cold bacon."

"I brought ketchup."

He hesitated for a moment, looking intently at the bottle of bright red sauce. He shivered overtly before taking it.

"Thanks kiddo," he said, affecting a smile.

She turned away, then suddenly realised her mistake. Bright red sauce. Bright red blood. She felt herself welling up, her stomach turning over, at the thought of Seffi's demise and was about to apologise to Ralph when the door clicked shut. He had retreated, clearly wanting to be alone with his grief and cold bacon sandwich. Randell had been right, brown sauce would have been the better option—why had she ignored it? Berating herself, she stood at the door for a minute deciding whether or not to knock, make amends somehow. Through the door she could hear the quiet sobs of Ralph. She felt terrible and her own tears now fell.

Composing herself she headed downstairs again where she found Randell washing up.

"You don't have to do that," she said from behind.

He saw her eyes were glistening, the lids red and puffy.

"Yeah, I know but Connor soon disappeared when he clocked it. There's not that much to do. You go put your feet up. I need to warm my hands anyway," he said.

"Thanks, I'm worried about Ralph."

"I know. We all are. It's gonna be raw for him for some time," he said softly.

Ulrica thought of her mum. "Yes . . . yes, of course."

"How about you?" Randell asked her.

"Not great, I wish Seffi . . ." Her voice broke as the tears started again. She stood there crying.

Randell quickly dried his hands and wrapped his immense arms around her, almost enveloping her.

She stayed in his arms for a minute, her head against his chest, and then spoke. "What about you? Seffi was your friend, too. And . . . Sullivan."

"One thing at a time," he reassured her. "When . . . I mean if Sullivan ever turns up then we'll deal with it one way or the other."

"Thanks, Randy." She sniffed, wiping at her nose and eyes. "You badly need a shower."

"Message received." He raised his arms, sniffing at his armpits, before looking at her. "I'd better not tell you your hair smells of bacon then."

Connor stabbed the needle into the vampire's forearm.

Once, twice, three times, four times. The heavily strapped and gagged Mitclani felt nothing, its nerve endings numb, long dead since its body had been turned. The syringe was empty. He jabbed it in again. Nothing. Up until now his experiments had yielded nothing. Just who was he kidding? Who among them would actually care?

He was beginning to think his efforts were useless. He felt sick to the stomach; he had hated Seffi at first but she had always been kind and respectful. He thought of the times she had done things for him: fetching him a drink, making his breakfast and dinner, how she would always try to include him in the conversation, tell his father off for being abrupt with him. And she understood his sexuality. A part of him wished it had been him instead of Seffi. It would have ended his pointless questioning, whether about himself or about his relationship with his dad, or the silly so-called experiments he was currently engaged in. It would certainly bring an end to the melancholia he felt on a daily basis. He knew Seffi would never be fetching him a drink during a night's work ever again, something she had always done gladly. It was a case of not appreciating what you had before it had gone. He felt like an idiot, again.

So, *now what?*

His father would be too stricken with grief to ever notice him now, let alone take note of his pathetic attempts at serious research. Even if he was to find a breakthrough, what would it matter? He thought of the outcome, what he was aiming to achieve, the cycle of life and death: a human is turned into a vampire, then the vampire turns back into a human, miraculously rejuvenating itself, the brain and flesh resurrecting, become healthy and alive once more, only to become a target of the Mictlani once again. Would it mean the successfully treated would become immune to being turned? And if so would the next attacking Mictlani know this and, instead of trying to turn them again, merely flick out their human heart, unhappy at being mocked? The returned undead being dead forever this time. A vet would only laugh at him, would put the animal out of its misery for fear of it suffering further.

*Shit.*

He sat at his workplace, pushed a few Petri dishes around, rolled vials back and forth listening to the tiny sounds that glass makes, mulling over his stupidity. But then if he did get a result . . . If he did, surely, that would be worth it. It would not be stupid. His theory was solid; he was only following on from previously well-documented and well-respected research. If the 'cured' person was killed at a later stage then that was fate. He could never control that, or even want to. It was not as if he was Baron Frankenstein. As a member of the Mitclani's eternal vampire clan a person was as good as dead anyway. Stuff what anybody thinks. No, giving up would be failure. And failure meant being ridiculed and called names that he did not like. And what else was there to do anyway? Sit around masturbating into a tissue like Randell?

He looked over at the vampire. "Right then," he told it. "I'll make them see what I'm all about."

The hessian sack—the sheets now replaced with something heavier—over its head twitched.

No, he told himself again, it was not a waste of time and effort. Just how long had the scientific community been testing and experimenting on a cure for cancer? Or HIV? Or any of Man's known terminal diseases? Those guys had millions of pounds pumped into their studies, the best medical minds and pristine laboratories in the world, and still it took time. Lots of it. Yes, he was on the cutting edge, alone, with second-hand kit and some base knowledge; he would have to think outside the circle and get a lot more books from the library to aid him.

It was not all bad news. Each failure taught him something new, didn't it? He just needed to eliminate everything else until he found the answer. But, he realised, he would need more data. He decided to grab some sleep; he would get onto it later. He would need all his strength and wits about him. And after some sleep he would go out and catch himself another, one with some blood left inside its stagnant body, another perhaps not-so-willing 'patient' to practice on.

## Chapter 18

"They're on the move," Felix said.

Since they had arrived in the square Felix had offered to take first watch. It was early afternoon now, the blue sky dappled with large clouds, the sun searching for a way through, and the square looked grey in the dull light. Restless, Ivan stepped forward, careful to stay in the shadows and not reveal himself—as Felix was close to already doing—expecting to see the two strange men they had clocked secretly watching things from the other house on the corner.

Instead of a pair, a 'scrawny old guy and the big Asian-looking dude' as Felix had posited, there was only one man on his own and he had come out of the house at the far end.

It was the bigger man, the one they had seen digging the shallow grave for the deceased woman. Ivan glanced at the crude burial plot, the soil and weeds dug over as if ready for the planting of next season's spring bulbs. He watched the man head out of the square at the opposite end, towards Beeston Place. He was carrying something long.

"Got himself a shotgun. A nice one." Instinctively, as if threatened by words only, Ivan grabbed the hilt of his short sword.

"Is there such a thing as a 'nice' shotgun?" Felix asked.

"Well, it looks . . . It's got a quality finish."

Felix shook his head. "Are your eyes really that good?"

"All right." Ivan mulled things over. "Have you seen our two night watchmen over the road move or show themselves yet?" he asked, his hand relaxing.

Felix nodded. "Yeah. Every now and then I see the top of someone's head. They're careful to stay back, not be seen."

"Do you think they are watching that house?" Ivan pointed to the house at the far end. "Or us?"

Felix picked at the wallpaper. "They don't seem to be showing any interest this way."

"Well, it's . . . Hold on."

"What?" Felix turned quickly.

"Another one coming from the house at the end."

They watched as the smaller man now, the rearguard spade carrier, left the house and hurried away in the direction of Lower Grosvenor Place.

"Looks like he's going fishing," Felix said, seeing the man with something long slung over his shoulder. "Why wouldn't they stick together?"

Ivan shrugged. He looked at his watch. "It's only two in the afternoon. Plenty of time before dark. They should be safe enough alone."

"That depends on where they're going. If they enter a building, could be a different story."

"Well, that's up to them," Ivan said. "Those two Mitclani must have taken shelter somewhere close by. They best be careful."

"Yeah, that dude has got some serious anger issues."

Ivan agreed. "That still doesn't tell us who our nosey neighbours are."

"Perhaps they got caught out and needed to hide somewhere quickly, what with those two neck-biters roaming about outside," Felix said.

"Neck-biters?" Ivan shook his head. "You'd have thought they would have made a move by now."

"Maybe."

Ivan continued. "Let's say they have hidden away, you can't imagine that house would have any food, certainly no snacks. Not if it's anything like this place." Ivan pointed at the state of the house they had settled in, overturned and looted for anything worthwhile by any number of wannabe survivors. "Surely they'd move on, at least go out for supplies, for food?"

"Even if they have plenty of supplies, you'd think any self-preserving human would only want to get as far away from here as possible before night falls again," Felix added.

To his left a spider crawled up the wall. Ivan spotted it and watched it continue on its way, ignoring its eight-legged antics; he was more interested in the four legs over the road and what they were up to. If they were even human.

"Yes, you would think that wouldn't you," he said.


Connor entered the courtyard.

He was of the opinion that they couldn't have gone far so he'd have to be extra cautious. Daylight being the handicap it was, a vampire would have no choice but to get out of the light unless it favoured tender, blackened and brittle skin. So, to save on the crispy, they needed a place to shack up. And this place was as good as any. Better even; it was close and large enough to hide away for a few hours.

He dodged between the skeletal frames of several horses, the skulls an odd pointy shape with a fixed grin of large teeth, more devil than equine once the flesh and skin had gone.

"Nice," he said out loud.

What looked to be smashed furniture, dining chairs and a coffee table, and a large screen television in several black pieces lay to one side of the courtyard. A liberated—why?—and dented car bonnet acted as a large tray, housing other electrical bits, including a rusting toaster and computer keyboard. Looters had obviously ransacked the place and thrown all the useless stuff from one of the four metal corner balconies that led to the individual apartments. A red and gold livery jacket lay wet and rotting on the tarmac. Old magazines, the cover photograph that of a beautiful woman, whirled in one corner, caught in the eddy of a breeze. The smell of rotting flesh had since come and gone now that the skeletons were dry and grey, picked clean by the birds and bugs. Weeds pricked through the tarmac where it met the stone edging, tall and flourishing as though competing for height with the aged trees.

In the centre of the courtyard he stopped and turned slowly, carefully scanning the balconies. He remembered what an old friend from college, an avid traveller, had once told him: "When you're out on your travels, always remember to look up. All the beauty, the architecture, the interesting stuff is up high. Ground level is where the shit goes down. Literally. Have you seen how many dogs there are roaming about in any one city? You'll see crap everywhere. So, remember, look up. Only watch where you're stepping." It was something he had done since, often watching people scurrying about the roads and pavements on their way to work, to the gym, or to pick up the kids from school. Their heads down, they missed everything. Architects deliberately put their most intricate and special designs up high on buildings so that only the discerning few would notice, their rarity in being seen making them more precious. He wondered if his friend had made it, or was he higher still, looking down on him now as he prepared to do what he knew to be crazy.

The courtyard had once been elegant, the home of the Queen's carriages and stables. The four large trees were the only thing of any note now, the leaves bristling with foliage. A mass of discarded pigeons lay dead beneath them, their throats torn and their tiny bodies sucked dry. A Mitclani aperitif, or the only source of blood available? Connor knew it meant nothing; they could have been lying there for days.

He wandered up the east stairs to the first floor searching for fresh evidence, anything that looked recently touched or broken. A door left ajar, something newly disturbed, or if he was really fortunate, a hand print. Walking to the first apartment he raised his heavy-duty dog pole, its slip-noose nice and loose, hanging freely, ready. In his right pocket, hidden deep inside his work trousers, a Russian 8mm Baikal pistol converted to fire 9mm ammunition rounds sat in readiness in case everything turned to shit. He hoped it wouldn't.

He checked his watch, the dial sitting passively on the hairs of his wrist: 2.37PM. *Plenty of time.*

Pushing the door open, he first sniffed, the scent of the Mitclani like that of a rotting compost heap—only minus the rats but with an extra ration of teeth—not obviously present. Again, it did not necessarily mean anything; the modern vampire may be odour sensitive and was just as likely to drop into a nearby pharmacist for a quick spray of deodorant. Outside the threshold he waited, his dog pole poised, feeling safer for being closer to the light; a silhouette come to catch you, the light-trick would obscure his prey's eyesight and give him the advantage. He wished he was as big as Randell, but then he had already caught a couple of vampires this way for his research. And he had managed to get them back to the house, unseen.

Once more he sniffed the air. Inside, the room was dim, bare of furniture; newspapers and cushions, broken plates cluttered the floor. What looked like an old jar of pickled onions lay broken in a collapsed and cracked heap, the spilled contents about it, lying like little lost and vinegary eyeballs. Connor peered at the floor, ignoring a semi-dried slick of tomato ketchup, and took a step closer. As he stepped onto the threshold he stopped, wondering if he had heard something. Maybe it was his steps, the hollow room echoing? No, he had heard something, spoken words perhaps. Quiet, maybe, but there. He was sure. He listened hard; if someone had left a radio on, it had now stopped. The chances of it having been on since the residents had gone and then gone off as he just happened to pass by could not be coincidence. Maybe he was hearing things. He gulped as sweat formed on his brow.

He allowed his eyes time to adjust. *Come on Connor. You've got this.* He knew that during the day the Mitclani were weak, could be hurt by the UV and would do anything to stay put. It meant that while they were vulnerable they would do anything to stay away. But he had done this before. Of course, it presented a challenge but one he was prepared to risk. After all, dying here and now meant that he would not have to go home and deal with that lot in the house. It did not take a genius to realise he was not liked much. Ralph, his own bleeding father, barely spoke to him. And Randell was Randell; he was more brooding that hateful or hurtful. But then there was Ulrica. At least she talked to him, gave him the time of day.

He stood there thinking, feeling guilty about his idea. He would have to try and impregnate her sooner than later; the full moon was imminent and who knew what might happen then. Would any of them survive? Perhaps his idea would fizzle out to nothing. Being dead did that for a person, ended all their dreams and aspirations. For a moment he thought he might just ask her; she may actually have pity on him and allow him to do the deed as it were—it was all in a good cause. Then again, no. If she took it the wrong way, or he found he just could not 'perform' with a woman, what then, where would he put his face? Perhaps walking into a vampire's den during the day and meeting his maker was the best for everybody.

No, he decided, as much as he might hate himself, he was not going to give those fucking dogs back at the house the satisfaction of his death. They could put up with him a little longer yet. *They'll see*. Things would change soon enough.

He turned his attention back to the room. If anyone had been there surely they would have jumped him while he was distracted by his thoughts. Well, they had not. Did that mean nobody was there and that he was actually hearing things? Or were they biding their time, waiting for the precise moment to attack?

He stepped in.

Randell sat on the front row bench of the Anglican church of Saint Peter's on the corner of Hobart Place and Eaton Square.

The wooden seat was still polished, smooth and clean as he ran his palm along it. At the chancel end a crucified Christ bore down on him from above the apse. Behind him was a huge organ; tin, copper and gold pipes of differing heights and bores stood sentry-like above the door on metal struts, the whole thing wrapped in a framework of beautiful golden timber. Randell admired the workmanship, wondering at the juxtaposition of the potential of heavenly sounds: life's air pumping through man-made bellows facing the mewling and abandoned nailed Son as He struggled for breath with foundering lungs and pierced abdomen.

Not religious—all his life the news had shown him murder, slaughter and death in great numbers because of organisations that professed their belief in a divine power to be the true one—he enjoyed the solitude of the building, the ornate and precise architecture. The inside was large, with high ceilings, and it was quiet. The church offered him peace, if only by way of no noise. He looked up again at the man on the cross. The barbarity of Man had been relatively tame back in His day. Multiple wars around the world since then, the genocide of whole races, new and horrific ways of killing and maiming had even surpassed Man's avarice. Death had become big business in the last few centuries.

And big business had its own price it seemed; the bigger the house the sooner the residents had been murdered once anarchy took hold, the dying asking just where their hedge fund managers were to protect them. Even those with personal security guards had seen their trained and ready guards vanish below the fists and clutching hands of an angry and hungry mob. Then came the Mitclani and the Urbat in full force.

It was a group of Mitclani who had taken Sullivan. He and his brother had been trying to get out of the city, heading south towards the coast, after the mayhem began. After visiting their home one night they had found the place smashed up, their mum and dad gone. No blood, no bodies, just signs of a struggle. The house stank. Broken glass lined the carpet. They were about to begin looking for their parents when the howling had begun. Preternatural roars had broken the night's air, chilled them both to the core and, in panic, they had fled.

They managed to get as far as Tooting. Hungry and dejected they had entered Saint George's Hospital in the hope of raiding the vending machine for some sustenance when they were ambushed. A large man—or thing that stood and walked like a man with a wolf's face—had come at them at the T-junction of a corridor, teeth and saliva flying fiercely, the jaws snapping with vigorous malevolence. It had been the first time they had actually seen one in the flesh, and it was enough for them to do an about-turn and scarper back down the corridor to where three Mitclani lay in wait.

The darkened corridor had limited their experience of the ensuing battle in which they were caught, and, in-between the stuff of nightmares, they had seen little. A flash of teeth here, a grievous claw there. They had smelled the thick metallic tinge of freshly spilled blood before getting splashed in the viscous and sticky liquid. A sound much like that of a sea bass being dropped onto the fishmonger's slab had accompanied another dull clonk as a body, or bodies, slumped to the ground. Squeals and yowls became grunts and whines as foe met foe, their evil intent on killing each other centuries old, both ignorant of the human bystanders caught in the middle. One or the other, they would deal with the dismayed bystanders after the fight; to the victor the spoils.

Scrambling away from the sprawling daemons, wolf and vampire tangled upon the tiled floor, Randell felt his legs go from under him. He slipped on something wet, slamming his face into the wall. Pain coursed through his body. Dazed, he looked about, instinctively reaching for his brother. As his eyes focused he saw two bodies, gruesomely mauled and lacerated; the chest of one was ripped open, the skin around it almost translucent; the other, its hirsute hand gripping at a gaping hole in its thick grey-black neck; both finally dead, having killed one another.

He would have screamed had it not been for the release of his brother's grip as the remaining two vampires dragged Sullivan away. Randell was quick to his feet. Too quick. His head reeled and he stumbled, the blood-ridden floor causing him to stagger and slide to a halt in a heap. By the time his head had stopped whirling, and he had clambered to a standing position, the corridor was quiet. The surviving two vampires had gone and so had Sullivan. The quick hospital visit should have been easy forage for nourishment; instead he had only served his brother up for food.

Randell puked on the church floor. Those sucker-fucks had taken his brother, and probably tortured him, feeding off him for a while and then—a part of him was sure—they had killed him. He wanted to believe Sullivan was still out there, somewhere, being held captive. He reasoned that his brother was being kept alive for their purposes; there were so few humans left and if the vampires killed everyone, what then? How would they feed? If there was a possibility, however small, that his brother was still alive then Randell would keep looking. Unless he found evidence to say otherwise, or saw his brother's lifeless body for his own eyes. Only then would he stop searching. And spend the rest of his god-forsaken life hunting and killing those responsible.

He dragged himself to his feet, picking up the shotgun that lay on the bench beside him. He gave it a quick check and turned for the door. He passed under the six huge columns out front, feeling small as he descended the steps, and headed out onto Upper Belgrave Street. This afternoon he would search the houses and garages on Wilton Mews. It would not take him too long. That way he could get back way before dark and check on Ralph, see how he was bearing up, and also find out how Ulrica was coping. He did not like the two consoling each other alone, not after what had happened, and not with that spiritless Connor in the house.

## Chapter 19

Having found nothing of any importance, except a Blu-Ray copy of one of his favourite movies about a hitman and a young girl, Randell trudged back to the house.

The clouds from earlier had cleared, the evening sky cool and calm; it was about an hour until dusk. He eyed the square, looked over at the freshly dug grave inside the railings. Seffi would always be near. As long as they were able to stay in the house. The air smelled clean somehow; years of diesel fumes had been replaced by the stench of decaying and putrefying bodies but even that had dispersed. He could smell fresh earth. He looked at Seffi's grave again, and closed his eyes for a moment, seeing her as she was; helpful, genial, a mother-figure for those who knew her closely. Randell realised he had not actually known her that well, or that long, had initially been envious and resented her wealth after hearing that her and Ralph had lived in a similar house in Pimlico. He shook away the thoughts and sighed before banging heavily on the front door. He slipped the Blu-Ray disc back into his bag, noticing the garlic that had once adorned the door frame and the front of the house had gone, cleaned up ready for another fresh batch; Seffi's final chore.

Usually during the day the door was locked by three heavy-duty latches so that they could come and go as they needed. Because of the latest tragedy Randell had instructed Ulrica to lock and barricade the door from inside. Extra vigilance, just in case. The amount of clanging coming from within the house could mean only one thing: Ulrica was being left to open up on her own.

Randell muttered under his breath. "Come on Connor, give her a hand." He knew Ralph would be useless for a while. He'd have to cajole him out of his room in readiness for work tonight.

The door swung inwards and Ulrica greeted him, squinting. Inside, the house was dark, the air stale. Ulrica's eyes were red around the edges, the skin directly beneath still swollen.

"Hey, Randy. Could've used your keys."

He looked at her. "The door was supposed to be locked. *And* bolstered."

Ulrica said nothing.

"Hey, Ulrica. You OK?"

"Yeah." It was a drawn out response, as if she was not entirely sure herself.

He decided to change the subject, draw her mind away from her thoughts. "You've lost your dog collar." He attempted a smile, unsure of how she would take it.

The same drawn out response. "Yeah."

Randell shifted his bulk into the house and began the process of locking the door again.

"Don't get too ahead of yourself. Connor ain't back yet," she said.

He paused. "Where'd he go?"

She shrugged, her tiny shoulders bony with only a vest-top on. "Dunno."

Randell locked the three latches anyway. Habit. He put down the extra timbers, laid them to one side in readiness for when Connor returned. *Of all the days.*

"Well, he'd better be quick. I'm not leaving us open to who knows what. It'll be dark soon," he grumbled.

"OK." Ulrica turned and headed towards the lounge.

"Did Ralph check on the solar panels?"

The girl shrugged again. "Think he's been locked away in his bedroom all day."

"What, and you haven't checked on him?" Randell sighed.

She looked down to the floor. "Well, I tried . . . Aw, crap. I've got my own issues ya know."

She did not want to tell him how she had tried to speak with Ralph, how he had all but ignored her. She did not want to tell him how awful it had been hearing the man sob behind the door and just how miserable she had felt. Especially since the ketchup incident earlier. Talk about shoving it down his throat. She did not want to tell him how she had gone outside, sat next to where Seffi lay all alone in the square, in the warming sunshine, and 'talked' with her. And in doing so she had realised just how much she missed Seffi and so she sat, gently rocking, letting quiet tears flood her face. She definitely didn't want to tell Randell how she had taken a pencil sharpener, released the crude blade, and, lifting her short skirt to reveal her upper legs, had taken to cutting a series of lines into her thigh, each one slightly longer and deeper than the last.

Randell was about to say something harsh, then softened. "Yes. I know. It's fine." He walked to the bottom of the stairs. "I'll go on up and check on him. May as well be the dog, and bark myself."

She called to him. "Why are the solar panels so important?"

"How do you think we cook, light the place, and watch TV?"

"Nuclear power?"

He smiled at her, hoping the solar panels had not sustained any serious damage. He would have to find the damned generator if so, or they would all have to rely on candles and eat raw food.

"Close, but no. And talking of TV . . ." He reached into his bag. "We've got this to watch." He tossed her the Blu-Ray disc.

She held it up, reading the cover, then flipped it over. Miniature still scenes of actors' faces looked up at her. "Is it any good?"

Randell gawped at her. "What, you haven't seen it? Really? It's one of my faves, an oldie but . . . Anyway, what's your favourite: Monsters, Inc?"

"No. Bolt." She put her hands on her hips.

"Bolt? Bolt? What's that about, Frankenstein?"

"No, it's about a dog, and he's a famous TV star who has his own show in Hollywood but, when he's not on set he still thinks his amazing super-powers are real. It's so cute."

"A dog actor. Sounds riveting. Geddit? Bolt?"

"Whatever," she grunted. "Don't give up your day job."

"Ha ha. Already have. My job now is to check on Ralph." He started up the stairs. "Your job is to sort some grub for us. I'll be back down in a bit."

At the top of the stairs Randell halted, the still-obvious mark of Seffi's life-force stained the floor even after it had been mopped up. He went to Ralph's bedroom. The door was closed.

"Ralph," Randell said.

No answer. "Ralph?"

He waited a few more seconds and tried the handle. The door opened and he stepped in. The room was half-tidy; Seffi's side untouched. The other side was scruffy; screwed-up clothes lay strewn about in small mounds, a plate of food sat half-chewed on the floor, tools and sharpened sticks were stacked in the corner. The room badly needed airing.

"Ralph?"

A noise came from the en-suite. Randell knew the ex-vet had access to animal anaesthesia products, but would not do anything to harm himself. *Would he?* After all, he could do that with a host of knives or stakes and a whole plethora of implements designed to open up veins or plunge into vital organs. But then, he realised, it wasn't him who had just lost his love in such disturbing circumstances. Fearing the worst Randell reached the door in two bounds and forced himself into the small bathroom.

"Ralph." It wasn't a question, more a concerned exclamation.

Then the smell hit him.

Sitting on the toilet, Ralph stared up at the younger intruder. "What the fuck?"

"Oh shit," Randell squealed, squirming away, backing out of the bathroom. "I . . . You . . . I thought . . ."

"Can't a man even take a shit in peace?"

Back in the bedroom Randell held his arm up to cover his nose. "Sorry Ralph. I called but there was no answer." The sound came out slightly muffled.

"Wonder why that might have been."

"I'm sorry, really." Randell turned to walk out. "I'll leave you to it."

The voice from the bathroom was full of sarcasm. "Thanks, I'll find some communal toilets next time I need to go, maybe we can all have a quaint little get-together."

Randell shouted out. "Yeah, that'll be nice. Thanks. I'll look forward to it."

A voice of reason took over, the initial shock gone. Ralph called out. "What do you want anyway?"

Making for the door Randell stopped. "I wanted to check on you, you know, and thought you should know that Connor isn't back yet."

The toilet flushed and Ralph appeared. "Where did he go?"

"Ulrica doesn't know, she said she never heard him go out."

"What time is it now?"

"He's got about twenty minutes or so before—"

"Yes, of course." Ralph hesitated, dithering in the doorway, unsure whether to dash off as he was or grab his coat and kit bag. That meant wasting time. He started for the stairs.

Randell followed, glad to be away from the odour that still permeated the immediate vicinity. They both took the stairs two at a time. In the kitchen Ulrica was preparing some food, or what passed as food in her view. She was surprised to see Ralph moving with such intent. Randell was behind him.

"Hey guys," she said as Ralph ignored her and began to unlock the front door.

"Erm . . . Guys . . . What are you doing? I've got food. It's almost time to eat." She pointed at the plates. *It's not that bad.*

Ignoring her, Ralph continued in his quest, determined to get the door open. It looked like he hadn't realised just how much work was involved when in a hurry. With the door finally unlocked Ralph grabbed for a spare shotgun that stood, loaded and ready, in the oversized umbrella stand by the door. It sat below a shelf loaded with lighter fluid and spray cans, the contents of which were labelled *highly flammable*. They were surrounded by stacked boxes of matches—the safety type and extra long ones—and a multicoloured selection of disposable lighters.

Ulrica looked to Randell for an explanation. "Randy, tell me, where are you going?"

Randell sighed, not wanting to get in the way of Ralph. "It's Connor, we're—"

"What about me?"

Ralph stopped in his tracks, the voice coming from behind him so familiar. He turned to see his son standing there.

Connor, hands in his pockets, looked at them both. He shrugged. "What?"

"Where the hell have you been? We thought you were still out there." Ralph placed the shotgun down.

Connor pulled a face, shaking his head. "Nope. Back now."

Ralph glared at him. "Where did you go? You know we don't go out alone."

"Why not? He did." Connor pointed at Randell. "Look dad, it's no big deal. They don't like the daylight. As long as I'm back before dusk, where's the problem?"

Ralph realised his son had a point. Ulrica had not gone with Randell this time. But having Randell go alone was less of a worry to Ralph. Randell was big, strong, could handle himself.

Again Connor shrugged casually. "I'm back now. All safe."

They all stood staring at him. Randell's heart was thumping in his chest; he wanted to slap the nonchalant smirk off his face.

Connor rocked back and forth, from heel to toe. "I've literally only just got back. Look, and before dark." He pointed at the window, his actions pointless as it was heavily boarded up. "Didn't you hear me come in?" he asked. "Where were you?"

*Where were we?* Neither Ralph nor Randell wanted to think about their awkward situation in the en-suite only moments ago. Best left unsaid.

"It's all right," Ralph said, instantly dropping the matter. Connor was OK, at least. He nodded gently before turning to Ulrica. "Did you say you'd made some dinner?"

She sighed. "Yes. Better get it down ya pronto and then get prepared."

Randell patted Ulrica's arm as he passed her. "Thanks."

So, Ralph had been inconsolable for most of the day, retiring to his bed, uncommunicative and morose, and she had finally given up calling out to him and knocking on his door. But now, he was awake, alert. Was it the idea of Connor being out that had done it, or was he, quite literally, trained to be at his station at a certain time? Either way, it saved Randell having to entice him out.

In hindsight, breaking in on Ralph had been a stupid thing to do, but in that moment of clumsiness Ralph had focused, and it had got him talking. He had then panicked over his son. Surely that had to be a good thing? They all had their own demons to deal with, it seemed; hopefully the rest of them would make it through, come out of this unscathed if not each a little troubled. Ralph could then grieve for Seffi properly, Ulrica could come to terms with the revelation that her mother had been turned, Randell could keep up the search for his brother, and Connor could go on doing whatever Connor did, but tonight, now, there was work to do.

Randell turned to Connor. "You can help your dad secure the front door first."

## Chapter 20

As the planet shifted in its rotation, obeying the rigorous laws of physics—the day's events unfolding naturally, passing by unhindered and largely ignored as they had for countless millennia—the sun slipped below the horizon.

For yet another night London would be lost to the dark. As if turning up to clock in for a shift, the two Mitclani had entered the square instantly, stark determination in their strides. Serkan's face appeared to glow white in the gloom. He appeared grim, his patience at an end. The woman followed a step behind. Directly outside the house they stopped. Serkan placed one arm across his abdomen and placed the elbow of his other arm in his hand for support. He rubbed at the sides of his chin and mouth, feeling old oversized cuspids below the skin. He was contemplating his next move. As if he had not had all day to dwell on it.

"What do you suggest this time?" Hemma said.

He scowled. "Quiet."

She shook her head. "We can't keep just throwing ourselves at the same place; this isn't nineteen-sixteen you know."

He waved her away. "Leave me alone."

"I can, you know."

Serkan was not listening, simply glowering at the house, deep in thought. "There must be another way," he muttered to himself.

When they had first arrived on the scene a large waxing gibbous moon had lit their way. Ancient mystics had for centuries looked to the moon, using it as a celestial guide on all things. This particular phase, according to those who followed such lunar ramblings, foretold of things which were near the verge of completion. How apt. With this presage in mind Serkan had inspected the top of the house, the sides, the rear for any obvious weaknesses but, regardless of what the wise old men had once promised, they had not found any; the place was done up like a small fortress.

Serkan had been around long enough to have witnessed the real thing—a proper fortress; now merely historical sites, once a thing of pleasure, a day-trip for contemporary humans. Search as they may modern-day materials, coupled with contemporary methods of fixing, had hindered their every attempt at exploiting a vulnerability. The only obvious weak spots were the front windows. And they were guarded. But there was hope. A sick satisfaction of his own deeds made him smile. Tonight there was one less to defend it. "Maybe they were on to something back in nineteen-sixteen."

Hemma rolled her eyes. "Really?"

Serkan glared at her. "I'm not letting him escape. You're either with me . . . or against me." He eyed her with disgust. "Choose wisely. You may find yourself surplus to requirements if you choose the latter."

Hemma sensed his anger, felt his eyes boring into her. She touched his shoulder. "Of course I'm with you."

She knew she would never replace Agana, even during their acts of sex Hemma could tell he was distant somehow. There, but not there. During those moments of closeness was he thinking about her? She realised he had only taken to her because of her directness, her strength and resolve. Hemma had climbed the ranks quickly because of her simple brutality; rare in one so recently turned but exactly how a vampire should be: bereft of compassion, almost reptilian in thought. Humans were fodder, beyond that a pet cat was of more use. Regardless of her savagery, next to him she was a beginner. Having been turned she knew her place in the Mitclani pecking-order. She knew he would kill her on a whim if it came to it and deal with the consequences afterwards. If any came.

Serkan leapt up to the low half-moon shaped concrete balustrade of the first floor balcony, noting this time that there was a touch more room for a composed vampire than a rabid and unrestrained Tecuani, its wolf blood clouding its judgement. *Damned Urbat*. Dark smears stained the white concrete from where he stood the night before. The blood had dripped from his fingertips after he withdrew his killing blow. He smiled and beat against the window, testing its strength.

"Knock, knock," he said.

The window was solid; he could see just by looking at it how they had been reinforced further. A noise below him caught his attention, a scratching and scurrying, rat-like. He looked down at the pile of junk that lay against the basement's entry steps.

He smiled at what he saw, wondered if he was seeing things.

A man, middle aged—no, he was older than that—and bearded looked up at him. He was lying on his back attempting to negotiate the gaps between the old whiteware.

"Ah," the man said, realising he had been spotted from above. And was now in imminent danger.

Immediately, Serkan soared from his elevated position, descending atop the man with ease. He stood over him. "And you are?" He bared his fangs, wondering where Hemma was.

The man and his beard stayed put. He stared up, his eyes wide and white amid all the facial hair. "I wanted to share something with y—"

"Serkan." Hemma's tone was one of concern.

Pleased that his find had frozen like a rabbit in the headlights, Serkan turned to Hemma. "What?"

Two men, or rather a man and a teenager, walked towards Hemma. The man in front wielded something thin and sharp. He stopped, about ten yards from Hemma. The boy joined him, standing by his side, his weapon of choice longer again, and poised.

"Easy," Ivan said to Felix. He looked at the female Mitclani. "Tell your . . . friend over there, we'll take the man."

Hemma regarded them for a moment. "Why don't you tell him yourself," Hemma said.

Serkan stared at the old man beneath him, pointing at him. "You. Stay."

The man nodded up at him; he needed no other command.

Serkan crossed over to Hemma and her two new foes. "Ah, I see you have some new, what do we call them? Acquaintances."

"Not really," she said.

"We don't want any trouble. Let us take the man and we'll be on our way." Ivan nodded towards the house, where the man still lay.

The two vampires stared at the man with the sword. "Would you take a sandwich from the hand of a starving child?" Serkan asked.

"Depends. What's in it?" Felix said.

For years Serkan and his kind had watched humans do that very thing. Rich businessmen and politicians turning a blind eye to the needy. Choosing not to help when they could, only too happy to furnish their bank balances with more money, and their fat faces with expensive food—ninety-pounds sterling for a monkfish lunch—and alcohol while half the world starved. It was tantamount to taking food from a hungry child. Just who were the real monsters?

But with so few humans left, Serkan, as far as he was concerned, had found his supper and was not about to give it away to two strangers. He thought of the man, the grey beard, the lined face. No matter how bitter and tainted that supper might prove, it was sustenance of a kind. And right in front of him. Serkan was hungry and the man was . . . aliment for his ailment.

"You guys might wanna come see this," Connor said quietly to his housemates.

"What is it?" Randell asked.

"Look."

The initial knocking, the threat of another night's barrage, had quickly ceased because of what was now going on outside in the square. Randell peered through the cracks.

Two new men, strangers with weapons, facing off against the two Mitclani: Seffi's killer and Ulrica's undead mum.

"We have to go out and help them," Ulrica said.

"Help who?" Randell said.

"My . . . mum." She fell back and sat on the floor. Tears welled in her eyes.

"Who do you think they are?" Ralph said, his tone even. Since his minor altercation with Randell and the toilet Ralph had come round a little; he knew he was needed. He could always go back to his grief if he survived the night—it wasn't as if it was going anywhere soon.

"Don't know. Maybe just two people trying to survive," Randell said.

Connor nodded in agreement.

"Then they're the ones we need to help." Ralph looked to Ulrica. "I'm sorry Ulrica but that's the way it has to be."

Ulrica looked up. "Yes, you're right. Oh, crap." She swiped her forearm across her wet cheeks.

"Wait a minute," Connor said, peering closer now. "There's an old man lying down near the house."

"What? Where?"

"There."

Randell craned his neck, could just make out the man. "What the . . . ?"

The front door was already rattling and clunking as Ralph began to disassemble the inner defences to get at the locks. "Are we sure about this?"

"No," came the reply.

Heading outside after dark was one thing. Knowingly heading outside with two newcomers, two vampires and a strange old man was another thing entirely. A stroll in the sun may get you a slight tan, a parched throat. A stroll during the night would likely get you killed, that same throat torn asunder.

"Fuck it," Randell said. He reached for his shotgun, filling his pockets with lighters and cans.

Ralph waited while the others got tooled up. "Let's go. I'm locking the door behind us. Wouldn't want a squatter moving in while we're out. So stay close."

The locks yielded, chinking as the key threw the respective barrels back. The door, so quiet in the day time, creaked loudly as if to signal their approach. The four of them entered the square, standing at the front of the house, weapons raised in readiness. In front of them stood the two Mitclani, Seffi's killer, behind them were the two newcomers. The old man lay to their left. They ignored him for the moment; their focus lay on the two in the centre. Ralphs fingers twitched; he wanted nothing more than to kill the Mitclani there and then. Anyone watching would think a demented game of piggy in the middle was being played out in Victoria Square, in the dark, the two piggies sadly outnumbered but seemingly unarmed. At least six weapons pointed at the two porcine pretenders.

Serkan turned. His eyes flared when he saw the big man with the shotgun. "You?" he said, staring at Randell.

"Me what?"

Ignoring the two behind him with the swords Serkan gave Randell his full attention. "You murdered my Agana."

Randell looked at Ulrica. She was fidgeting wildly, the spray can and lighter in her hands shaking. He knew how she felt as he turned back to his accuser. "What's that, one of them fancy ovens?"

"You dare to mock me, after killing her."

"If by *her* you mean one of you sucker-fucks then she may as well have had a target on her back. You'll be next, mister . . . ?"

The vampire sighed. "Serkan. And you are?"

"Just a pissed off builder who—" Randell's words were cut short.

Ivan was becoming impatient. "Listen, we only want the man," he shouted, the tip of his sword bobbed to the right, indicating the man on the ground.

Serkan took a step back to Hemma, his eyes still on the four from the house. The big man for all his bluster was now twitchy. He would deal with him soon enough. First though . . . Without moving he whispered to Hemma. "I'm going to turn around and face the two behind me; at the same time I want you to turn around and face these. Now."

As one they turned, swapping views. She now faced the four from the house, eyeing them each in turn. There was definitely something familiar about the girl.

Serkan spoke, looking directly at Ivan, his voice sharp but assured. "I don't know who you two are but this is not your fight. I implore you to leave now. You said yourself that you don't want trouble. Well, neither do we. So, off you trot, and take this . . . boy with you." He nodded towards the lad at his side, pointed to his raised blade. "I'm not sure he knows how to use that."

Felix bit his lip. He looked to Ivan for instruction but only saw him fixed on the gobby vampire. He held his blade steady.

"I know how to use it, granddad," Felix said as calmly as he could.

"Do you know?" Serkan turned his attention back to Ivan. "I suppose it's an age thing. You know, he really should be more respectful of his elders." At the word elders Serkan had made his mind up to attack. And was all set to do so when yet another body entered the square.

A large Asian man staggered into sight, his gait clumsy, unsure. "Barclay, you there mate?" Sani said. The man was either drunk or scared shitless. "Barclay?"

The old man on the ground called out. "Over 'ere."

Seizing his chance Randell pulled the trigger, the number 4 shot burying deep into the calf of the man who had introduced himself as Serkan, causing the Mitclani to lurch back a little. At the same time Felix dashed forward, slicing at the vampire. For once, Serkan's left hand was too slow and as he turned, righting himself, the blade struck, glancing down and away; he was one finger less, the little one gone. Connor followed Ralph as they advanced on the Mitclani woman who in turn had backed off. Ulrica stood behind, too afraid to face her now-vampire mother, adrenaline causing her to shake all over. Randell fired again at Serkan before popping the barrels to his 12g over/under and reloading. Red hot shot crashed into Serkan's back causing him to squeal in surprise, more shot flying straight on by and narrowly missing the two sword-wielding strangers. Randell knew it would not kill the fucker but it would injure and hinder him and with any luck he would lose his concentration and then, what with all the manic sword activity going on, hopefully lose his head

The fighting continued, attackers and attacked trading places in the mêlée, the six assailants now standing together, albeit cautiously because the four from the house still had no idea who the strange swordsmen were. All they knew was that they all had a common enemy and that, with the greater odds against them, the Mitclani were steadily being repulsed despite their ferocity.

Ralph was looking at Randell who had his hands full dealing with Serkan while trying to miss the lad with the blade. More than anything Ralph wanted to abandon his post and go and shoot the bastard who killed Seffi right in the eye, take out his defiled brain. That would mean abandoning Ulrica's side, leaving her vulnerable, and no matter how strong his desire he could not bring himself to do that. He raised his own shotgun, aiming at the woman who now came at him. As Ralph did so, Ulrica screamed and knocked the gun to one side as he squeezed the trigger. The blast rocked Ulrica's vampire mother, the shot only skimming the side of her right shoulder. The woman pitched backwards, swiping violently at her gun-toting attacker while he was momentarily distracted. The shotgun came away, released from Ralph's grip. It rattled on the tarmac. The woman kept on coming, this time for the girl. Reaching out in frustration and anger she grabbed at Ulrica's neck.

"You're coming with me," she bellowed.

Seeing the young girl in trouble Felix joined the fray. He brought his sword down, this time more carefully and far more adeptly. The woman fell back, cut free, her discerped fist still gripping the young girl's throat, the arm severed halfway along the forearm. The Mitclani mum fell back to the floor, her eyes wide, and she screamed—not in pain but shock; the limb would be gone forever, the dead flesh unable to knit together even with the world's best surgeons' efforts.

Serkan and Ivan were in a standoff, both facing each other, each unsure of the other's next move. The man with the blade appeared to have the advantage.

Seeing Ulrica and Ralph in difficulty and disarray Randell stopped firing and began bundling Ulrica back towards the house. He eyed her young severing saviour as he led her away while Connor stood watch.

"You might wanna help your friend," Randell said to Felix nodding over to the two still at it.

Ignoring his clobbered shotgun Ralph got the door.

Having regained some composure Sani ran over to Barclay who was still lying on the ground, and dragged him to his feet. Together they made off in the only direction they could. It was fate alone that sent them out towards Lower Grosvenor Place because, entering the square from Buckingham Palace Road, another tribe of Mitclani appeared, perhaps eight to ten strong.

Randell stood at the door and they all entered. Directly outside the house now, the two swordsmen watched the square fill with more vampires. Randell sighed, considering the swordsmen. What should he do—leave them outside or left them in? He was unsure but ultimately had little choice.

"You two," he called to them. "Inside, now."

Felix and Ivan flicked a look at each other, then back at the house, careful to keep the Mitclani within their sights. Serkan made a move forward, but Ivan countered quickly, bringing his blade within inches. "Ah, aahh." He jabbed and Serkan stepped back again.

"I'm locking up any second. Your choice," Randell shouted.

Eyeing the unwelcome horde and the two they had been battling, Serkan and his woman on the floor, Ivan realised he and the lad had nowhere else to go. He quickly nodded at Felix. They backed off and hurried into the house, sheathing their weapons, slipping past the bulk that was Randell. Serkan stood his ground; there was little point pursuing them into the house. Inside, it would limit his options and his space. He would be like a trapped rat surrounded by weapons. The odds were better out here—for now.

After locking up and re-barricading the door Randell took a look outside. Above, the waxing moon was approaching its full lunar phase—a day away, two at most he guessed. With so many vampires outside now, having any Urbat turn up would be . . .

Well, all hell would be let loose.

## Chapter 21

The four householders looked at the two swordsmen.

The two swordsmen eyed their new housemates. Each group waited for the other to speak.

Outside, shouts and jeering could be heard. They all knew they need not worry about the vampires outside for a while; they currently had their hands full with the unannounced new arrivals. However, once they sorted their differences out, it could mean an even heavier barrage and full-on attack if they were to join forces. Randell had counted maybe seven or eight of them.

"I counted eight," Ivan said, as if reading Randell's thoughts.

Randell nodded.

"Let's get the pleasantries over with," Ralph said. "Tell us, who are you?"

"My name is Ivan."

Felix looked up at Ivan. Ivan nodded. "I'm Felix."

"Felix," Ulrica repeated. She rubbed her bottom lip with her forefinger. She appeared dazed.

Ignoring her and feeling a little embarrassed Felix continued. "We're vampire hunters, we hunt vampires."

"OK, that makes sense . . . Not," Ulrica said.

"Why?" Connor said.

They all looked at him as if he had said something stupid.

Connor continued. "Look, killing them is one thing, why would you want to hunt them?"

"Everyone we've hunted so far we've had to kill," Ivan said.

Randell spoke up. "So, it's basically the same thing. Vampire hunter equals vampire killer?"

The man shook his head. "Not exactly," Ivan added. "First we approach them and give them our terms. If they disagree, they die. Simple as that."

"And what are your terms?" Randell looked at Ralph.

"That they stop killing humans."

"Good luck with that," Connor said.

For once Randell agreed with Connor. He turned to look directly at Ivan. "How exactly do you expect to stop the Mitclani feeding off humans?"

"It's pretty brave of you, what with your sword and all," Ulrica said, butting in, eyeing Felix.

Felix faced the floor, trying to avoid the girl's gaze.

Ivan looked at Felix—a simple attempt at warning the youngster that their new comrades may not like the next bit— but the youngster still hung his head. Ivan shrugged, ready to grab his weapon if things went awry.

"We are . . . vampires. Mitclani."

"What?" Randell jerked his shotgun up. He aimed it at Ivan, figuring he would take down the adult and deal with the boy after. Eliminate the immediate threat first; something he had learned the hard way.

Felix snapped his head up, his gaze now on the two bigger men. He grabbed for his sword.

Ivan held out his arm, hindering Felix's advance, trying to keep the situation calm. He had to let his hosts see he was genuine, and that he and the lad meant them no harm.

"No Felix," he said, sternly. "We're here as guests."

Ralph raised a stake, taken from the umbrella stand, as Connor took a step back. Ulrica stared at Felix.

Randell held his shotgun rigid, his finger ready at the trigger. "Guests?"

Ivan nodded. "Yes, you invited us in."

Ulrica agreed, her voice high-pitched in surprise. "Oh, crap. We did."

Randell watched Ulrica. Her face was perplexed but something in her eyes showed curiosity. He was pleased to see her interacting; the two strangers were distracting her. After all, it was only moments ago that her mother's severed hand had been wrapped around her throat. He knew it would all come back to her soon enough; then they would have to deal with the fallout.

Ralph didn't want to be near any Mitclani. He turned to his group, eyeing them each in turn. "I think we should just finish these . . . sickos now."

Ivan instinctively reached for his short sword; he would not die tonight, not at the hands of this ragged pack. But neither would he kill them. He would, though, defend himself and the boy.

"Everyone stay calm." Connor declared, and held up a torch.

All hands stayed where they were. Eyes flicked back and forth. Then there was laughing; short, quiet giggles. Everybody looked towards the source of mirth: Felix.

"What's so funny?" Ralph said, irritably.

Felix pointed at Connor's torch. "Is that an LED torch?"

Connor's head shook. "UV, and it'll fry your ass if you move."

"But it's LED."

"So?"

"So, LEDs hardly emit any UV light; they don't even attract flies or bugs, that's why the food industry uses, sorry, used, LED lights. Even museums, they used them so's not to damage paintings and artefacts," Felix said.

"And your point is?" Connor said.

"The point is that it won't harm us."

Connor aimed the torch at the know-all young vampire.

"Go on, turn it on," Felix said.

"I will."

"Go on then."

Ivan broke in. "Look, kid, stop goading him."

The hall lit up as Connor hit the on switch.

Nothing happened. Other than Felix being highlighted, lit up like he was on stage, about to perform. His skin was worse than white, veins trailed their blue highway about his translucent face. His eyes were black.

"See," Felix said.

"Enough of the horseplay," Randell said. "Connor, turn it off."

Connor dithered as he pretended he could not find the off switch. He shone it deliberately at Felix still.

"Connor." This time it was Ralph.

The torch went out. "Worth a try," Connor mumbled.

"We need some clarity. Everyone, put down your weapons. Now," Randell said before turning to Ivan and Felix. "You don't mean to hurt us, do you?"

"No."

"Then tell us why you pulled your swords on those two outside. And who was the man on the floor, by the house?"

"Serkan, the one out front, he wants to kill you. It's as simple as that. You have blood and he wants to feed. We, on the other hand, want to help. The man on the floor was a just a human. A man. So was his friend. What they were doing there is anyone's guess, but I'd say it's highly suspicious given the danger they were willing to put themselves in."

"And where did they go?"

Ivan shrugged. "Don't know. As far away from Serkan as possible, if they know what's good for them."

"And the woman with . . . Serkan?" This time Ulrica spoke, her eyes leaving Felix and fixing upon Ivan.

"I think her name is Emma . . ."

"Hemma," Ulrica said. "You mean Hemma."

"Yes, seems she was turned by Serkan."

Ulrica dropped to the floor, sobbing, her head in her hands. Ivan turned to Randell.

"It . . . She is . . . Was, her mom," Randell clarified.

"Yes, and you chopped off her mom's hand." Connor jeered at Felix.

"Oh, shit," Felix said. He crouched in front of Ulrica. "I'm . . . um . . . sorry." He put out his hand, placed it on her shoulder.

Unflinching at Felix's touch, the girl kept sobbing.

"She's not her mother anymore," Ivan said quietly.

Ralph ignored him, he had his own agenda. "Why didn't you kill this Serkan? He took my Seffi." He hung his head.

Ivan was left to guess who Seffi was. "I don't know if you noticed but we were outnumbered. And there's a few more of them out there now."

"Yeah. Are they with Serkan?" Randell said.

"I don't know. Why don't you take a look."

Randell went to move but Ralph stopped him. "I'll go." Ralph headed up the stairs to get a better view from the first floor window.

Ivan sniffed, thinking back to his day at the zoo a few nights ago. "You know this place smells like an animal house."

"Yeah, well, cleaning's not been high on the agenda," Randell replied.

"You better take a look at this." It was Ralph calling out from upstairs. His tone was serious.

Randell and Ivan started for the stairs.

"Why do you want them to stop killing humans?" Randell asked as he took the first step.

Ivan eyed him closely. "If they keep going, the human race will be snuffed out. Then what?"

Randell nodded, thinking of the atrocious acts humankind had perpetrated over the centuries, stuff he had read or seen on TV over the years. "Wouldn't be a bad thing. Go on."

"But that means there will be no food left for them."

"So they die."

"Yes. But, the thing is, vampires cannot feed from other vampires, but the recently turned don't know that. So they'll probably tear each other apart before perishing."

"Good," Randell added.

Ivan thought about his words. "Felix and I will die too."

"So, the Urbat win the day?"

"No, they die also. There's no humans left, remember? No food source for them either."

Randell was nodding. "Oh. Yeah. So?"

"So, unless we want total extinction, we have to negotiate a truce. One where we can live in peace, so we all stay alive."

"And just how do we do that?"

"The idea is cooperation. Man can give blood, and the Mitclani can use it. We all benefit," Ivan said.

"And the Urbat?"

"They already have a loose truce; lock themselves away for the full moon. Why shouldn't vampires do the same?"

"The Mitclani?"

"Yes."

"It makes sense."

Ivan smiled. "And everyone's a winner."

They were at the top of the stairs. Ralph was peering through the cracks in the window.

"Out there," he said.

Randell and Ivan stepped forward to see. Serkan was mid-throw, launching a severed head at another member of the intruding vampire gang, the leader's caput gone kaput.

"He doesn't care who he kills," Ivan said.

"We know," Randell said.

Ralph stayed quiet.

"Once he's done with them, either killed them or chased them off, he'll turn his attention back to us."

"He seems to have a fucking hard-on for Randell," Ralph said.

Randell eyed the older man. He felt responsible for Seffi somehow. "I . . . I wasn't to know."

"If you hadn't killed his woman, then maybe . . ."

Ivan turned to Ralph. "He'd have caught up with you all sooner or later. There's only so much fresh blood still left in the city. If Randell here took out Agana then he's already doubled your chances of getting out alive. She was vicious. She made Vlad himself look like a beginner."

Not wanting to dwell Ralph quickly changed the subject. "And why don't you want to kill us?"

Ivan repeated what he had told Randell, regaling to him the obvious: that the devastating after-effects of the Underworld conflict had resulted in so many deaths that there were now so few humans left, and those who were left were dwindling rapidly as the vampires either killed or turned them. By getting the Mitclani to sit down with the remaining humans and come to some sort of agreement was going to be tough. For all their intelligence and age-old wisdom the Mitclani were simple, wanted only to feed and kill, but, unlike the Urbat they did it consciously and not in a wild blood rage. Could they not see there was only one way it could possibly end? Extinction of one's food supply meant extinction for oneself. Unlike the Maori of two-hundred-years ago or the Asmat tribe of Papua, Indonesia, the Mitclani could not subsist by eating their own kind. And there was little by way of protein in an undead vampire body to benefit a ravenous and starving werewolf. It was more likely to kill the hungry wolf as it ingested the vampire's tainted flesh. So, the bugs and trees would get the planet. As, perhaps, it should be.

But, if the talks were successful, it could see a return to blood donation, some for medical reasons, the rest for vampire consumption. After that the Urbat could be approached in hope of bringing an end to all conflict, although that may prove extremely difficult as the pack elders still saw the Mitclani as a cancer which needed eradicating entirely. The Urbat may seek peace with the humans but never the Mitclani—too much bad blood had passed between them over the centuries. But it was something Ivan and Felix were willing to try. They were Mitclani, vampires, who wanted, like any other species, to survive.

Nodding in acquiescence Ralph listened realising that if it could be achieved then maybe Seffi would not have died in vain; who would mourn her if they were all dead and gone?

"But that crazy fucker out there is never going to listen," Ralph said.

Ivan agreed. "Then we kill him."

"Aren't there rules about killing your own kind? Consequences?" Randell asked.

Shrugging, Ivan answered. "Not for Serkan, he's a law unto himself now. Nobody dare challenge him."

Ralph peered into the square again, seeing the crazed Serkan making mincemeat of the others before saying, "You know, throughout history dictators, potentates and megalomaniacs have all eventually paid the ultimate price of their actions. We'll have to make sure he follows in their footsteps."

Of the eight new arrivals four were already dead. Their bodies lay strewn in broken humps, two of them headless, one's chest torn open. The last had something long and gnarly sticking out from its brain cavity, a branch maybe. The other four were backing off, one holding another as they limped away in retreat. The fight for food was over; Serkan, the apex, lord above them all. He turned to face the house, his eyes like melanite in the maturing moonlight.

Would he carry on and continue to attack the house or would he have had enough for one night, pull back and tend to the woman with the severed arm? Randell realised that the undead did not need to rest, only keep away from the sun's rays. He asked Ralph the time.

Reading his thoughts Ralph replied, "Four hours until sun up. There's plenty of time left yet. I for one hope he does have another go." He looked at Ivan. "We've got back up now, and I'm ready to rip that motherfucker limb from limb."

They watched as Serkan eyed the house, staring intently, his face a scowl of utter hatred. He turned and went to Hemma's aid, raising her up. His arm around her for support, they walked out of the square, in the direction of Lower Grosvenor Place, where the two men had exited earlier. A wounded vampire would heal quickly enough, arm or not, but she would need strength in the form of red liquid.

"The two men, they may not have a sufficient hideout, or the strength. We'll have to go." Ivan made for the stairs.

Downstairs Ulrica was holding on to Felix, her arms wrapped around him. Her tears had ceased. Hearing footsteps Felix tried to turn his head but the girl clung on tight.

"We've got to go out again."

Felix nodded, taking the girl's hands in his own and lowering them. "I have to go."

Ulrica's reddened face nodded back at him.

"You lot stay put. If we're not back before sunrise, we'll find a safe place to see the day out and return tomorrow evening. If we don't return . . ."

Randell went to Ulrica, placing an arm around her gently. "What about the four defeated vampires? They'll still be out there," he said.

"If we see them, we'll offer them our terms. If they decline, then . . ." Ivan looked at Felix. "Get your sword ready."

Ralph nodded at them as he unlocked the door and let them back out into the night.

## Chapter 22

Having experienced a brief idea of home life with the others back at the house—a safety they had not felt for some time—going back outside as the night further darkened the doors and entrances of the disused and barren buildings left them feeling strangely vulnerable; they would have to be extra vigilant and keep their wits about them and their guards up.

The four stupefied vampires had retreated further than Ivan and Felix had anticipated. It had taken them some time to find them but now he and the boy faced them.

Approaching them, his eyes keen to the dark and wary of Serkan springing up again, Ivan wasted no time in telling the four of them exactly who he was and precisely what he wanted. For a moment it seemed they were thinking it over but in typical Mitclani hotheadedness and reckless stupidity they had dismissed it, instead complaining of the comrades they had lost to Serkan's rage.

"Your comrades were dead anyway," Felix said.

"Undead," the newly self-appointed leader and spokesman said. His face was young but his eyes were asymmetrical and he wore a tatty jumper, the colour of insipid lager, his hair pulled tightly back and bunched up in a bun. His pre-undead beard gave him the look of a week-old llama.

"Whatever." Felix shrugged. "If you don't listen to reason you'll meet the same fate."

The leader jeered and attacked, his pace fast.

But Felix was faster, his sword cutting through the air with sharp precision, his blade connecting briefly with white flesh at the vampire's right temple. A second later the blade exited below his would-be assailant's left ear lobe. It had not quite taken the whole head but had just managed to severe the spinal connection to the fool's brain. It would serve its purpose. The top of the head slid to one side, the eyes twitching left and right as the ridiculous beard and body slumped to the pavement.

It was an impressive move; the boy finally coming of age.

The others moved forward as one.

Ivan sighed. "Why will you not listen?" he asked the remaining three.

"Because we're Mitclani." This one's voice was deep and defiant. She stepped forward, her face slim but androgynous. As a human she would have been quite fetching.

"But you're not. You've all been turned. And recently by the looks of you. True Mitclani are elders, ancient beings, vampires who have survived the centuries."

"Exactly. They have survived centuries. And we will, for centuries more," the youngest-looking of them all said, his voice almost falsetto. He wore a black Def Leppard t-shirt with some kind of triangular imagery emblazoned across the front.

Ivan shook his head. "But you won't. You can't, don't you see, there will be nothing left. No blood."

"The elders will provide," said the last of them, a grown man in his thirties when he was turned, his head bald, his trousers and shirt slim fitting and tight. His black brogues were scuffed and had not seen polish in a while.

"With what?"

Ivan looked at the ragged bunch. Full of bravado and their own self-importance. For what? Either way, it would be their undoing. Ivan had had enough. It didn't seem to matter what he said or how much he implored them to see sense they were not going to listen. He could go on talking until his tongue fell out. There was only one thing for it. Ivan raised his sword, giving Felix a laconic nod.

Together they stepped forward, their minds clear as to their actions. Ivan only wondered whether Felix would take out one or two, leaving him the remnants; the boy was learning quickly, had shown maturity and poise. The sooner the boy could handle himself the better. And he was proving to do so. Killing speedily and decisively increased one chances of survival, and it meant one less worry for Ivan. If nothing else, another four less vampires in the world would at least give any remaining humans the tiniest of advantages.

"One last chance," Felix said.

"Yes," Ivan added. "What's it to be?"

Ignoring their former colleague, whose body lay still in front of them on the tarmac, the three stood rigid. A final act of solidarity or simple perverse obstination? Ivan thought about the fight earlier in the square: they had run then—it was a normal act of survival—so why not again? Something told him they had come to the end of the line. They had, or he and Felix had. Whatever the outcome, it would soon be resolved.

Blades hissed as they sliced the air, a deadly dance performed with terpsichorean precision. Bodies jostled in the moonlight as, momentarily, the blades found skin, muscle, sinew and bone. Then free air again.

In a matter of only a few seconds Ivan and Felix stood alone, the shimmy of night still once more. It was one job out of the way. Not the outcome they had hoped for, but an outcome nonetheless. Now all they had to do was find the two humans and avoid Serkan and his woman.

Barclay glared at Sani. "What the hell were you thinking?"

Sani was dragging a wardrobe across the floor, leaving heavy lines in the once-plush and deep pile of the carpet. Shoving it against the door he turned and faced his comrade. "Looked like you were in trouble."

Barclay looked away. "I . . . I had it handled."

"I know, but . . . you was outnumbered." Sani nodded, happy with his answer.

"I was that, my friend."

Barclay hauled himself into a chair. It was a Chesterfield; whoever the owner had been they had clearly appreciated its comfort for it now had worn edges across the arms with a divot in the seat pad, the material dark and greasy. The room was decorative, covered in rich textiles and finishes. The chandelier that hung from the ceiling, once a showpiece of times forgotten, was now bedraggled and broken, many pieces missing, broken away and smashed. The room smelled earthy, damp, as if moss was steadily invading the room, the walls, the carpets.

Earlier on in the day Barclay had intended to do a test run; managing to worm his tiny frame through all the obstructions that barred the way to the basement rooms of the house in Victoria Square. It had taken some doing, even for him, but on finally getting to the old door, manoeuvring himself into some sort of comfortable position that would allow him some comfort and give his arms a bit of movement, he had used an antique hand drill he on the lower wooden panel of the door. Taking his time after fitting the wood bit in the chuck he had, in near silence, stitch-drilled the panel all the way round. He had picked up the drill, second-hand, from a bric-a-brac shop in Camden; the drill bits were all brand new and sharp—doing the job by hand, he knew, would be hard work and so he would need all the help he could get. Anybody listening would not have heard a thing and if they had would probably pass it off as a mouse or a rat—no real threat.

And it was not a threat. Not to life anyway. It was just a way for him to get in and get out with his rightful booty. He inspected his work once he was done—it would only need a single sharp kick when the time was right—and then, after catching his breath, he had begun his return wriggle. The job had taken longer than he wanted and it was dark as he squirmed out of the final obstacle. He had calculated that the job may go over and that he could lose the light but had hoped that, by using only minuscule movements to creep away, he could use the dark as his ally which would allow him to get back to number twenty-three unseen. What he had not reckoned on was that, at the precise moment he had crawled out into view, he would be spotted by a roosting vampire. He also had no idea that the typically quiet square would suddenly become so populated and that a battle would escalate so rapidly. The diversion of the battle had at least allowed him and Sani to make their escape unobserved.

They were now safe inside a house on Palace Street. "We've got to get that money."

Sani looked at his companion. "There's diamonds too."

Barclay nodded, knowing only too well. The job had been their greatest achievement, if one did not include the time behind bars they had both served. Prison had been relatively simple for them both. Sani was big and strong, an intimidatory presence. Most people who met him were immediately dismayed by his mighty bulk, saw him as persona non grata, and did not want to be anywhere near him. Because of that they were left alone to serve their time. And they had, mostly.

The prisons had been the last bastion of human life. Bars that kept prisoners in also kept vampires and wolf-men out. That was until the levels of humans had dipped so drastically that there was no other option for the Mitclani to quench their thirst, and so the prisons were attacked aggressively. The attack was frenzied, had lacked concentration and purpose, and wild eyes hungry for blood had allowed Sani and Barclay to slip through and get away, sitting it out until daylight. It had not taken them long to adapt to their new surroundings; stealth and patience had always been their best virtues.

Growing up on the streets of South London had been tough. It was a steep learning curve that one learnt at an early age if he or she wanted to survive. Barclay's father had left when he was small and his mother was often three sheets to the wind, so he had been left to fend for himself. Gangs had grown rife and the government had all but turned a blind eye on all the muggings and the stabbings. That meant lawless streets where either a weapon or having the means to buy your way out of trouble was the only way of survival, way before the Urbat or

Mitclani came after them. He was small and sinewy, had evaded trouble by simply running or, when cornered, had given up whatever spoils lined his pockets—usually cash or the odd fancy watch he had pick-pocketed on a visit to the West End. The trouble was, the gangs all knew this and often came for him when they were short on funds. So Barclay had no choice but to improve on his evading techniques. It did not take him long to realise his deftness in breaking and entering.

Sani had come from a large family but had been ostracised early on due to his autism. He was naturally big and, having thrown his weight around with his parents or siblings one too many times, had been taken away and placed in a home—a place for 'bad lads' he was told. Only he was not bad, not in the real meaning of the word, just misunderstood and never given a chance. Life was all about the now; nobody seemed to have any patience any more. People were fickle; soon bored with one thing they turned to another, and another. And so on. No one had time for him. Until he met Barclay, and Barclay immediately saw an opportunity for protection, a huge ally who would do pretty much what was asked of him, almost obliviously, and for no personal gain. His bulk had come in handy for any door or lock that Barclay could not get through. He would simply coax Sani into using his muscles to do it for him. Yes, it made a noise, but they were quick. In and out. Having Sani by his side also meant he got to keep a lot more of his takings. He was not into using people and Barclay would always front up fifty percent of the proceeds to Sani for his efforts. He had begrudged it the first couple of times but soon realised that getting to keep fifty percent of anything because of

Sani's sheer size was better than being left with one-hundred percent of nothing.

He was thinking of that now. And, he had decided, they had waited long enough. They had both been through too much. Anyway, possession was nine-tenths of the law. And there was no law left, although he had once spotted a recently burned vampire, a baton proudly protruding from the once-policeman's face, the skull below shattered, the brain crudely pierced. No, they wanted their rightful plunder. And in acquiring it—getting into the house was going to be tricky after Barclay's almost-failed reconnaissance and preparation attempt—the next time they met the angry vampire they would be in a better position to do a deal with him. Hopefully appeal to his calmer side.

Of course, it meant they would have to be in possession of the swag first before any deal could be made. First thing in the morning they would make their way back to Victoria Square. Sani could wait over the road as before while Barclay wrestled his way back into the basement, kicked in the pre-drilled door panel as quietly as he could, make his way into the kitchen and get at the units. If he could manage all that without being caught then he and Sani could finally get what they desired.

The vampire convulsed, the veins in its face and neck bulging. Connor watched and waited.

Nothing.

*Again.*

He had lost count of how many different concoctions he had tried now. His notes would soon tell him once he bothered to look but he was beginning to lose heart. Since his father had lost Seffi, Connor was hoping that the grieving man would open up to him. Maybe not fully but at least a little. Surely blood was thicker than water? He recalled the thick red oozing from Seffi's chest. Maybe not; blood was blood. In most cases it thrusted life-giving oxygen into its happy owner's veins; in others, it merely sustained their lives as they experienced pain and misery. The happiness of one's psyche was determined by life's beauty and luck, or the harsh lessons it learned along the way. One day he hoped his father would bridge the gap left in his soul. It was not for the want of him trying.

He thought again of the TIMP2, of how he was ever going to obtain it once his diminishing stock had all gone. Seffi was dead, one female less, but that did not matter, she was not the right choice and had seen her menopausal days go by a long time before her demise. He wondered if her sex-drive had diminished, or had she and his father . . .

He shook away the thought, favouring instead to think of Ulrica. OK, Ulrica was currently in a state, depressed after finding out about her mother. Well, maybe Connor had an answer to bringing the mother back. All Ulrica needed to do was to lay back and think of England—he preferred to think that she would enjoy the moment, take pleasure from seeing his erect manhood as he slid it into her, driving it deep with the firm intention of, once he was all done and the baby had been delivered, driving the vampire out of her mother. He thought of his ex-boyfriend, realising Ulrica, at least sexually, did nothing for him. Would he even be able to get it up? Then again, she was a little tomboy-like in lots of ways; he only had to use his imagination. Shut his eyes. It would have to be done, for his trials, for the sake of humanity.

And it would be a joyous moment, grandchild saving grandmother the moment they entered this world. Some people had to wait years to donate organs to unappreciative and apathetic relatives, too busy posting a sob-story about themselves on social media than worrying about the poor soul who had donated it after paying the ultimate price, but that did not matter as long as they had not missed the latest episode of ball dancing morons on TV.

He wondered if Ulrica would be up for it. No reason not to be. She was not romantically involved with anybody. But what if she was involved with someone? She could get pregnant all the merrily. He would be happy with that, save him the trouble, the sour thoughts. But that could be years from now. Far too long. All right, so she was close to Randell but he was more of a big brother to her. The problem he faced was that she had shown that new young vampire with the silly Japanese sword too much attention. He decided he did not like the wanna-be ninja. *Felix*. Anyway she could fancy him all she liked, the boy's semen, like his all the rest of the fluid in his vampire body, was dead. She could massage the boy's prostate for all she was worth it was not going to happen. It would not work, would be a partnership from hell; Connor was sure she would soon realise that a permanently flaccid penis accompanied by shrivelled and desiccated testicles was not so much fun after all. He knew he would not find much joy in them.

He smiled at the image in his mind, noticing that his latest catch, the vampire he had newly captured and brought back on his dog noose, was quietly observing him. The thing was heavily bound, its convulsions from earlier over with for now. His previous experiments—something he had done wrong, measured the dose incorrectly, administered it too quickly or at too soon intervals—had killed the last one. He had no idea why the thing had perished, only realising he would be consulting more medical books at this rate. If nothing else he had potentially discovered another way to rid them of the vampire scourge. Finally at rest it lay there slowly decaying beneath a sheet. The smell was becoming stronger. *I'll get rid of it tomorrow.*

"What are you looking at?" Connor said, feeling as though he was naked and being scrutinised by unwanted eyes.

The eyes blinked up at him.

Connor reached forward and covered the vampire's face with a sack cloth.

## Chapter 23

Felix and Ivan had used all their tracking skills to follow the two men but could find no sign.

Ivan did not believe for a minute the two men possessed such aptitude after seeing the smaller of the two caught so easily. The second much bigger man had then trundled outside into what was quickly becoming a potential war-zone with such apathetic disregard for his own safety that the rest had stood staring in utter disbelief. If nothing else it had interrupted and stopped an impending attack on the house. Only luck, and drawn weapons taking action, had seen the two humans escape with such ease.

Ivan sniffed the air deeply. Usually he had a good sense of smell, and was hoping to get a whiff of their sweat, their stale body odour or over-deodorised armpits, perhaps a taste of cologne. After all, neither of the men looked like they had taken a shower lately. Not tonight though. He wondered if there was a slim chance that the two men were recently-turned Urbat, waiting for a full moon.

For some reason, inexplicable as it was, a vampire could not sniff out a werewolf, their lifelong enemy. It was something that had always fascinated and disturbed Ivan as to why. Wolves were canines—dogs—and as dogs they would sniff each other to ascertain identity and rank. He recalled that most of the dogs he had ever encountered during his days of life, a time when he was a legitimate human with no cares other than how the bills were going to be paid or what was for Sunday dinner, had actually stank. The reek of a dirty dog would stay on your hand long after you had stroked it no matter how friendly it had been or how happily it had wagged its tail or how much it licked you. And the bigger the dog the more it smelled, so it stood to reason that a man-sized wolf would possess a stench that even a vampire, with a dried-out nasal passage, could sniff out from a good distance.

"This is useless." Ivan said the words to himself while Felix searched a doorway and its entrance.

They had set off down Buckingham Gate in the hope of picking up the trail of the two men. As they passed the ransacked palace they turned right at Birdcage Walk deciding that the men would most likely have steered clear from Saint James's Park, opting instead to stick to the multitude of buildings; at least attempted to get as far away as they could in what little time they had.

What looked like a recently forced door at the Swaziland High Commission had piqued their interest. If not the men then perhaps Serkan and the injured female had passed by, could even be inside. For all they knew either party could be anywhere in the city, in this building awaiting discovery or sitting at the other end of Birdcage Walk in a huge clock tower overlooking the Thames and Westminster Bridge.

What had surprised him was that he had not had even a mild hint of Serkan's whereabouts; the forced door was the first real sign of anything.

"Be ready Felix," Ivan said as he shouldered the door aside and entered.

It turned out that Serkan and Hemma were overlooking the Thames, or would have been had they ventured to find any windows.

They had realised they needed to get far enough away to avoid detection and so, because of Serkan's old-fashioned sense of style, he had chosen the grandest building he could find at such short notice to use as his latest hideout. The Tate Britain had large rooms and few windows—ideal for keeping out the sunlight. But not for the benefit of vampires; it was for the delicate artefacts and paintings that needed protection from the sun's UV rays.

After dressing Hemma's arm and shoulder wound—the shot had made more of a mess of her clothes that the dead flesh beneath—he let her rest knowing she would live. He traipsed the corridors and rooms, mulling things over in his mind. Just how was he going to get into the damned house? Every attack so far had yielded little result. The arrival of the other Mitclani in the square had halted proceedings. It had been his best opportunity yet. And why were two other vampires now rebelling against his cause? With swords to boot. Then there was the prostrate man and his large friend; just what the hell were they up to?

Inside Room 1840 he stopped, careful to stay clear of any light that may enter from the ornately arched rooftop windows. In front of him, Sir John Everett Millais' Ophelia. It was a favourite. The subject lay there beneath the weeping willow, drowning, her face still above the water. Not too many visitors would have had the good fortune to have met the painting's model: Lizzie Siddall, wife of Dante Gabriel Rossetti. Yet, he had, many years ago. She would have been twenty-years-old when he spotted her on the paved pedestrian thoroughfare of Cranbourne Alley while he had been out looking for a bonnet on a cold and dark late afternoon in November 1849.

The bonnet was for his mother, or so he had said. It was a simple cover up as he needed to revisit the scene of his feeding exploits from the night before, just to make sure the police had not picked up any leads; he had discarded a body in the tangle of filthy streets, the windows there too dirty to see out of and witness anything. The police had dragged away the leftovers of his midnight feast with few questions asked, leaving only whispers in darkened corners of how the victim had met their demise. Like, where was all the blood? Or, could it be the ghosts of Frederick and Marie Manning, the recently convicted and hanged killers of the Bermondsey Horror? He wondered why, some thirty-nine years later, during the autumn of 1888 in the East End the police had not captured anybody then. Then he realised even he and his kind had not managed to find the killer known as Jack. The man—or woman some had surmised—known as the Ripper was as elusive as he was deranged. Serkan knew the murders had not been perpetrated by his own kind but, by the way the bodies were so mutilated, perhaps a rogue Urbat had run amok for a few months. It was an interesting theory.

He thought back to the young girl he had met all those years ago on Cranbourne Alley: Rossetti's muse. He could have had her, sucked her veins dry but the death of a woman like that would turn too many heads, get too many inquisitors involved, each one asking questions, delving into her final movements. And turning her was never really an option, Agana would have seen to that. It was not that he found her terribly pretty, but there was something peculiarly attractive about the young Miss Siddall, something that drew a man's eye; she moved with an air of great confidence, a fearless swagger, while portraying a placid and unguarded vulnerability. He could see why the Pre-Raphaelites wanted to paint her. She reminded him of Agana; that was the real reason he had decided not to feed on her. That and too many killings in the same area always drew too much attention. And, had he made the opposite decision, well, he may be looking at an altogether different painting now.

*Agana.*

He turned in anger and kicked at a statue, a man wrestling with a snake. The darkened bronze figure toppled to the ground. Immediately Serkan saw, or rather heard, his error as the metallic man and the snake rattled loudly upon the floor. *Damn.* He had no desire to draw any attention as day broke; they would be sitting ducks, stuck in a crypt with its own art galleries.

*Calm, Serkan. Have patience.* He would not allow himself to die today, he would lie low, accept that Hemma would only be of minimum assistance because of her injuries, give up on any of his own kind helping him, kill more if they stood in his way—he would face up to any allegations later (of course he would)—and have another night to get Agana's killer. It meant taking a bigger risk than usual. Tomorrow night was a full moon, the ever-increasing moonlight always a dead giveaway when stealth was needed, and the possibility of any unwanted wolf adversaries turning up, the Tecuani, was all too real. He wondered where the one from the other night had gone. It was obviously an older one, able to change on any given night, not wait for the moon to hit its bright monthly phase. Thinking back to when he was watching it he realised now that it was desperately hungry and weak; any other time, heavy rain or not, it would have ascended the building with ease. It could be holed up now, cold and naked, lying alone in a building, back in its human form, waiting for death to find it. He doubted he would see that one again anytime soon.

Never mind, he would deal to any full moon freaks, cross that bridge when he got to it, if they came out to play. Sacrifice Hemma if need be. Things had gone on for too long. Agana's killer was living on borrowed time. One more day. *One*. This time he would make that fucking builder's mate pay. Bastard was the size of a truck.

*Yes. A big ugly truck.*


Their careful search of the Swaziland High Commission came up blank.

Heading back out they went door to door, house to house, building to building, along one side of the street. Apart from an intricate set of stark white rooms and offices a couple of doors down they came across nothing of any importance, no traces of either human or vampire or wolf. They must be looking in the wrong place. London was too big for two people on foot to find anything other than a severe dose of plantar fasciitis.

The night dragged on.

They came to a halt at Westminster Chapel. Inside, the air was stale, dusty. In front of the organ pipes sat two massive video screens and below that a circular stage with pickup microphones complete with stands surrounded a traditional drum set. Rows of pews sat empty, the band made up of no one (alive, at least), waiting for an audience that was never coming to the gig. This time their search would take longer.

And so it did. The place of worship, however, was empty save for more dust, cobwebs and spiders. After coming down from the tower they stopped on the second floor tier of pews at the south side. It gave them a good vantage point, overlooking the whole of the chapel, enabling them to spot an intruder immediately. Felix lay down on one of the blue padded seats, taking a rest. The vampire had no heartbeat but could still tire from overall fatigue—a fatigue that came about if one did not fill up the tank as it were. Ivan sat on the pew behind him.

Ivan was looking at Felix. The boy was pale, severely so. A vampire's pallor was one of wanness; it was the way of things but Felix's skin was a sickening grey, diaphanous. His once vibrant eyes were sunk and dark around the edges, the pulp of young healthy skin well and truly gone. He had to face it, the boy was sick. He knew Felix needed food. He needed blood, they both did. He thought back to the last time they had fed. It may well be that they had made the decision not to kill humans but a simple fact remained: they needed blood to survive. None of them knew quite how blood revitalised a Mitclani body; just that without it a vampire grew weak. Would that weakness eventually lead to complete expiry for one of the undead? It was a question no vampire had ever answered. Giving in to blood was the easy and obvious answer.

Careful not to single the boy out, Ivan addressed him quietly. "We need to feed."

Felix spoke to the ceiling. "On what?"

"You know very well what on." Ivan thought about the teenagers they had found at the Shaftesbury, how they had taken some of their blood, what little was left, before putting them out of their misery. Although he hated himself for it, it had been an act of kindness. The thought didn't help him feel any better.

"Yeah, OK then, but where from?"

Ivan shrugged. "There's only one place we know for sure where there's people."

Felix sat up. "You mean back at the house. Those people, you think they will go for it?"

"Have you got a better idea?"

The lad smiled, thinking of Ulrica, the girl in the dog collar, the girl who wouldn't let go of him. "I suppose I could take just a little. If she agrees." He lay back again, hands behind his head.

"She'll agree, I'm sure." Ivan leaned over the back of the bench and ruffled the boy's hair.

The two hunters stayed as they were for some time. When Ivan finally stood, Felix stirred, knowing it was time to get going again.

"Felix. Up and at it. We need to get down from here."

Ivan's words were not what Felix had expected. *What does he mean?*

"Don't ask me how, but we've let the night get away with us," Ivan continued.

Opening his eyes Felix could see light coming in through the south windows, from directly behind them. *Daylight.* He ducked down again, making for a shaded area further along. It did not help much; the building was large and open, bright and airy. They needed to find a smaller room, somewhere far more secluded. He thought of Ulrica, of the blood that coursed through her veins, of his hunger, of the Mitclani's primal need. He would have to wait a little bit longer than anticipated.

They both would.

## Chapter 24

The eighteen-wheeler truck had taken out the corner of the British Red Cross shop.

Like teeth ravaging soft neck flesh and opening up the carotid, the facade and brickwork splashed to the ground, the truck bouncing over the rubble that sprayed out onto the tarmac, as Serkan steered it away from Buckingham Palace Road and onto Victoria Square, the Nova Building behind the only witness to the Mitclani's deliberate carnage as Serkan pressed his foot against the accelerator pedal in order to get the speed up.

Derelict and long-discarded cars bounded into front walls of buildings and houses, ricocheting off railings, shattering windows as the massive weight and inertia of the truck slammed them out of the way, forever gaining momentum. As it passed, the side railing of the square was ripped away from its moorings and folded up like a concertina, collapsing untidily against its will as the driver and his eighteen wheels dragged it away, leaving the statue of Queen Victoria unguarded and defenceless. She would not be amused.

The driver of course ignored all of this, only revelling in his deliberate vandalism, his foot hard down. The vampire driver willed the truck forward. *Faster*. There was to be no quarter given as heavy rubber churned up the freshly-laid soil that covered Seffi, her final resting place now more that of a demolition derby.

Serkan looked across at his passenger, grinning dementedly at Hemma. At that moment the truck slammed into the corner of the house, instantly denying his target of its walled fortifications. Blocks crumbled and broke away as the two of them were thrown forward with the impact. A cloud of dust filled the square, billowing high and wide, as the two vampires straightened themselves inside the shattered cabin. Serkan and Hemma were fine, if one discounted half of her missing forearm and hand, and the slivers of timber from the custom-made retro-fitted wooden dashboard embedded deep into Serkan's forehead and right cheek.

Inside the house, Ralph, who had only just left the kitchen after pouring himself a drink of water, was thrown forward into the hall. For a moment, the sound of the collision and crashing house debris surprised and bewildered him. He felt bits of bricks and fragmented wood fall on his back and head. Brushing it away he looked back at where the kitchen had once been. Water sprayed into the air, the sink torn away from its mooring of copper pipes, the worktops buckled and splintered. Tins of food, pots and pans and cutlery littered the floor as cupboard hinges broke and doors fell open.

Randell sprang down the stairs, rubbing at his eyes with one hand, attempting to buckle up the belt to his jeans with the other. "What the fuck was that?" He spotted Ralph lying by the front door. "Shit, you OK?"

"Yes, think so. Mind the glass." Ralph pointed at his drink, now conscious of his dry mouth. "Damn."

"It's too fucking early." Randell peered outside. It was pre-dusk, too early for a vampire attack. When he saw the truck—the cabin windows were covered in mirrored window film to match the expertly painted art on the truck's wings and bonnet—he realised the vampires would be protected from the light. And they were still inside the cabin.

"Quick," Randell reached for the front door. "Help me get out while it's still light. I'll drag the fuckers outside. And blow their brains out."

Ralph jumped up, the thick hairs on his arm covered in blood. "Damn blast."

The door, free of its shackles, would not budge. "Fuck." Randell looked about. "Where's Ulrica, Connor?"

"Ulrica, upstairs I think. Connor, probably the basement."

"Are they both asleep? Didn't they hear anything? The whole fucking house moved. Surely, they must have felt it?"

Ulrica had felt the house shift as the truck hit but was sat on the toilet. *Aw, crap.* She could not believe it. For her it was the time of the month. Why tonight of all nights? Pursued by vampires she would be a dead give-away to the Mitclani during her monthly period. And with the full moon due this evening it meant that any number of Urbat could soon be joining them. She finished up and headed out, calling out for Randell, hoping for the best but fearing the worst.

Randell called up to her. "Down here." He grabbed his shotgun.

Heading outside Randell wasted no time and jumped up on the truck's side, slamming his fist into the driver's side window. The glass flexed but stayed as it was. He hit it again.

"I know you're in there you fucking maggot," he shouted at the glass, spraying the window with thick spittle. He lurched onto the crumpled bonnet and stamped at the windscreen. It jarred his leg. "Fuck it."

By now Ralph was at the side of the truck. Seeing Seffi's final resting place desecrated, disturbed so violently, he flew into a rage. In his hands he held a baseball bat and he hammered at the side door where Randell had just been.

Forgetting any of his upbringing, his education, training and profession, he went wild. "I'll cave your fucking head in, you bastard," he screamed.

Ulrica hesitated at the door, afraid of what she'd see, of what she had to do if her mum was out there.

She was about to head out with them when she heard Connor behind her.

"Hey, Ulrica," he said. "I could do with some help downstairs."

This was it, his chance to get her on her own while his father and Randell dealt with the vampires outside. It was light out so he knew they had the advantage and the racket told him it would be over soon so he'd have to be quick.

She was looking at the two outside as they beat and shouted threats and expletives at the truck's cabin. They did not appear to be getting very far. Whoever had pimped-up the truck had done a good job, the glass was not giving way at all. If only Ralph and Randell could get through, let in the light before darkness fell, it would render the occupants weaker and more vulnerable to attack. Perhaps then it could be all over. Ulrica knew her mother, or what was once her mother, would be inside the truck with her . . . whatever he was. Tears fell as she came to the understanding that whatever happened, Hemma, her mother, would have to be extinguished. She only hoped it would not be her who had to set her free. And if it was she hoped she would have the strength and resolve to carry it through. *If you love something, let it go.* It was time to kill, or be killed. The thought did not soothe her at all. After all, why should her mother, indeed herself, be saved when so many had perished; she was not special. Nobody was. Life was not fair. Had never been. There was no balance, no karma. Good and evil existed side-by-side; love needed hate to be noticed, life needed death to be appreciated. The woman she once called mum would have to suffer a second—and this time permanent—death. *I love you, mum.*

She turned her attention to Connor. "What's up?"

"Nothin' much, just don't think you want to be going out there. Probably safer down here."

"OK."

They headed on down.

"Take a seat," Connor said, ushering her towards the sofa. "Want a drink?" He rubbed his palm with his thumb, the skin tacky with sweat.

Drink was the last thing on her mind; her mother was about to be killed. Maybe she was better off down here, away from it all. Randell could tell her all about it later. She could always hide in her room for a few days. She missed Seffi.

Connor could see the girl was unhappy. Could he actually do this? "Thought it'd take your mind off . . . you know . . . things."

"Aw, crap. Go on then."

Connor poured her a tot of Jack and handed it to her. He slid in next to her and took a swig from his own glass. He hoped Randell and his father would still be a while. Give him some time to . . . No, it's not right. For either of us. But what of his experiments, his cure. It was within his grasp, if only he could summon the act. He knew it was wrong but sat there anyway trying to convince himself that the others would forgive him one day, maybe even thank him for it. He looked at her; she was leaning forward, both hands around the tumbler.

"What about your dad and Randy?" she said.

"It's still light out, they'll be fine."

She frowned. "But the house is wrecked."

"Yes, that's why I said to come down here. It's safer. Drink up," he said to her.

She took a gulp, rinsing the liquor around her teeth before swallowing. She grimaced as it hit the back of her throat, warming it rapidly.

He did the same.

He looked at her, hesitating, unsure of what to do or say. He felt it was something he had to do, despite his sexual orientation. It was not all new to him. As a growing teenager, trying to find himself in a still-prejudiced world, he had made out with a girl, had gone all the way even, but had felt nothing. He realised it was something he had done because society had expected it from him. Boy meets girl, and together they live happily ever after. What bollocks that had turned out to be. For him anyway. The people who viewed society through rose-tinted spectacles had conveniently forgotten about the high levels of divorce and would be sorely disappointed when they found out that this boy wanted only to meet another boy and just live his life, not being pestered, and without being the victim of prejudice or hate.

He took another slug of bourbon. The drink would help them both relax. He would just need to ply her with some more. He sat back, right next to her, his leg touching hers. He scratched at his groin.

She turned and made a face. "Ew. You OK there?"

"Yeah, yeah. Just an itch."

She grinned. "Well, you be careful with that inch."

"Itch, not inch."

"Aw crap, did I say inch? I'm sure you've got more than that." She put her glass down.


In the middle of their frenetic, mostly pointless, attack on the crashed truck, Ralph and Randell had not initially heard the new voice as it entered the fray. "Get inside, both of you."

Randell looked down, seeing four legs, the owners' bodies and heads huddled beneath heavily embroidered curtains, lined and clearly expensive. They were bright pink and looked incongruous in the deserted dull streets.

Ralph turned. "Ivan?"

"Yes," came the muffled reply. "Do as I say, it won't be long before we lose the light."

In their frenzied haste none of them had actually realised how close to darkness it was, how the day was fast slipping away, giving way to the vampires' single true ally.

Hemma was rubbing her arm, just above the sever point.

She wanted to scratch at it. She sat watching the irate man on the truck's bonnet as he pointed his barrel at the windscreen. "Er . . . Serkan?" she said, turning to him now.

"What?" he snarled. "Let him. It won't get through. The fool's attempts are futile. Relax, my dear, it won't be long now. We'll soon have the darkness on our side."

*Bang.* The windscreen pitted as the shot splayed out from the barrel, staying put.

Serkan smiled, his visage one of utter smugness. "See."

At that, the big irate man outside with the shotgun turned and climbed down. Serkan heard him cursing as he went.

"Where's he going?" Hemma asked.

Serkan peered out of the side window where only moments before there had been another angry man slamming and bashing at the door with a baseball bat—as if that would do him much good. This man had gone too, the crashing now silent. He watched as the two men met at the front of the house where two more men waited, a heavy vividly coloured blanket or something resembling a poorly designed tapestry covering their faces and upper bodies.

He sighed, looking at Hemma. "You can forget rubbing that arm. It's gone. I need you on full alert. Talking of your arm, or what's left of it, it seems those two sword tricksters are back. I'm sure you'll want to pay that young pretender a visit, give him a little payback." Serkan made a chopping motion with the side of his hand against his neck.

Hemma only nodded, her face restrained as quiet came down over the square.

Dusk came and still they sat, in silence, encased within the truck, biding their time. As the outside light finally faded and nightfall proper began to set in, Serkan turned to Hemma. "I am truly sorry about your arm, my dear, I am. But right now I need you at your strongest. But remember, whatever happens, you leave the big one to me."

He gently patted the military-style sling bag on his side and reached for the door latch.

Inside the house once more, Randell and Ralph locked the front door and began to bar the kitchen doorway using junk and busted worktop, disrupted blocks and the heaviest furniture they could find.

Everything they could muster went on to the pile, the kitchen sink already lodged somewhere in there involuntarily. Looking outside for one last time they saw that dusk had descended during their toils. They breathed hard, knowing the assault would come soon.

Ivan and Felix threw their makeshift covers on the floor, and Felix was about to say something when an explosion upstairs rocked the house.

The grenade blew in the first floor landing window, with debris and dust skidding down the stairs. In the hall downstairs they all ducked, diving instinctively for cover. Another grenade followed, making more noise and more mess.

This time the stairs caved in, surrounding them in rubble.

His hearing worse for wear, Randell shouted for names, hoping he would hear the replies. If they came. They came back at once. Everyone was still with him.

*So far, no casualties.*

Randell looked back and forth, up and down, his brain working overtime. "Shit. What now?"

The others all looked about, at each other, scurrying around on the floor in the house's detritus.

"Wait, where is Ulrica?" Randell said, his heart quickening. "And Connor?"

Ralph dropped his head. "I think Ulrica was up there." Where was his son?

Rushing to where the stairs should have started Randell began shouting "Ulr—" His voice was lost as yet another explosion hit. More plaster and dust rained down on them. He dived backwards, careening into Ivan and Ralph. "Shit, that was close."

Eyeing the basement door, it was Ralph who uttered the obvious. "Only option is down."

"But we'll be trapped down there," Ivan said.

They scanned the area; the kitchen barred, the stairs all but gone, the rest of the house off limits.

Ralph looked at Ivan. "Got any better ideas?"

"Where the fuck have they got grenades from?" Randell was reloading his gun, thankful that the ammunition stash was still intact. And readily accessible. He could only hope that Ulrica was safely tucked away upstairs, somewhere safe and out of harm's reach. He'd get to her soon. He'd get to Connor later. *We'll be back for you, girl.*

"Bit late to worry about where that head case does his arms deals," Felix said.

Another grenade hit. This time the front facade of the house and its pretty little balconies slipped away from their moorings, falling in a heap at the base, the dust fallout billowing into the square and sprinkling young Victoria's tiny right foot. Any other time it would have been a blessing, extra blockades for would-be intruders to get over; a hole in the kitchen left by an artic' lorry piloted by a crazed vampire rendered the additional obstructions superfluous.

It left them with no choice.

They headed down.

## Chapter 25

To say he was filled with mixed emotions when he saw the four of them appear in his basement rooms was something of an understatement.

Connor was relieved to see everyone alive still—not so happy to see Felix—but despite the assault going on at ground level he felt that he had been unfairly invaded. Downstairs was his domain, his private space; none of them had ever shown any interest. He certainly did not want anyone down there now. Not yet. Not until he was ready.

Immediately Randell pushed his way to the front. He spotted Ulrica sitting suspiciously close to Connor.

"Are you OK, girl?"

Ulrica looked up. Almost in a daze, she said, "Mum?"

Randell went over to her, kneeling in front of her. "Ulrica, it's me. Are you OK?"

Ulrica smiled and lay back in the soft chair. "Yeah, we're fine. We were . . ." Her words drifted away as she spotted Felix. "Oh, hi Felix."

Standing to face Connor, Randell barked at him. "What the fuck are you doing?"

Connor flinched, squirming back into the soft cushions of the sofa as the large bulk of Randell moved towards him.

How could he ever tell Randell the truth? He couldn't. They didn't need to ever know. Besides, nothing had happened; Ulrica had embarrassed him with her inch comment. He felt like a fool.

"I . . . I brought her down here . . . for safety," he stammered. It was partially true at least.

At the simple explanation Randell immediately softened, Connor's fears needless. "Yes, of course. Good. Good man."

"Good thinking, son," Ralph added, he, too, oblivious.

Connor couldn't quite believe his ears. His father had actually recognised something he had done, something all on his own—something for the good. With one simple sentence—albeit, a half-truth—he had won the approval of both Randell and his own father. They had observed his logic, his actions seen as heroic, maybe. No, he shouldn't fantasise. But it was a start, if only he could build upon it. He needed to keep a clear head. Now all he had to do was keep them all from entering the next room.

By now Felix was sitting next to Ulrica, quietly and slowly talking with her, the alcohol in her system making her drowsy. Randell was speaking with Ralph and Ivan about their next move. As far as anyone was concerned they only had the one move: defend their position and get out alive. It sounded much easier than it was going to be.

The noise above them continued. It would not be long before they either died down here, beneath a pile of eventual rubble, or had to head outside to face their attackers. At night. But there were six of them; they outnumbered their adversaries three to one. They could still do it. First, though, they needed to avoid all the incoming missiles.

Leaving the rest to discuss tactics among themselves Connor sat back down. He stared ahead, his mind a blur. What to do? On looking down he noticed one of the kitchen unit kick-boards was dislodged. It stuck out, along its length, by a couple of centimetres. He frowned; he couldn't recall ever seeing it before now. Then again the house had been grievously bombarded like never before. Stupidly he made a mental note to fix it before realising he actually had the pick of any house he desired, as long as it was secure—he would need to survive—and that this house would soon be demolished.

Another blast rocked the house.

And another.

The noise of the blast slowly subsided, the splash of falling debris fading as the final remnants of brick parts and plaster rained down.

Silence fell as dust filtered under the door, invading the room only slightly.

The quiet that followed seemed to last forever but in reality only moments had passed. That was when they heard footsteps above. Hard and deliberate, intimidating, the steps moved along the hall to what could only be the top of the internal stairs. Stairs that led directly to the basement.

"Ready yourselves," Ivan warned the others. His short-sword was already at his side, his knuckles white where he gripped the hilt.

Before he had raised the weapon and before the others had even responded to his words the door imploded. It hit Ivan full in the face knocking him to the floor, his blade snapping in two as he went down, the blasted door on top of him. Immediately Felix ran over to him, crouching by his side.

Wasting no time he lifted the door and dragged the older man free. Together they made their way towards the back of the room.

The others followed, backing away together.

"Quick, the next room," Randell shouted among the mayhem, his hand on the door handle.

It did not move. Locked.

He turned to look at Connor. "Where is the fucking key?"

Connor jumped, fumbling in his pockets. The footsteps from before had returned, only this time they were coming down the stairs, slowly and carefully. Click . . . Clack.

Randell turned and fired into the gap where the door used to be. Without a weapon, Ralph grabbed for something, anything, hoping for something sharp. His hand settled on a kitchen knife. He lifted it and regarded it. The word *Gourmet* adorned the metal—he wanted to kill the vampire intruders, not eat them.

He looked across at Randell. "This'll have to do."

Randell only nodded, his shotgun still pointed at the door. He had one cartridge left.

"Ulrica, next to me," he shouted.

Having left Ivan propped against the wall while he recovered, Felix grabbed Ulrica's wrist and dragged her closer.

Serkan stepped into the doorway. His eyes were wide, and black, his hair completely grey with dust. He appeared calm, as though he was relishing the moment.

"My, my, isn't this cosy?" he said.

He was met by a blast of shot as Randell discharged his final cartridge. They watched as the Mitclani monster reeled backwards into the stairwell.

"Connor." It was Ralph, shouting at his son. "Get this door open now."

"Yes . . . I . . . Just give me—" Connor fumbled with the key, dropping it. He bent to pick it up.

"Today Connor. Fuck's sake." Randell shouted.

Connor fell to his knees. Managing to retrieve the key, get it the right way up, hold it steady, insert it and turn the lock took some concentration. It made it harder when he heard the voice of the intruder again.

Serkan lifted himself up, inspecting his abdomen. The door frame had taken half of the blast, his torso and dusty clothing the other. He gazed at the fools all huddled around the doorway. "You've ruined my clothes."

"Good," Randell said. "Any time now Connor."

The familiar click of a lock was a welcome sound. Connor stood, hesitating, his hand on the handle, the unlocked door still closed.

"Open it," his father said.

Doing as he was told, Connor opened the door and went through, allowing the others to follow him. Toes hit heels and legs tangled as they all flocked through into the only room left, their last sanctuary. The final battle would be fought here.

Randell bundled the quickly-sobering Ulrica through the door as Hemma stepped up to stand beside her new man and master.

In the next room, the door locked once more behind them, Randell stopped.

And stared.

The scene was one of utter disbelief, the room was done up like a set for a third rate hospital sitcom, kidney trays filled with utensils, strange machines and test tubes, bloodied rags. The set was complete with strapped mannequin on the bed.

The mannequin, its face covered, moved. *Oh, shit.* More like complete with real live patient.

Randell's eyes met with Connor's. "What the fuck is this?"

He stepped closer, ignoring the continued beatings now coming from the other side of the door. He pulled the sack cloth away, waiting for some silly animatronics dummy to appear, to scare him, or make him laugh. Instead, the face was pinched, gaunt, eye sockets deep and hollow, their blackness exacerbated by the gauze-like grey skin. It could have been a zombie from any number of flicks he'd enjoyed over the years. The mouth, like the limbs and torso, was strapped down with thick leather. A small knife slit had been pushed through the covering of the mouth, its edges stained black with old blood. It was a feeding hole. Apparently, the 'doctor' would not want their patient to starve. Next to that was another shrouded figure. Randell pulled back the cover to reveal a well-and-truly deceased vampire, its undead-but-now-fully-dead discoloured body decomposing steadily, cheeks deeply excavated, the eyes sunken.

Connor flinched. "It's not what you think."

Felix and Ivan looked at each other, at Connor.

"What, that you're experimenting on them like some sick fuck. You get a kick from this?" Randell looked down at the vampire, the feet in shackles, the torso, the head and mouth, the arms, all bound tightly; the hands free but severely restricted.

*The hands.*

Randell halted, standing numb, staring at the vampire's digits. It was faint, barely noticeable because of the dull gossamer skin, but it was there. He rubbed at his own finger, recalling the memory. One night, three or four years ago, he and his brother had been on a drinking binge when they were cajoled into having a tattoo each. It had started out as a silly dare, a drunken game. Inebriated and unable to think clearly—and after counting what little cash they had left after a night's drinking—they had both opted for a simple black inked third-eye symbol, an eye set inside a triangle, on the base of their middle fingers. Only Sullivan in his intoxicated state had taken a firm stand—you can't rub it off you know, this stays with you forever, he had said—and insisted that the artist do it the other way up, despite the tattooist attempting to explain that he was looking at it upside down and that it would be all right once finished. Sullivan was not having any of it, the alcohol in his system knew better, and so the artist with his needle had done it the way his customer had insisted upon. They had laughed about it for weeks later.

It was something Randell had not thought about for some time, let alone looked at. But there it was, that same third-eye symbol, in front of him now. His head reeled. *What?* He looked at what only minutes before he'd thought was a mannequin, eyed its face, the fastened mouth, recognising the contours, the hairline, the scar he'd given his brother during a brotherly fight that had quickly got out of hand. *Sullivan?*

*But how, when?*

The room came back to him, the sounds, the people. Connor was standing to one side, biting his lip, Ralph was frowning and Ulrica looked half cut. There were two others he could barely remember the names of. And some fool banging incessantly on the door. He was about to tell whoever was at the door to politely fuck off before his current situation revealed itself to his benumbed brain: it was Serkan and his woman at the door and they were not going to give up anytime soon.

He and his comrades were in the final room in the house, trapped in the basement, and the dinner bell was sounding.

Randell quickly made for his brother's mouth strap, ripping it away, avoiding the teeth just in case. He regarded his stricken brother. He had looked better. "Sully? Sully, you in there, bro?"

The door burst in.

How they had done that so easily was the obvious question running through Randell's (and probably everyone else's in the room) mind, until the giant Asian brute—the one who had clumsily come to the aid of his much smaller friend in the square—entered the room. Serkan and Hemma followed him in, Serkan's sharp mitts firmly gripping the man-made battering-ram around the back of the neck.

Serkan scanned the room, shoving Sani to one side. "Well, well, this is even cosier. Such a convenient place to choose as a mortuary."

All weapons, what was left of them, pointed at the two Mitclani as one large Asian man crawled away, out of reach.

Eyes flashed left and right. Nobody said anything. Just waited. Ulrica gulped, spying her undead mother's severed arm. It no longer looked sore, just grim. *Not my mum, not my mum.* She repeated it in her head, over and over. *Not my mum.*

"Um, can I come out now?" A tinny voice, coming from behind them.

Everyone stopped.

And turned.

**Chapter 26**

In the far corner of the room the one and only cupboard door creaked open.

Huddled inside was one of the men they had seen in the battle from before, the small older one that Serkan had found lying on the ground. And, as small as he was, just how the man had actually managed to squeeze himself into the diminutive cupboard was anyone's guess.

Ralph turned away from the two intruding vampires and raised his chef's knife. In lieu of any other weapon he pointed it towards the cupboard inhabitant instead. He waited, his fingers stirring nervously about the handle.

Bewildered, the room was quiet, subdued, each waiting for the other to say something.

The man in the cupboard spoke again. "Er, hi." He was nodding now from his improvised hideout. "Anybody mind if I leave you all to it then?"

Randell threw a look at Connor. Connor shrugged, his mouth turned down.

"Not one of yours?" Randell said to him.

Connor shook his head. "No."

Randell pointed to his brother, the incarcerated Mitclani on the table. "Just this one then, my brother?"

This time Connor's eyes met the floor. He nodded twice.

"Why?" Randell asked; thoughts of his brother made him ignorant to the room. Whatever was going on—he would ask questions later, get the details, make sure he left nothing out—this was between him and Connor.

"I've been trying to save him," Connor said, so quietly he was all but mumbling.

"You mean experimenting?" Randell added.

"No. Well, yes, to reverse the effects, to make him human again."

Coarse laughter filled the room. It was Serkan, loud and mocking. "Oh, well, my, my, this is just so . . . so absorbingly heart-warming."

"If you mean two species trying to work out their differences," Ivan said, his broken short-sword held firm and true, "then yes, it is."

"Work out their differences," Serkan repeated. "Looks more like torture to me. More in the style of Josef Mengele."

Randell shot Connor another look.

"No, really." Connor turned to face Ulrica, for some support. "I was hoping to cure your mum, too."

Randell was having none of it. "I should kill you where you stand."

"You can't do that, Randell." Ralph said, sticking up for his son. "Is this true, son?"

Connor nodded once more.

Serkan turned to Hemma. "Isn't this fun?"

Randell knew Ralph was right. Connor was a little shit but he was one of them, and if there was a grain of truth in what he said then Randell knew he needed to be less opinionated and at least give Connor the chance to explain the science behind it. That is if he would even understand what it was Connor was telling him.

A shout filled the room, angry and loud. "Enough!" Serkan looked around the room, at each of them in turn. "Do you think I'll let you kill him, where would be the fun in that? No, no, no, no, no. It's my job to kill you all." He stopped as he eyed Felix. And smiled as he remembered Hemma was by his side. "That one's yours, my dear."

"Whatever," Felix said.

"Well kill you all," Hemma said.

"Bring it, Ulrica said.

"Yeah," Randell said, before repeating the girl's words. "Bring it."

Tensions and hackles rose, the room now one boiling pot of certain doom as they faced each other. Whatever happened next would be messy indeed. There was no time, or even choice, for fight or flight. Or even freeze. It was fight. To the death.

"You, get your arse out of here now," Randell said, his words meant for the man in the cupboard.

Like a sorrowful contortionist whose audience had not appreciated his act, Barclay scurried forward, bag in hand. "'Ere you go, guv'nor," Barclay said as he approached Serkan.

Serkan frowned. "What?"

"It's payment innit," Barclay continued.

"For what?" Serkan was puzzled.

"For makin' us twos into what you are."

And that was it, Barclay's big plan; the deal he wanted to make with Serkan was that he and Sani would hand over their treasures, their valuables in turn for being turned. Plain and simple. After figuring out that they spent much of their waking lives during the night and stealthily dodging all others during the day it made perfect sense. And they would have strength, agility and power along with it. The man would be crazy to turn away all those beautifully cut diamonds, and all that free cash. *Now that's what I call blood money.*

Serkan took the bag, eyeing it carefully. He looked inside, saw bank notes and glittering jewellery. He nodded. "Ah, now isn't that terribly charitable of you."

Barclay smiled, winking at Sani. *A done deal.*

By way of thanks there came a flash of sleeve, a rapid movement of limbs and digits, scarcely discernible, and at the end of it Serkan held his hand aloft. In it, the heart of the little man still beat, neat and bloody. It was a deft trick that he never seemed to tire of. "I'll take that instead, thank you so much."

Barclay gawped at the heart-snatching vampire, his face one of bewilderment, his brain mystified, as if astonished at the nimble moves of the man he had come to deal with. He blinked several times and was about to utter something when he slumped to the ground.

Seeing his friend and partner-in-crime die so rapidly and unceremoniously Sani lunged for Serkan, thinking that if he got hold of him he would rip the bastard's head off. Instead, lightning-fast and hardened fingernails slashed at the big man's throat opening up his carotid artery. Serkan stood as the release of Sani's pressurised blood showered him. Serkan opened his mouth as a child might to the warm summer rain.

Soaked in crimson, the Mitclani spoke, his teeth eerily white. "And what good is money or diamonds or whatever else you've got in that stupid bag of yours? Now, if you had come offering me the head of a traitor or, better still, my Agana's killer, then . . . maybe we could have talked." He spat a large wad of red onto the big man's back as he fell.

It was true. What good was money, material things? The economy was done. The only thing of value now was food, water and life—the basics. Nothing else mattered. Yes, a solid and age-old allotrope of pure carbon, once cut and polished nicely, looked nice on a ladies finger or hanging attractively from a pierced ear but it was hardly a necessity. Serkan was more inclined to use the diamond to open up someone's throat rather than wear it for a night out on the town.

Zipping in behind the large Asian man's falling and dying body Ivan seized his opportunity, and attacked. He went at Serkan with renewed vigour, his short-sword shorter still, the end jagged. The blood-red Mitclani was too quick, easily countering Ivan's assaults, dodging and batting his arm to one side time after time. Seeing him in trouble Randell went to his aid and, turning the shotgun on itself, he used the handle as a club, taking wide swings, trying not to take out Ivan in the process.

Connor stood back, protecting his test results, his gruesome table of mixed imaginings as the havoc around him continued. Ralph stood in front of his son, the knife braced in his hand, ready if or when one of the attacking vampires broke through.

Felix was about to help out Ivan and Randell when Hemma came at him and Ulrica. The vampire mother pounced, wailing and cursing, her one good arm reaching out, her fingers finding purchase. And a neck. Hemma bit down hard, her teeth tangling on Ulrica's dog collar. She tore at it, snapping the studded leather before spitting it away. Ulrica screamed as her so-called mother drove her fangs into the soft flesh. Like a parasite, stuck fast as a tick, Hemma sucked at her daughter's neck, relishing the young and fresh blood.

Ulrica gurgled out a squall as Felix smashed into them, his only option in prying them apart.

The vampire, releasing her bite, rolled across the room as Ulrica hit the deck with Felix on top of her. In seconds Felix had regained his composure and was hoisting the wounded girl back to her feet. He held his sword aloft, expecting another attack.

Dazed, Ulrica whimpered, reaching for the puncture marks. She stared at her mother.

Hemma's mouth and chin was flooded with blood, red and glistening. She smiled a deranged smile at the girl, her dull eyes flashing, lit up as though seeing for the first time. She licked her lips, then gazed at her daughter as though the blood had some meaning.

Felix stood his ground, waiting for the next attack, knowing the Mitclani would feel renewed in her vigour now she had fed.

The woman's smile faded, replaced by a frown. A grimace followed as agony flashed across her face, and she let out a scream. The momentarily bright eyes turned grey, then black as thick globs of dark blood leaked from their corners, the eyeballs losing shape and form, crumbling, mixing with the gooey black liquid, leaving a charred paste on her cheeks. Blind, she screamed again.

In mid-fight with Ivan and Randell, Serkan had not seen what was going on with his latest lover. He did not see as she raised her severed arm, the action to claw at her eyes lost on the suffering Mitclani's psyche. Hemma dropped to her knees as more dark liquid—part red, part black, the smears brown—oozed from her mouth and nose and ears, and down the inside of her legs. Like a diver coming up too quick her spine began to curve, causing her to hunch over horribly. Another scream caught Serkan's ear and, dropping his attention, he was caught in the arm by a ragged blade. He scrambled away from Ivan, grabbing for Hemma. By now Hemma's clothes, her back, was sodden as any interstitial fluid that was left inside of her began to excrete itself from any and all orifices.

Felix stood with Ulrica, holding her up while she palmed her neck wound. Together they watched the strange phenomenon.

It was in that moment, seeing the vampire suffering with its body twisting and wrenching into shapes that seemed impossible, that Connor realised his mistake. His whole pantomime with Ulrica had been doomed before it had even started, even if he had managed to get it up. He had forgotten one crucial element. It was the most fundamental of things; it meant his experiment could never even get off the ground. How could Ulrica ever be the right choice? He had been looking in the wrong place since the beginning. *What an idiot.*

Unable to do anything to help, Serkan slipped behind her, using Hemma as a morbid and makeshift shield. She was gone anyway, the sooner the better for her, he may as well use her wrecked body to defend himself. It was a good idea, in theory; what he had not banked on was the amount of fluid being released. In seconds it had flooded his eyes, obscuring his view. Still not comprehending what had happened to his partner he threw her twisted body to one side as he felt the Mitclani life drain from her. He caught a blow from Randell, the blow knocking him to one side as Ivan thrust his weapon forward in deadly fashion, missing his target by millimetres.

Sick of all the horseplay Serkan went berserk. It was his turn to attack now. And attack he did, with full force. He grabbed Ivan's arm, squeezing it tightly, disarming him in one swift move while Ivan shouted out for help. The shout was cut short as Serkan slammed the crooked blade through its owner's Adam's apple. Once in there, Serkan shoved it home, hearing a familiar crack as the scraggy ended weapon snarled with gristle and bone. The swordsman went down.

The next blow was a violent backhander that found Randell's jaw, knocking him almost insensible and sending him halfway across the room. Serkan stepped over Ivan's body towards Ralph, parrying with the older man and his stupid kitchen utensil.

"Dad," Connor shouted, stepping up as Serkan lashed out. Connor reeled backwards, falling on his backside, his face and upper arm deeply slashed. He sat back against the wall as Felix shifted Ulrica into the far corner, away from all the fighting.

And then, almost as quickly as it had begun, it stopped.

Ralph took an uppercut that did not sit too favourably with his brain and, as it rattled inside his skull, his legs gave way.

Seething, blood and spittle spraying into the air in front of him, a livid Serkan stood facing them. He glanced at Hemma's aberrant and convoluted body. He had a notion he had seen this before somewhere. He shook any thoughts away, his attention turning to the young wanna-be medicine man who was the most likely candidate responsible for Hemma's demise. He would save the big thug till last, relish it, knowing Agana had finally been avenged.

He stepped forward. It was time to finish this.

## Chapter 27

Serkan regarded the room, and its occupants, sizing up his next move.

In front of him lay Hemma's gnarled and partly liquefied body, meat and fluid commingled in a heap, like a victim trapped in a lava flow. He shook his head. *Oh dear, Hemma.* Both of the thieves were dead, having not sized up their situation correctly, for putting their trust in him. Like he would want a random bag of money and jewels—he would take what he wanted as and when the mood took him. The younger man, the mad scientist hopeful, was sitting injured on the floor, rapidly wrapping a bandage around his bicep. The older man, unconscious after taking a fierce blow to the chin, lay next to his son. They were both alive but out of the fight, for now. The fighter, Ivan, was dead, slain by his own sword, the jagged end having pierced his brain stem. His friend, the young Mitclani miscreant, was with the girl; she too, injured. That left one more—the one he had come for.

He was surprised the big guy had already recovered from the backhand, had clambered to his feet and was up and with it; he had grabbed the table and was pushing it like a gurney, his still-tied up brother attached to it, into the corner of the room.

253

Serkan frowned at the man's petty actions, at watching the big man attempting to protect his brother. *Please*. Did he not know his brother was now one of them now and, like Hemma, would devour a family member in mere seconds, at his command? *Devour*. The word made him realise he had used up a lot of energy and now his body craved more blood. One of the thieves he had killed could provide him with some much-needed sustenance. He dived onto the smaller of the two, sinking his fangs in. Once done, feeling stronger, he would free the vampire from his bonds on the table and the two of them could then lay waste to this room, together.

His feeding was cut short as strange noises filled the room.

A chorus of screams, wails, gurgles, and howls pierced his ears. Looking up he saw Randell bent forward over his brother's body, the big man's body shaking violently. Had the brother managed to wriggle free, and was he—as a vampire was inclined to do—now attacking the big cocksure bastard, brother or not? The girl, too, was wrestling away from her young vampire friend, screaming at him, her face distorted and dark. The wannabe medical student and his father were also writhing on the floor, yawping and yammering, their injuries either more painful than Serkan had first realised or . . .

Something else entirely was going on.

He lifted his face in revulsion as the screams and howls turned into something more intense, the writhing and reeling giving way to an audible show by way of clicking, clacking, snapping and cracking, ripping and twanging. A refrain of lamentations followed as bodies heaved and squirmed in the small space. Whatever was going on appeared to be easing.

He stood and stepped back, looking about the room. The basement room, with its tiny boarded windows needed artificial light at all times meaning that without a clock it was difficult to tell the time or even what the weather was doing. Things inside appeared different and far removed from outside. And then it dawned on him.

Outside, the full moon hovered in the southern sky. As always it shone bright and beautiful, the one celestial sight that no one never ever tired of.

Inside the room clothes tore and split, limbs cricked and snouts stretched leaving in their place wet noses, coarse grey hair, elongated ears, and razor sharp claws.

The high-pitched wails and yawls from only moments before had now ceased, turning to a low rumble of menacing growls. Randell, Ralph, Connor and Ulrica had made their monthly change, their bodies morphing hideously into something supernaturally unnatural. Instead of locking themselves away as they knew they should, they had found themselves in a battle with a belligerent and arrogant Mitclani vampire who thought he was better than everyone else. In his bluster that same vampire had completely missed the obvious. They were Urbat, his hated Tecuani, and as fully grown wolves with the power of the full moon would now be ignorant and unaware of any of their previous injuries.

That meant they would be strong. Four of them.

A pack.


Somehow recognising what Ulrica was screaming at him as she began to change, and knowing just what would happen to him if he stuck around, Felix fled.

Before it was too late. It was dark, albeit bright outside, but as long as he was careful he could get away, avoid any other Urbat that happened to be out tonight. With no other option he would have to take his chances. Staying there with Ulrica only meant a most violent end. No, he would hole up somewhere in the city far enough way so as not to be found and afterwards seek out Ulrica and her friends later, letting them first return to human form. It was far less dangerous and appealing. And if she asked why he had returned he would tell her that he had to come back and deal with Ivan's body.

The four wolves stood to face Serkan, Mr Mitclani, the vampire of vampires, now so small in front of all their hybrid sinew and muscle.

It all made perfect sense now. Hemma had bitten the girl but as he well knew the canine blood was toxic to vampires, lethal. It attacked the Mitclani body at cellular level, making it turn against itself. It happened rarely but when it did it was quick, it was painful, and it was final. There was no vaccine, no cure. No coming back. Hemma had unwittingly been killed by her own daughter.

"Fucking dogs." Serkan spat the words at them. Then turned and ran.

Randell, his wolf-man physique vast, followed. Serkan was quick, was already outside in the square, but Randell's strong canid legs pushed him forward. A little older maybe but in full wolf form Ralph was not far behind. A claw struck Serkan's left shoulder throwing him towards the fence of the tiny square. His feet left the ground and he crashed against the railings.

Leaving him no time to recover Randell struck again, his claws taking out layers of clothing, skin and muscle from Serkan. This time the vampire bounced as he went straight down. Unbeaten, Serkan reacted. He jumped up and leapt over the railings. In the centre of the square now standing in front of Victoria, belittling the statue, were the two other Urbat, Ulrica and Connor, the pack sticking together, all eager for the kill. Serkan dodged to his right, the spoilt earth from the truck ride beneath him. He slipped, twisting his ankle as he sprang forward. This time he went down on his own.

Randell watched him crawl away, towards Seffi's violated grave. But Ralph was already there, his white-grey skin and hair slick with sweat and grease, lustrous in the moonlight. It would make a fitting place for revenge. The werewolf, that for most of the month was a retired and beaten down veterinarian trying to stay alive in a world gone mad, bent over the Mitclani's face-down body. Ralph grabbed the vampire's hair, halting any escape.

Serkan's words were lost in the soil. "Do your worst, you hyena-faced hybrid."

Ralph slammed his clawed canescent fist through the vampire's skull. Bones crunched and Ralph's fist exited the vampire's shattered face, the undead brain forced from Serkan's dome.

For a moment the wolf-man studied his freed hand, his arm still encased within the vampire's head; would he remember when he came round in the morning that he had used these same hands, countless times over many years to save animals, to love, care and nurture them back to health, to never kill? Then again Mitclani were not animals, so maybe they were fair game?

Ralph let out a long howl as the other three wolves closed in on the body and tore it apart. One sniff told them the meat was rotten and that they could not consume it; there was no nutrition for the powerful brawn that the Urbat body harnessed. They needed to satiate themselves. Find red meat, with real blood coursing through it.

Morning found them back in the basement, covered with blood, the two overly-optimistic-but-largely-deluded thieves' remains chomped and ripped apart beside them, bones stripped of meat.

All were human once more.

Ulrica immediately started crying when she saw her mother's body.

Connor was silently bemoaning his stupidity; in the middle of all the chaos, seeing Hemma writhing, her wricked body suffering, he had realised that like him, Ulrica was Urbat, the wolf blood flowing through her veins would never be any good for his experiments. He needed pure human specimens, not one that only appeared human for most of the month. Somewhat ashamed, but thankful his previous actions had been all but forgotten, Connor comforted her, throwing his arm around her.

"She's safe now. At peace," he said. At that she turned and hugged him tightly, her tears still flowing, her face puffy and red.

On the table, still strapped up, lay Sullivan. In their savage state they had forgotten all about Randell's brother. Randell picked himself up, patted Connor on the back as he passed, and headed over to his brother. He released the strap from his mouth.

"You OK?" Randell said.

Sullivan spoke, his voice dry and hoarse. "Yeah, still here. Hungry."

"I can give him something if my fridge hasn't been damaged," Connor said, leaving Ulrica to grieve.

Randell turned to him. "Thanks."

Connor nodded, inspecting the fridge. "Good news, it's OK."

Looking at his brother, Randell spoke. "Now, if we let you go, you're not going to turn on us are you." It was not a question.

"Course not, bro." Sullivan eyed Connor. "Can't say the same about him though."

Connor gulped. "I . . ."

Shrugging, Randell said, "He was trying to help. Anyway, you allowed him to capture you, bro. I'd say it's pretty much your own fault."

Sullivan nodded. "That's my big brother speaking."

Randell smiled. "Yeah, and don't you forget it."

After releasing Sullivan they allowed him to feed on a fresh bag of donated red stuff.

"Here, think this one is Raspberry flavour," Randell said as he passed his brother another bag.

Realising his brother might need some time to adjust they left him alone in the basement. Ralph and Connor had taken to getting several large suitcases together. Randell may have had experience at building but the house was beyond repair; it was easier to find another, and reinforce that.

Regaining his confidence around Sullivan, Connor showed him Hemma's body, giving him a brief account of who she was before explaining to him that this is what happens if he was to ever swallow Urbat blood. If nothing else, it made him feel safer being alone in the basement with a Mitclani. He went on to tell him about his experiments—he apologised several times—and how it was theoretically possible to cure vampirism.

"Perhaps," Connor said, "one day, if I had help, and a pregnant mother and child."

"Can you cure your own monthly cravings?" Sullivan asked.

"Not that I know of."

"Then if you can't cure yourself or Randell, then I'm OK with who or what I am. He'll just have to change his shifts and sleep during the day if we're ever to go out together."

Ulrica was pleased to see Felix return.

They had almost finished their move, rushing to get away from Victoria Square as the day dragged on. He helped to carry a box for Ulrica, of what she called 'accessories', the contents—an assortment of dog collars—spilling over the top. He noticed one had a heart locket attached to the front.

They found a suitable house just south of Eaton Square on Eccleston Street. This time there were houses on the opposite side of a regular two-lane A-road so no chance of anyone driving a truck straight at it. Over the next few days they buried Hemma and Ivan and Seffi, after exhuming her, in Eaton Square Gardens. Ralph did not want her remains to be too far away. Felix said a few words, coming out of the house as night took the silent city once more, explaining how, after losing his father to the Mitclani, Ivan had found him and mentored him, had taught him to survive. Ulrica cried some more but, through gargled gulps, told them how she dearly hoped her mother was at peace. And Ralph said goodbye again, his eyes glazed and wet.

There were still vampires around, the Mitclani an ever-present threat, and there was the added danger of a stray Urbat finding Sullivan or Felix one night. Then there was the monthly peril of changing. They would have to lock themselves away for good measure—unless they were under attack of course, and hope that Felix and Sullivan got out of the way, lying low in a private hideout that only they knew the exact location of. It was nothing they couldn't work out.

Randell and Ulrica stepped out into the dark, Felix and Sullivan at their sides.

They could have taken Connor or Ralph but they had decided that it was not fair to leave only one person alone in the house to protect it. After all, they were a pack, they performed better together. And Ralph needed to reconnect with his son. Leaving them alone all night might just propagate some long lost love. It was going to be more dangerous, searching by night, but they did have safety in numbers. They needed to find humans, and quickly. Would they ever get as far as Northampton, or Scotland? They may have to. The donated blood bags that Connor had collected along the way were quickly running out, even when rationed out. A long-term solution was needed. Willing blood donors living side by side with Mitclani and Urbat. For the greater good, the future, if there was to be any.

They stopped at a building on Sloane Terrace.

Something about it had made them all halt. At once. Was it the brass-bottomed double doors, clean and firmly shut, the barred windows adjacent? Or the fresh-looking bloodstains on the front porch steps?

After finagling with the lock for several minutes they stepped inside, their soft footsteps squeaking on highly polished tiles. Through the darkness they could make out a large entrance hall. Unidentifiable paintings and works of art adorned the walls looking like huge black squares. To Randell's immediate left was a grand staircase. He guessed it was marble. In front of them, at regular intervals, elaborate columns ran along the length of the room.

Sullivan was about to say something when the lights flicked on, temporarily blinding them all.

Four figures, their outlines blurred, their bodies silhouetted, stood opposite. They were either wolf, vampire, or hopefully, human. At least the odds were the same. Felix thought about Ivan, of how he would tackle the situation. Whoever they were he hoped that they were prepared to listen and engage in conversation. If not . . .

The sound of weapons being drawn echoed around the walls.

Ulrica blinked, squeezing Felix's hand. "Aw, crap."

## The End

## ACKNOWLEDGEMENTS

Thanks to my dear Elisabeth for allowing me time to shut myself away with my creations, only to continually scare the living daylights out of me by bursting in with the many cups of tea, coffee and biscuits it took to get this thing down on paper. A nod also goes out to Michael Portillo for signing for me a copy of Colette Hooper's book: Railways of the Great War with Michael Portillo.

Printed in Great Britain
by Amazon